T

Thicker Than Blood

Thicker Than Blood

Penny Rudolph

Poisoned Pen Press

Copyright © 2005 by Penny Rudolph

First Edition 2005

10 9 8 7 6 5 4 3 2 1

Library of Congress Catalog Card Number: 2004117562

ISBN: 1-59058-148-2   Hardcover

Poisoned Pen Press
6962 E. First Ave., Ste. 103
Scottsdale, AZ 85251
www.poisonedpenpress.com
info@poisonedpenpress.com

Printed in the United States of America

To Ralph, my best friend, my biggest supporter:
thanks for putting up with me

Acknowledgments

Special thanks to:

Rob Kresge, Mike White and Pari Taicher for their critique and advice

Bob Rich for his fine editing

Madeline Dwyer and Ira Rimson for their help landing the balloon

Chapter One

Rachel could recall the last time she saw Jason as if she were watching it on a movie screen. Jason was always larger than life.

The weather was warm, the air heavy, the metallic odor of old motor oil permeated everything—a perfectly ordinary morning, except for the flat tire.

Nothing about Jason Karl was ordinary.

The offending flat was on his company Cadillac and he had summoned her to change it. She remembered his tapping a shiny wing-tipped toe and generally implying she was taking too long. He didn't seem to mind relegating the tire changing to a woman. Perhaps he hadn't noticed. Rachel both appreciated that and was offended by it.

Jason jerked his wrist forward to stare again at his watch, and something thwanked into the upturned hubcap at her elbow. Los Angeles road sludge had turned the concrete garage floor the color of old mud.

Flicking a glance upward, she saw him frowning across the roofs of the cars left by the people who paid her for the privilege of parking. InterUrban Water District leased space for its employees and for its fleet of company vehicles. Jason was InterUrban's general manager.

"Lose something?" She deftly fitted the spare tire in place and fumbled for a lug nut.

He glared down at her. "Don't tell me something is missing. I have to get on the road."

Brushing a damp strand of straight dark hair from her face, leaving a sooty streak on her cheek, she poked a smudged index finger among the bolts in the hubcap and fished the interloper out.

"Cuff link," she announced, glimpsing the etched image of a turtle before holding it out on the palm of her hand. *No, not a turtle.* The remnant of a tale from her childhood stirred in some dusty corner of her mind. *A tortoise.*

"Damn." Jason took the cuff link gingerly, not thanking her, careful not to soil his hands. "Goddamn thing is always falling out."

"Nice design. Unusual." Rachel's arm began to ache from holding the wheel; she went back to work replacing the nuts.

He jabbed the silver stem at the neat openings in his shirt sleeve. "Indian. The prices they charge, you'd think they'd at least make things right, so they stay put. Indians don't give a damn. They could daub paint on a rat turd and everyone would rush to buy it."

She tapped the hubcap into place, stood, stretched her legs in grease-speckled designer jeans.

Without a word, Jason got into the Caddy, backed out of the parking space, and disappeared into the hot Los Angeles smog.

⌒⌒⌒

Across the street, in one of InterUrban's two executive suites, Charlotte Emerson was watching four scrub jays raucously claiming rights to the bird feeder outside her office window. As one bird dive-bombed another, she was thinking that human behavior made the jays look sweet and courteous.

Her six decades in the water business had been a series of wars. Not mere quarrels, not disputes. Wars.

Before her time, Los Angeles had drained the Owens Valley, but that hadn't been enough. So Charlotte had been in on tapping the Colorado River, had watched hundreds of miles of aqueducts built. She turned back to the stack of reports on her desk. Now the Colorado wasn't enough.

The gleaming teak desk top reflected her perfectly, the royal blue suit that set off her pale complexion, the sublimely casual grooming that gave her an appearance at least fifteen years short of her age.

Dan Emerson had been a thundering force of the thirties and forties, one of the giants who had pruned and shaped the state and given Southern California the water that made anything possible. Charlotte had worked at his side, had helped him bring forth from a desert the world's eighth largest economy. And the largest water agency in the world. InterUrban.

Until now, at seventy-six, she had hardly given a thought to retiring. But she couldn't go on forever. She would just win this last battle. And when this term as chairman of the board was done, she would…what? Maybe take up the piano again, read all the great books.

Morning sun glittering in her pale hair, Charlotte leaned back in her chair and closed her eyes. She wasn't as sure of herself this time. But it had to be done. This one would be her legacy.

With a small dry laugh, she opened her eyes and reached for the phone. She should call to be sure the car was ready. Imagine, a woman running a parking garage. Well, more power to her, Charlotte thought, and began to dial.

On the garage's street level Rachel sat on a stool in the glass cubicle watching a thinning stream of cars depart. It was nearly six and most of the regulars had collected their cars like pets from a kennel. She perched there in the late afternoon in case someone had locked keys in a car or discovered a dead battery.

Rachel aimed to keep her customers happy. This parking garage was her last chance.

The few remaining cars belonged to the workaholics. She waved at the driver of a Pontiac and began her rounds of the gates, pushing buttons to lower metal doors across five. People who worked late in the nearby offices knew the sixth exit would be open until ten.

Back in the booth, she drew out the middle phone book from a neat stack in the corner, opened it, and eyeballed the old thirty-eight lying neatly in the space she had carved from the center of the thick mass of yellow pages. She just wanted to be sure it was still there.

The revolver's short barrel made for terrible aim, but she could shoot well enough to make someone bent on trouble reconsider his plans. The gun wasn't registered. Marty, her father, had won it in a poker game.

She put the phone book back and left the booth to trudge through the fifth-level parking area to the apartment she'd had converted from a storeroom. Empty, the garage echoed like the disturbed tomb of some forgotten pharaoh.

An orange tabby with the face of a prizefighter and the demeanor of a duke came stretching and yawning to greet her when she stepped inside her living room.

"Evening, Clancy," she said, and went straight to the kitchen area to scrub her hands with something from a plastic container labeled *Gunk*. Leveling an appraising gaze at the small mirror above the sink, she scoured the grime from her cheeks until they reddened.

After a frozen dinner of fettuccine Alfredo so flavorless that even Clancy gave the noodle she offered him just one desultory lick, Rachel dumped the plastic dinner tray in the trash and made her way back down the five levels of the garage. Not sure where she would go, but feeling she must go somewhere, she stepped onto the sidewalk.

"There you are, dear girl." Wheels on the supermarket cart rasped and squeaked as the old woman pushed it toward Rachel. The cart held neat stacks of clothing, a rose-colored blanket that looked nearly new, and a couple of aluminum pie pans.

"You were looking for me?"

"Indeed I was, dear girl. Indeed, I was." The woman was short and so round she might have been made of sofa cushions. Her salt-and-pepper hair was cropped short as a Marine's, but it still managed to stick up here and there, giving a bizarre hint of punk.

"Found something." Gleefully, the woman waved a deck of cards. "Know what this is?"

"Sorry. I don't gamble. Besides, I'll bet the deck is marked."

"No, no, dear girl. These are fortune cards. They see the future. And then they tell Irene." She tapped her ample chest and chirped, "Yes-yes."

Irene sat down on the sidewalk with amazing agility, settled the rough cotton skirt around her, patted her knees, and eyed Rachel with delight. "Sit, dear girl. Sit with Irene." She shuffled, then held out the cards to the still standing Rachel. "Cut."

On the third floor of InterUrban headquarters, Hank Sullivan glanced up from his desk and was startled to find the window dark. Lately he always seemed to be working late.

Something was happening in the water industry, some shift in the wind. And this morning Jason had called to say he was sending down yet another rush project.

Hank took off the glasses he needed now for close work, and rubbed the bridge of his nose. A shock of pale brown hair tumbled across his forehead. At forty-two, threads of grey were creeping in. Eyes closed, his face had the look of a boy's. Open, the eyes were blue and sharp.

If his rangy limbs were clad in denim instead of the Nordstrom suit, he might have looked like a rancher. He had little love for suits. Three minutes after he picked one up at the cleaners, it sprouted wrinkles. But as the senior water resources engineer, he was spending more and more time attending meetings.

His eyes lit on the face of the miniature desk clock and the time jolted him out of his chair. Nine fifty-five. The garage would be closing. Not pausing to put on his suit jacket, he threw it over his shoulder. The wrinkles be damned.

Rachel frowned at the round little fortune teller with the spiky hair.

Irene was still holding out the cards. She cocked her head like a plump brown hen. "Come-come, dear girl. Lots of tomorrows ahead. Don't it make sense to know what they hold? Cut," she said again.

Rachel drew a small wad of dollars from her pocket. "I have to get the garage locked up. But thanks anyway."

The woman unfolded the bills with gnarled, bird-like hands. "Thanks be for this. I owe you a telling." She wheeled her market basket and pushed it up the sidewalk.

Rachel strode through the almost empty garage. It wasn't part of the contract, but the water agency's cars were the only ones that regularly overnighted there and she liked to count noses, or back bumpers as it were, to be sure no one had left a door open or lights on.

On level C, she scanned the small fleet. All twenty-six were in their places like roosting hens.

The trunk lid of the car in space C-18 was slightly ajar. Pausing a moment to close it, she noticed a long scratch along the side of the vehicle in the adjacent space—a DeVille, one of the five kept for top executives. The rank and file drove stripped-down Chevys. Had some jerk been scratching fenders with a key? She'd lose customers if that happened too often.

Rachel ran her finger along where the mark crossed the door. When she reached the front of the car, she realized that the scratch had not come from a key. The car had hit something.

Dim light bounced from the front fender, which bore a dent so broad and deep she thought the metal must be rubbing on the tire. Part of the bumper had torn away and one headlight was gone.

At the upper right of the dished-in fender were small irregular splotches of dull brown. She bent over to study the smudges. *Blood?* Little prickles raced up the back of her neck. *Of course not.*

She was still peering at the stains when the lights went out.

Chapter Two

The ocean of blackness that swallowed her came so swiftly, Rachel froze where she was, barely breathing.

No glimmer, no glow of light showed anywhere.

Disoriented, she swayed a little. A sound welled in her throat, but her mouth was too dry, her jaw too rigid to let it out.

Something rasped against the pavement. *Feet?*

Yes, moving slowly toward her. She crouched, crawled under the car.

The ripe smell of oil made her dizzy. Her arm struck the muffler and she jerked it back. The metal was still warm. The car had not been sitting there long.

The rasping came again, but the pulse of her own blood in her ears was so loud she couldn't fix its location.

A man's voice split the quiet. "Anybody here?"

The car's chassis creaked as someone touched the back of it. The steps went on, then faded.

Rachel's mind spun. Even if the spots on the fender were blood, and she was suddenly certain they were, they had nothing to do with her. And no ordinary mugger would bother tampering with the electric lines.

Something in a saner part of her brain suggested that lying there all night breathing oil fumes would only make her queasier.

Ducking her head, she crept out from under the Cadillac and followed its cool metal body to the bumper. Now she must be in the driving aisle. The elevator was near, and just beyond that the stairs.

Hugging the wall, hands feeling the way, she had reached the door to the stairwell when something grazed her elbow.

A grunt. A hand grasped at her arm.

The legs would be slightly to the right. She shifted her weight, brought her knee up, hard.

A whoosh issued from a mouth she couldn't see. He was just beginning to moan when the light flooded back as quickly as it had departed.

Sprawled on the pavement was the doubled-up shape of a man, eyes shocked, mouth contorted. No gun was in sight, no knife, no brass knuckles, just a suit jacket under his right shoulder.

She bent over him. "You okay?"

The growled response was not flattering.

"Sorry. I thought you were a prowler, a stalker, maybe a serial killer."

He struggled to his feet, planted them wide apart, gingerly shook out the suit jacket and brushed off his clothes.

She held out a hand. "Rachel Chavez."

He folded his arms over his chest, the hardness only beginning to fade from his eyes. "Hank Sullivan. You want my rank and serial number?"

"I said I was sorry. I panicked." She dropped her hand. "What are you doing here?"

"Looking for violets. Isn't this the flower market?"

She tossed her hands in the air and turned to the stairway exit.

"The gate is probably closed by now," he snorted irritably.

"It's still open," she called over her shoulder.

"Hope you're right." He moved toward the ramp.

"I'd better be. I haven't locked it yet."

He turned, shot her a frown.

"I own the garage."

He stared a moment, shrugged, and stiffly marched off.

At the gate, Rachel fiddled impatiently with her keys waiting for him to drive out so she could lock up. Streetlights threw a purplish veil over the office buildings. A breeze chased a piece of litter along the curb. The power failure had swept the dented fender from her mind, but now it loomed again. Should she get a flashlight and have a better look?

Rachel jumped as a hand touched her elbow.

"Sorry," he said loudly, stepping back so quickly she couldn't stop a laugh.

"Me, too. Really, I am." She looked up the ramp into the garage. "So where's your car?"

He hung his head like a small boy. "I can't open it. I seem to have locked the keys inside."

"That," she said, "I can fix."

He followed her to the glass booth and waited while she reached inside for the slim-jim, but the hook where it usually hung was empty. Then she remembered. "I had it in my hand when I went home."

He pounded a fist lightly against the glass wall. "End of a perfect day. Guess I need to find a phone. I'll call a cab."

"I assume you can wait two minutes. I live right here."

"In the garage?" His voice cracked a little.

She started toward the elevator. "Better come along. You'll have to show me where the car is."

In her apartment, the television was still on, the news report winding down.

Clancy rose from the sofa, stretched, yawned, and eyed Hank as if appraising his ability to scratch ears and work a can opener.

Behind Rachel, Hank took in the collection of plants and books. "Never would have guessed someone lived here."

"You gotta admit it's a great commute."

Seeing him in clear light, she decided the face was nice, but the straight sandy hair had a mind of its own.

She crossed the room to the kitchen counter where she had tossed the jimmying tool. When she turned back, he was looking faintly amused or surprised, she wasn't sure which.

"How on earth do you happen to own a parking garage?"

"My grandfather built it. The hours aren't great, but anyone can run a car park. Think what I save on the Saks' bills."

The blond anchorwoman on the television screen was rearranging her fluid features to a look appropriate for unpleasant news. "This just in from the newsroom. Jason Karl, the general manager of InterUrban Water District, was found dead late this afternoon, on a country road about a hundred and forty miles east of Los Angeles. The sheriff's department is investigating what they say appears to be a hit-and-run accident."

Chapter Three

"Jesus, that's my boss." Hank's words rushed out and stopped.

Rachel's mouth opened twice before the sound came. "Jason Karl? I just saw him. I just changed his tire."

They both stared at the screen, but there were few details beyond the fact that Jason's body had been found next to his car on a desert road northeast of the Imperial Valley.

"You knew him?" Hank asked, surprised.

She shrugged. "Not really. Just a client. My most important one. Will this affect your job?"

Hank paused. "I have no idea."

"Was he a friend of yours?"

Hank's eyes darkened. "It's probably safe to say Jason was no one's friend."

She gazed at him a moment. "Well, guess we better get your car open."

This time, she took along a flashlight.

It didn't occur to her until they were passing the long row of company cars. She stopped so quickly that he was several feet ahead before he noticed and turned around.

"Oh my God," she whispered, eyes wide, hand over her mouth. The overhead light edged her hair with tiny flashes of red.

"What is it?"

She didn't move or change expression.

He ambled back and put his hand on her arm. "What's wrong?"

"The car," she said in a hoarse whisper. "The fender."

"What car, what fender?"

If she had stopped to think, she might have kept it to herself. But she reached for his arm and led him to the damaged car. "Is that blood?" she said quietly, pointing at the fender.

Hank knelt to examine the dent. "Hard to tell. Could be." He stood again, dusted off his hands, then wiped them on his trousers. "I heard that someone driving one of our cars hit a deer. Maybe this is it."

"Oh." Rachel's thoughts raced, stumbled over something, bogged down.

They found Hank's green Mustang looking lonely and deserted on level B, the jimmy did its work, and he thanked her.

At the gate, she watched Hank's car exit, then locked up.

Back in the apartment, she readied herself for bed, spit out the toothpaste, and stared at herself in the mirror. The brows rose over suspicious eyes. She could almost hear her mother saying, *What a nice young man.*

Probably got a wife and six kids, she told the voice in her head. *Besides, you were never one for nice young men. You married Pop.*

Her mother, Madeleine, had adored Rachel's father, whose family had made a small fortune farming, but Madeleine's austere parents had never quite forgiven their daughter for marrying a Mexican. Marty was only half Mexican, of course—the other half being Irish—but to the Feinbergs that didn't matter. He was still a gambler, a joker, and a Catholic.

Rachel climbed into bed only to lie wide-eyed in the dark. *Besides, I'm perfectly happy as I am.*

Was she? A sordid mess behind her and, if she were really lucky, she could go on working eighteen hours a day in a parking garage and be too tired to sleep.

A garage where one of the cars was used to kill someone.

She sat straight up in bed. The water agency usually sent over paperwork about dents and scratches and she arranged repairs. There had been no recent papers.

And I can't even go to the cops.

The streetlights made a pale glow at her curtainless windows like a movie screen before the film rolls.

Rachel tore off the covers and went to the kitchen.

The box of crackers was almost empty and smelled salty. She poured a glass of low-fat milk and sat down at the counter in the dark.

Soon, very soon, someone would quietly get the damage repaired and there would be no evidence at all that the car on level C had killed anyone.

But maybe it was just a deer. Maybe the repair order will come tomorrow. Besides, it's none of my business.

Rachel rose to go back to bed, thought better of it, pulled on her blue terry robe instead, and picked up the flashlight. First she would have another look at that fender.

In the yellow beam of light, the dent looked even deeper than she remembered. Crouching next to it, Rachel ran her finger over the naked metal. The blood, if that's what it was, was like a daub of dull brown paint.

She shone the light through the passenger window. Nothing odd there. She could search it of course. InterUrban left keys for its vehicles on peg-board hooks in her booth.

The light flashed across the side mirror. OBJECTS IN MIRROR ARE CLOSE THAN THEY APPEAR. There was an extra space after CLOSE where the stenciled R had come off.

She gazed again at the fender. *Is it blood?*

The flashlight beam glinted on something in the cleft where the hood met the fender. Something was wedged there, a nail or tack of some sort. Rachel wiggled it back and forth, but it wouldn't come free. Finally, she took a key from her pocket and pried the object out. It made a dinging sound as it hit the pavement at her feet—a bit of twisted metal about the size of a quarter.

Stooping to pick it up, she examined the sharp, pointed shaft that had caught in the crack. When she turned it over, a prickling began at the top of her head and moved swiftly down her spine, filling her body with ice water.

The metal bore the etched image of a tortoise.

Chapter Four

At noon the following day, Rachel climbed the stairs to the garage roof.

She had added the helicopter pad soon after opening the garage. Nearby businesses, from banks to medical complexes, used it. As with parking, the water agency was her biggest helipad client.

Normally, it was Lonnie's job to meet the helicopters, but she had sent him to pick up sandwiches for lunch. He'd been gone more than an hour.

She opened the door and a fierce downdraft of heavy air almost pushed her back down the stairs. Grabbing the narrow metal railing, Rachel squinted and leaned into the wind. The relentless beating of the blades was deafening; it sounded like the beating of a monstrous heart.

Covering her head, she waited while the chopper touched down, then crouched down and darted to the cockpit. The pilot handed her a parcel. She barely got back to the railing before the helicopter began rising.

The air finally stilled, leaving the rooftop stiflingly hot. Running a hand through wind-mussed hair, Rachel saw that part of the parcel had torn away. Through the inner plastic lining, granules like sugar were visible. The torn label showed only a return address for Rosen Chemicals.

She glanced at her watch, wondering where Lonnie was, hoping she didn't know.

The stairwell seemed black as pitch after the blinding sunlight and she narrowly avoided colliding with someone in the dimness at the bottom of the steps.

"Sorry I'm late," Lonnie gasped, breathless. No taller than she, and thin, he weighed in at about one-ten. Nose and chin jutted from a face the color of milk gone bad. He held up a bag. "Jeez, that Italian sausage reeks of garlic."

"Good."

"Not for me. Garlic kills my stomach."

"I got the package, catch your breath." She handed the parcel to him, took the sandwich bag and reached inside. "It's cold, Lon. What took so long?" The sandwich shop was only three blocks away.

"Sorry," he said again.

She waited for an explanation that didn't come. "Lon, don't do this."

Clean and sober, he was bright, clever, and could outwork three men. And she owed him. She owed him big. The last thing Rachel wanted to do was fire him.

"I'm clean. I swear it." He looked at the package she had given him. "What happened ? The address is gone."

"The return address is a chemical company. Only place I know that gets shipments of chemicals is the water quality lab."

Lonnie peered through the torn cardboard at the contents. "Looks like—"

"Sugar, crystal, coke, but somehow I sincerely suspect it is none of those."

"Right." He glanced at her, then with a show of haste and efficiency, hurried off.

Rachel sat down in the stairwell and ate her sandwich, hardly noticing what she was chewing. Finished, she stood, tied the tail of her shirt in a knot about her waist, thinking an icy Fat Tire beer would sure taste good. She settled for some M&M's and went to sit fidgeting, accomplishing nothing, on the scarred drafting stool in her booth, until almost closing time.

First that damn tie tack. No question, it was Jason's. The design was identical to the cuff link he had dropped in the garage. She should do something, tell someone.

And now, Lonnie. She couldn't ignore what was going on with him.

Her fist pounded the counter, causing the four window envelopes in front of her to dance. She tore them open and was pulling a large book of checks from a drawer when the phone at her elbow rang.

"Rachel? It's me."

A surge of pleasure gave way to a rush of anger. She shoved it down. "Pop?" She hadn't seen him in months.

"How's my girl?" He didn't wait for an answer. "You free for dinner?"

She was almost afraid to ask, "You doing okay?"

"Fine, fine."

She waited for him to say more, could almost hear the nervousness in his silence. "Dinner. Okay. How about the Italian Fisherman?"

There was silence on the line, then, "Pasadena's a little, uh, far."

Rachel sighed. That meant he would be playing poker and didn't want to have dinner too far from Gardena. "Okay, where?"

"How about the club? Seven?"

Oh, Pop, she thought sadly. "Okay."

She stuffed her paperwork in a box and went up to the apartment to wait for freeway traffic to thin out.

Sprawled on the worn sofa with Clancy on her lap, she wondered what to do about her father. He'd been in a downward spiral since her mother had died.

Madeleine had been thrown from a horse.

Marty had phoned Stanford and got Rachel out of class. In some dark corner of Rachel's mind, fear had begun to collect like the first drops of storm water. She raced home.

"Of course, she'll get better," Marty said as they shared a dinner of lukewarm takeout chicken in the dining room of the huge old farmhouse. His eyes seemed to have sunk into his head, leaving a pair of dark craters.

When her mother's condition didn't improve, Rachel dropped out of school. "Next semester she'll be better. I'll go back then," she told Marty.

She and Madeleine spent hours in the sun on the patio where the view was mostly row upon row of crops and the levees that ringed their island, like a range of little mountains, protecting the land from being swamped by the water in the river channel.

Marty had never bothered to disguise his lack of interest in farming. His own father had amassed a good deal of land in the Sacramento-San Joaquin Delta, and made a lot of money from it, but Marty had little taste for rising at four, preferring to turn in, rather than out, at that hour. Ever since Rachel could remember, he had alternated weeks in Vegas with weeks at home.

The days in the farmhouse dragged on. Madeleine got no better.

Bored, and drained by it all, Rachel left her mom with Marty and went shopping in San Francisco. A few days later, she woke up aching and hot with fever. "Just a virus, or something," she told Marty.

Three weeks later her mother, having caught Rachel's virus, followed by that stealthy assassin, pneumonia, was dead.

Why did I have to go shopping? What did I think I needed?

Brittle and ashen as a cutout parchment doll, Rachel began taking Madeleine's codeine to help her sleep.

Marty, always a heavy drinker, but never a drunk, seemed to forget how to stop. In the dim, joyless evenings, he would sleep wherever he fell. Grateful that he hadn't gone back to the casinos, Rachel didn't scold him.

One hot August morning over breakfast, she announced she was packing for school. "We have to go on with…." She stuttered to a stop.

Marty was still as stone.

"Are you ill?" she asked.

The silence rattled like a dried gourd. He stared at the plate of eggs he had barely touched. His eyes were lumps of coal in the ruined ashes of his face. His mouth opened, but he couldn't seem to speak.

Her head filled with cold air.

Finally, "You can't go back to school." The words had been torn from him like a dry bandage from a terrible wound. "There's no money. It's gone…. The whole wretched farm. Everything."

Chapter Five

The parking lot at the poker club was jammed with cars. Rachel parked, wondering why she had agreed to meet her father there. She should have insisted on somewhere else.

Marty rose from a red-vinyl booth when she entered. It was from him Rachel had gotten her almost black hair, her high cheekbones.

She winced a little at his appearance. His thick hair was now white, there were smudges under his eyes, and his clothes looked like ten-year-old Kmart specials. But when his arms closed around her she almost felt like a child again. Unexpected burning pricked at her eyelids. "Hi, Pop. Good to see you."

Marty lowered his head. "I wasn't sure you'd come."

She dropped her eyes. "Why?"

He jerked a finger at the surroundings. "I mean here, to the club."

"Well, the food usually stinks," she said, sitting down. "But I figured that if you got into a game, you'd stand me up anywhere else. At least I knew you'd *be* here."

"Haven't seen my little girl for what? Eight months? And the first thing she says is she thinks I'd stand her up?"

She leveled her eyes at him. "I don't think it, Pop. I know it."

"That was years ago."

"Three years. Almost exactly. I was in trouble. You told me you'd come."

He ducked his head and peered with great interest at the menu. "I know, okay. I know. But that game was…. I've never had another like it. I thought I was going to win enough to get the farm back. For you. It was for you."

She sighed, but said nothing. The fish they ordered was greasy and overdone. Rachel ate what she could and put her fork down.

Marty glanced at her. "Not like the channel cat we used to catch in the Two Forks, is it? Your mama didn't approve, of course. We had no business going fishing. You should have been studying. I should have been working." He grinned like a small boy. "But we all sure ate a lot of that fish."

The lamp that hung over the table made a rectangle of light between them. She watched him through it. "Nothing will ever be quite that good again."

He glanced down at the table, then back at her. "There's still plenty of time for you to hear the tortoise sing."

The statement tore a laugh from her. Her first-grade teacher had assigned animals for the kids to imitate. Rachel's was the tortoise. "I made such a fuss about that damn tortoise. I was so insulted. But you said—"

"—the tortoise is a wonderful creature, with a lovely voice," Marty finished her sentence, a long-missing twinkle beginning to kindle in his eyes. "When the moon is full and the night is warm and the tortoise has reached his goal, he lifts his head, closes his eyes, and sings."

"I believed you. Back then, I believed every word you said." The singing tortoise made her think of Jason's tie tack.

Marty's face had gone solemn. "You're doing okay now though, aren't you?"

"Well enough, I guess. Thanks to Grandpa."

Marty looked down, then at the wall. "Who would have thought that prissy Marvin Feinberg had built something as common and greasy as a parking garage. In LA, yet. Not in his beloved San Francisco."

"Well, if he hadn't, and if Mom hadn't left me enough to pay the back taxes, I'd still be living in that dreadful little room, flipping burgers for a living."

"But you're okay now?" Marty asked again as the waitress cleared the table.

Rachel folded her arms on the orange plastic place mat. Her water glass was fogged with vapor. She drew an X on it, then brusquely wiped it clean. "I'm not using, if that's what you mean."

Marty nodded and leaned back in the booth. "Good. I knew you weren't."

Her expression stiffened. "No, you didn't, Pop, or you wouldn't have asked. So, I'm okay in that way, but I do have a sort of weird problem."

Marty was watching her intently. "Like what?"

"The head of InterUrban was killed a couple days ago. The cops think it was an ordinary hit and run, some drunk who didn't stop. Maybe it was. But I think the car that did it is in my garage." She twisted her napkin into a rope. "It belongs to the water agency's fleet."

Marty's anxious blue eyes examined his daughter's face while she explained why she was so certain. Then his brows drew into a straight line. "You can't get mixed up in that. It's not your problem."

"I wasn't planning on getting mixed up in it. I was thinking of phoning in an anonymous tip. Like tonight. Whoever it is will be getting that car out of there real soon."

"But it would have to be one of the water people, wouldn't it? Your biggest customer. And the cops would come to the garage. They'd want to talk to you even if the tip was anonymous."

Circles of pink bloomed on her cheeks. "But how can I know and not tell anyone?"

"Listen to your old Dad on this, sweetie. Pretend you never saw it."

"I guess," she said slowly. The two words hung in the air.

"Damn right. You're getting along real well now."

She gave a small hiccup of laughter. "Compared to three years ago, things are fantastic."

His eyes skidded away toward the entrance to the poker room. "I was wondering...."

Abruptly she thought she knew why he had wanted to have dinner. "How much?"

"Just a couple hundred, Rachel. Even one hundred would help."

She ran her tongue along her bottom lip. "I don't have a couple hundred to spare. The liability insurance on the garage is due."

He looked away. "Okay, okay. I shouldn't have mentioned it."

She took her purse from the seat beside her. "I can do a hundred, but that's about it. She hesitated, annoyed at the tears clouding her vision, then counted out five twenties on the table.

The pathetic look in his eyes blurred her vision more. She handed him another twenty from her billfold. "That's for this sorry excuse of a meal."

She watched her father's forlorn smile flicker and go out. His face seemed more deeply etched, more haggard each time she saw him. He sometimes played cards for forty hours without sleep. How much longer could he go on this way?

Rising from the booth, Rachel straightened her clothes. "You're a sorry SOB, Pop, but I love you." She leaned over, kissed him on the cheek, and left.

By the time she got back to the garage, it was full dark.

Rachel made her rounds, locked up, and was heading for the elevator when someone began banging on one of the metal doors.

"The garage is closed," she shouted.

"I know, I know." She knew the voice: Hank. "Late again," he called. "I don't suppose you'd let me get my car out."

She made a face, but unlocked the door. He loomed before her, taller than she remembered, his shirt and hair purplish in the streetlight.

"I can't make a practice of this," she said. "The insurance, for one thing."

Something about his expression stopped her annoyance. "Okay, I guess I owe you something for not filing an assault and battery. I'll wait while you get your car."

He hung his head, and started up the ramp. "Thanks. I sure didn't want to call a cab."

"What are you doing working so late?" she called after him. "Don't you have another life?"

A van full of cleaning people had pulled up across the street in front of InterUrban headquarters by the time Hank's car appeared at the gate. She waited for him to pass, but he stopped, rolled down the window and called, "Got an idea."

She tried to see his face in the dim light, but all she could make out was the shock of straight blond hair swinging across his brow. "Oh?"

"You're right. I'm working too much. It's getting to where I'm just not running on all cylinders. And every night for the past four nights I've dreamt about going fishing."

"Good idea. Get some rest."

"Wouldn't have to go far." He fiddled with the steering wheel.

She waited, then bent down to look in the window. "You want to leave your car here overnight sometime? That would be okay."

"I thought maybe you might come along. You look like you're under a little strain yourself."

She straightened up slowly. Her hand wandered to her face. "It's real hard for me to get away. No one to look after things."

"Just a thought." The streetlight made a triangle on Hank's jaw. He put the car in gear.

Rachel listened to the tires squeal as the Mustang rounded the corner. A free-floating anxiety washed over her and she wished she hadn't told him about the blood on the Caddy's fender.

Chapter Six

The steel door had barely clanked into place after Hank's exit when a voice boomed from the other side, "Rachel! You here?"

She pushed the control to raise the door.

Built like a paperweight, close to the ground and formidable, Bruno Calabrese was pacing the sidewalk with his usual pent-up energy. He gave her a perfunctory kiss on the cheek. "Why you living like this when you could be an old man's trinket?"

Rachel rolled her eyes at him. "You're only fifty. What are you doing here? Don't tell me the water board meeting lasted this late."

"I tried to find you earlier, but you were gadding about."

"I still don't understand why you come to InterUrban meetings. They do city water. What do they have to do with farming?"

"No more than cats have to do with mice. If I don't watch out, one of these days I'll go out to irrigate and my pumps will be sucking air. They'd steal every last drop."

"Can't be that bad."

"Worse. Gotta keep an eye on the thieves. Little trick I learnt from your grandpa. And he would never forgive me if I didn't keep an eye on you, too."

Once her grandfather's protégé, Bruno had done everything Enrique Chavez had told him to do, right down to marrying ten square miles of the best farmland in the Central Valley. His wife died young and Bruno was still happily farming the land she left him.

It was because of Enrique, long dead by then, that Bruno had sent his own attorney to bail Rachel out of jail three years ago.

Bruno regarded her with a frown. "This really is a crazy way for a nice girl to live."

"It's not so bad. Come up and see what I've added."

"Holy Mary," he said when she opened the door to the apartment. "You got new bookshelves." He whistled. "And a thousand books."

"The books are old. But I finally got around to building the shelves. You into books, Bruno?"

"When have I got time to read? I gotta be up at four with the cantaloupes. Nice for you, though. Better you should be a teacher than a grease jockey."

He strode across the room, his stocky body rolling on the balls of his feet like a prizefighter, and examined the shelves. "Good job. But why would a woman want to use a hammer and saw?"

"Because she couldn't afford to hire it done." Rachel took a ceramic pot from a cabinet. "Coffee keeps me awake. You want some tea?"

"Sure."

As she ran water into the pot he said solemnly, "Why I am here, I got a proposition for you. Actually, I got two, but if you take the first, you don't need the second."

"Okay."

"I think, you and me, we oughta get married."

Rachel barely saved the pot from crashing to the floor and didn't turn her head to Bruno until she was sure the worst of the shock had faded from her face. Then she laughed lightly. "You been fooling around with a controlled substance?"

"Nope. I'm dead serious."

"But…." She pulled on the hem of her bright green tee shirt. "Why?" She finished weakly.

"Is that the only teapot you got?"

"It makes perfectly good tea."

"We oughta get married because your family's mostly gone, except for your Pa, bless his heart, but I bet dollars to doughnuts he's usually asking for help instead of givin' it."

Rachel lifted one shoulder and let it drop.

Bruno went on, "I got no wife, and you got no china."

"China? What does china have to do with anything?"

"You think china don't have to do with anything? It has everything to do with it. What are you doing standing there? Make the tea. I tell you a story." Bruno paced, waving his hands as he talked.

"I was eleven years old when my Mama shook me awake and told me to get dressed. That was in the old country, Italy. We got packs strapped to our backs, and we walk, all the way up the mountains, then down. Now me, I was always short, and I didn't have much muscle yet, and my pack, I didn't know what was in it, but it was damn heavy. Mama had food in hers and Papa had clothes and tools, so I figured mine had to be real valuable. Lira maybe. Silver, gold. Even when that pack rubbed blisters, I was proud they trusted me to carry it."

Rachel set water to boiling, listening intently, partly because she'd never heard this story, partly it kept her face busy lest the shock still show.

"We go clear over the mountains to Genoa and get on a ship. I was still carrying that pack around every day because we didn't have anything grand, like a cabin. We were on that ship a lot of days, and then more days on a train. Finally, Papa said we were in California and this was home. That was okay by me. I was plenty tired of carrying that pack. That night I found out what was in it."

Rachel handed Bruno a mug of tea and he looked into it as if reading the leaves.

"That was just about the biggest little bombshell of my life," he mused.

"What was in it?"

"My grandmama's china. Not lira, not silver, not gold, not even food. China."

"You're joking! They made you carry *dishes* halfway around the world?"

"That's what I thought. But I was a kid. I was wrong. That china was just as important as food and clothes, maybe more important than lira."

Rachel stared at him. "Excuse me! I don't think so. I've never known anyone who couldn't eat off a paper plate."

"That china was all we had of our old home, our past. What I carried in that pack was tradition. It's why I'm a farmer. Old Enrique, he understood that. His own father, his grandfather—farmers, like mine. He must be spinning in his grave to think you been thrown off his land. Come back. If you can't go to his farm, come to mine."

Looking at the cup, not at her, he ran his finger around the edge, then held it up. "This cup, it's heavy, made of mud. You got no china."

Rachel blinked. For a moment, no words came. She owed him too much to be flippant. She couldn't tell him she felt no loss of tradition, that for that matter, her mother had come from a Jewish family in San Francisco.

But he's a good-hearted, decent guy. He knows me. Even the worst of me. I'd be taken care of. I'd be rich.

She peered over the rim of her mug and smiled gently. "Let me think about it."

"Sure. You think on it."

Bruno drank his tea and changed the subject to his favorite complaint, environmentalists. "We give them land for wetlands. We give them water. What more do they want? My arm? My leg? No, they want to put us out of business."

He peered at her and stopped. "Rachel, sweetie, you look tired."

"I am. It hasn't been a terrific day. I saw Pop. He looks awful. He hit me up for some money."

"Son of a gun. Marty was a good kid. But your grandpa, he spoiled him. Me, I never had no kids. Maybe I woulda done the same. But it's a blessing Enrique is not alive to see him now."

"Pop never got over Mama."

"Fine woman. You are like her, I think."

"You wouldn't believe how wrong you are." She was surprised to hear herself blurt: "You know Jason Karl was killed?

Bruno nodded. "Hit and run. Dirty coward. Jason and me, we weren't friends—" He frowned at her. "That's got nothing to do with the agency's account with you, does it?"

"I think the car that ran over him is parked right here." She pointed at the floor.

"Rachel baby, you're not in any trouble, are you?"

"No, no. I'm fine. It's just that it seems like the right thing would be to call the police, but Pop made me swear I wouldn't."

"At least Marty still has some brains left. You stay out of it. None of your business. You want I should have Aaron call you and explain why you don't want to get mixed up in something like that? You want to hear about all the do-gooders who got their noses whacked off by cops?" Aaron Reiner had been her attorney.

"No," she murmured. "I don't need to talk to Aaron. You're right."

"Good. Now I got this proposition for you."

Rachel squeezed her eyes shut. "I know."

"Not that one," Bruno cut in. "This is for while you're making up your mind on the other. I got some money I want to put into this God-forsaken flophouse for cars. Partners. We could expand. Do some towing. Triple-A maybe."

Rachel ran her hand through her hair. Her forehead was damp. She needed a shower. "I don't know."

"You don't know? Piece of cake."

She rested her head in her hand. "Maybe. I just don't know."

"Rachel, the other, take your time, I'm not gonna pressure you. But this is a walk in the park. Good for you, good for me."

She closed her eyes and rocked back and forth. "Can you give me some time? I'm too tired to think."

"What's to think? Just say yes."

Something surged inside her: "Bruno, you're a dear, kind, wonderful guy. I owe you my life. And I love you. But I don't think we should get married, and I like my business as it is."

"Sorry, kid, I shoulda known better. You had a bad day. What can I say? I'm a dumb Dago. My wife, that's what she used to say. Take your time. Think about it."

Chapter Seven

By the time Bruno left, Rachel wanted nothing so much as to put her head down on the counter and sleep. But in bed, sleep did not come. Her arms, legs, head, felt made of lead. She was almost too weary to turn over, her eyes burned with fatigue.

Insomnia was something new. Even when she had plummeted into despair that night she was in jail—before Bruno made her bail—she had slept.

A little after midnight, she got up. With Clancy blinking at her from the arm of the sofa, she fixed some warm milk, moving about in the dark like a burglar in her own home for fear that light would wake her more.

The air in the apartment seemed thin and dead. She opened a window. The night had not cooled much. Maybe it would help to go outside, just for a few minutes. She threw on a tee shirt and jeans, took the elevator down, and slumped her disheveled body onto the small white bench in the narrow patch of green in front of the garage.

Magnolia trees that graced the entrance to the water district headquarters across the street had shed their blooms and the carpet of petals along the sidewalk looked like the aftermath of a ticker-tape parade. Lights in the offices were going out one at a time. The cleaning people finishing up, Rachel decided.

She leaned back and turned her face to the sky. The stars were barely visible in the haze above the city. It had been a night like this, the air swollen with unseasonable humidity, when she had nearly run that family off the road in Oakland.

Someone touched her arm. Rachel flinched away, opened her eyes.

"Honey? What you doin' here?" A woman wearing glasses, a black woman, was towering over her. "You're the gal from the garage, aren't you. Can't sleep here. Ain't safe."

Rachel shrugged off the hand. "I'm okay." Then, realizing where she was, she bolted upright on the bench and looked about. "Really, I'm fine. Sorry. You a cop?"

A deep laugh bubbled up from somewhere in the woman's mid-section. "Don't I wish! I just run the cleaning crew, honey." She cocked her chin at the van parked across the street. *Merry Maids* was written in script across the side. "We're not real merry, and we sure ain't maids, but we do a bang-up job of cleaning offices." She examined Rachel's face. "You don't look real good, honey."

"Just tired, really."

"Tell you what. I could use me a sit-down, and the rest of them aren't quite through over here. Why don't you just scoot yourself over a little?"

Rachel slid to the side. "I don't usually sleep on the street."

"Don't guess you do." The woman relaxed onto the bench, stretching her legs out and crossing her ankles. "How come you doing that tonight?"

"I was too tired to sleep."

The woman nodded. "I know how that is. 'Specially when we got something big on our mind."

"I don't—" Rachel shook her head sharply. Then, in the way that even the most private people sometimes confide in strangers, she said, "I guess you're right."

"Of course I'm right," the woman said lazily. She leaned her head back and the eyes behind the glasses closed.

Rachel examined her thumbnail. "You wouldn't believe it."

The woman chuckled dryly. "There's damn little I ain't seen or at least heard."

Rachel drew in a breath, paused, let it out. "A guy I sort of know was killed, maybe on purpose." A car passed, its lights making the black street look watery.

When Rachel described the tie tack, the tortoise and why she was certain it was Jason's, a low whistle came from the sprawled-out form next to her.

"You telling me that water company over there—that place where I scrub toilets and empty trash—has got itself a murderer in its midst?" The woman turned her head, purplish streetlight glinting from her glasses, but she didn't sit up.

"I guess that has to be one possibility."

"Damn rhinoceros-size possibility, if you ask me. Horn and all." The woman turned and looked Rachel in the eye. "Well, honey, it seems like you got to do something. You got to go to the cops."

Rachel rubbed her fingertips across her forehead. "If I do that, I could be buying myself a major stack of trouble."

"How so?"

Rachel knotted her hands and dropped them to her lap. "I'd rather not say."

"Mmmm," the woman nodded, sagely, then asked calmly, "You a criminal or something, yourself?"

"Of course not," Rachel sputtered.

"Then maybe your reasons are a little bit small."

Rachel studied the steel arm of the bench. "Look, I do have reasons, honest-to-God big reasons why I can't go to the cops."

"Like what?"

"Like for one thing, I don't trust them, and they wouldn't trust me."

"Why not?"

Rachel gazed at the pinkish-purple haze that passed for sky in the streetlight and smog. "I'm an alcoholic and an addict," she began. "I've been sober and clean for three years and two days and," she looked at her watch, "about twenty hours. My mother died and my father bet the farm—literally—in Vegas, and lost it. I started taking some of my mom's codeine. When that was gone, I had to drink. A lot." She drew a ragged breath.

"But being hung over and strung out all the time wasn't exactly great, so one night, I got me a noseful of some really terrific stuff. I wondered where it had been all my life. Here was the ultimate answer: Drink till you fall down, then snort a little coke or crystal and, wow, you're ready to go again. And you make the nicest friends."

A knowing chuckle came from the woman next to her. "Oh, yeah. Got some of those nice folks in my neighborhood."

Rachel plunged on. "I guess I was lucky. I got arrested by some mean-minded cops. I had run a father and his two little kids into a ditch on the freeway. Thank God it only shook them up and made some bruises." Rachel was staring at a point in mid-air. "But the father had a cell phone and my license number.

"I only had a blood alcohol content of point-one-six when the cops pulled me over. I was barely beginning to feel good. But I had five ounces of crystal on the floor of the back seat. After all, if you drink as much as I did, you need a lot of speed to wake you up. They thought I was a dealer. That was enough to get me free room and board at County."

The silence drew out like a spider's silk thread.

Rachel cleared her throat and went on. "An old family friend hired a wheeler-dealer attorney who got me off on a technicality. It seems that I was so drunk I had not understood my Miranda rights." The drizzle of tears she'd been holding back escaped, leaving a wet path down her cheek.

The woman beside her barely stirred as she spun out the rest of the story. When she finished, Rachel wondered if her companion was asleep.

But after a moment, "That's a reason, all right," the black woman said laconically. "But it ain't good enough. Unless the cops are still wanting you for something."

"No, it's over now, but they don't forget. You ever take a look at some of the gorillas they call cops at Rampart? Would you trust them?"

The woman raised her chin. "I guess I would."

"Why?"

"I'm just putting in time evenings with the Maids, waiting till my number comes up for the Academy."

"The Police Academy?"

The black woman nodded solemnly. "When I was a kid, I never owned a doll. Not one diaper-wetter, not one Barbie. Nope. My brother Marcus and I played cops and robbers. He was older and bigger, so most of the time he made me be the robber. He never let me have the hat or the holster or the badge. He went to the Academy soon as he turned twenty-one. Now I plan to get me a badge of my very own. I know some cops are thugs, but most are decent like Marcus. And you got to ask yourself, what if someone killed you and the one person who knew it wouldn't say anything?"

Rachel had been twisting the hem of her tee shirt. She gazed at the wrinkled fabric in her fingers, then dropped it. "Maybe it was just a genuine hit and run. What if the person who was driving didn't mean to kill him and is just too scared to say anything?"

"I guess that's possible. But you got no call to protect such a one." The woman glanced across the street. Six or eight people were milling about the sidewalk. A boy was crossing the street toward them. "They're done. They're waiting on me. Got to go." She heaved herself off the bench.

The boy, when he arrived, announced happily, "All done! Done. Done."

Rachel peered at a face as round as a doughnut, the eye sockets narrow, the brows close above them. Chinese, she thought. Chinatown was only a few blocks away.

"This here is Peter," the woman said.

"Nice to meet you, Peter. I'm Rachel."

Peter's head bobbed up and down energetically. A smile all but split his jaw from his face. "Pleased. Pleased."

"You go on back. I'll be right there," the black woman told him. "Look both ways," she called after him. "There's cars all night long in this city."

She turned back to Rachel. "They're re-tards. Sweetest people in the world. Today they call them 'special people' or '*de*-velopmentally disadvantaged,' or some such high-sounding words. But they don't mind the word retard. They don't understand the other words. It's just so much noise in their ears. They know they're different. They're simple in a good sort of way. They don't keep trying to pretend they're something they're not, like the rest of us do."

"They clean offices?"

"Sure do. The ones the Community Foundation decides are ready. Good workers, every single one. They love earning their own money."

Rachel gave her a weak smile. "Well, thanks for listening—I don't think I caught your name."

"Don't think I threw it." The woman chuckled. "Friends call me Goldie, it's okay by me."

For the first time in many hours, Rachel's mouth made a real smile.

Chapter Eight

Rachel snapped wide awake and cranky with the first rays of the next morning's sun. "Three hours sleep is worse than nothing," she grumbled to herself.

She kicked off the covers and padded to the kitchen in bare feet only to find the can of Folgers empty. Exasperated, she flung it into the trash and opened another. The jagged lid caught her right thumb, and her elbow hit the newly opened can, spilling the coffee to the floor. She banged her fist on the countertop, which made the blood bubble up in the cut on her thumb.

Gritting her teeth, she went through the motions again. The wait for the aging Mr. Coffee to brew seemed interminable.

She took a sip, then set the mug on the counter and studied it. "China," she muttered. "I like pottery." Unsure whether she meant "China" literally or figuratively, as Bruno had described it, she took another sip of coffee, leaned back, propped her bare feet up on the counter, and stared blankly at the place where the wall met the ceiling. *You're losing it. Lucky someone decent found you on that bench.*

Suddenly, her weary body shot past the merely awake state and revved up with tension. She sat for a while drumming her fingers on the arms of the barstool, then decided that running might help.

Five minutes later, in shorts, tee shirt, and a bright purple sweat band, she shoved a bagel into the toaster, fidgeted until it popped up, then jammed it between her teeth and headed for the door. She was still licking the crumbs away when she reached the ground level.

A light was on in the booth. Inside, Lonnie was slumped over the desk. Normally, he opened the garage for her at seven.

Swallowing the urge to slap him senseless, Rachel opened the booth door and gently shook his shoulder. "What are you doing here at this hour?" She was answered by a gurgling snore. "Lonnie! Wake up." She shook him harder.

"Whaa—!" He came awake, eyes wide with surprise. Pallid cheeks shone through a day's growth of beard.

"Look," she said, taking both his hands in her own and peering into his blank, foggy eyes. "I know what you're doing and you have to stop. Like now. This minute."

He stared at her a moment. "No, you're wrong."

"Lonnie, I've been there. I know the signs."

He shook his head. "Honest to God, Rachel. I just couldn't sleep last night."

"Neither could I, but it wasn't from using and boozing."

He glanced away from her, ran long, narrow fingers through hair that stuck up every which way. "How come you're always hounding me?"

Rachel had gone to high school with him. They'd been from two different worlds, had not known each other well. But four years ago, when she had plumbed the depths of her problems, he had recognized the signs and dragged her to AA. When he was struggling back from his own fall off the wagon, she had given him a job.

"I'm your conscience. I'm supposed to hound you." She knew that wasn't true. Hassling only makes a drunk or an addict withdraw further or get angrier.

Lonnie lifted eyes filled with sincerity; oddly, they now seemed clear and sharp. "Look—I swear to you—I've been feeling sort of rotten, sure. The damn finance company repossessed my car.... Okay, I admit I've been wanting some stuff real bad. But I haven't done it. Really."

"Your car? When?"

"Last week."

"Then how have you been getting around?"

"Burt loaned me one of his." Burt was a thin, totally bald man who chewed an entire box of toothpicks during every AA meeting.

"How much do you owe on the car? I'll advance you the money."

Lonnie shook his head. "No, really, I can handle it. Sorry if I've been a jerk lately."

She leaned both hands on the desk. "Lonnie, I care about you."

"I know, I know. If it weren't for you, I'd still be lying in the gutter where you found me."

He had helped her begin her own recovery from booze, then two weeks after she had opened the garage, she found him sprawled unconscious in a corner, his nose scarlet and dripping, his breath reeking of cheap wine. Rachel had put him in her car and driven him to AA.

She crossed her arms over her chest, hoping he was telling the truth now, but not believing it. "So what can I do?"

He gave her a steady gaze. "You can believe me when I tell you I'm clean."

She dropped her eyes. "Okay. If I'm mistaken, I apologize."

He noted the scuffed pair of Reeboks on her feet and mustered a thin grin. "Now go on and run. You haven't been exactly laid back lately, yourself. I'll open up."

⌒⌒⌒

The dry bed of the Los Angeles River was not the best place to run but it was nearby, fairly flat and safe from traffic. As Rachel ran, the snarled string of thoughts in her head began to unkink and fade. A knot of people peered at her from the rim of what had been the river. There were, she knew, several settlements of homeless folk along the railroad tracks and beneath the freeway underpass.

There, but for the grace of AA and Bruno.... She was beginning to sweat. She dropped her pace to a walk for a few dozen yards, then began a slow jog. Ahead, a couple of boys were shoving each other about. She slowed, but they scrambled out of sight. She was picking up her pace again when something hit the center of her back with the force of a cannonball. Gravel bit into knees and elbows as she hit the ground.

Someone grunted, grabbed her arm and jabbed a hand into the pocket of her shorts.

Chapter Nine

"Stand up. Slowly." The voice was that of a calm and confident woman. Rachel thought it was speaking to her and tried to rise.

The hand withdrew from her pocket.

"Move away from her. Put your hands on top of your head."

"What's that, a toy gun?" a young male voice sneered.

"No. It's small, but believe me, it's deadly."

Rachel heard the sound of feet running, but they didn't belong to her assailant. "Bullshit!" The boy spat. "That fucking thing is for babies," he jeered, but he was moving off and didn't look back.

Hands were gently moving over Rachel's legs and arms. "You okay?"

Gingerly, Rachel sat up. "Just knocked the breath out of me, I guess."

The woman sat back on her knees. Long black hair hung about fragile features that would have suited a dark-eyed Dresden doll.

Rachel swayed slightly.

The woman steadied her. "Head still spinning?"

Rachel nodded. "I think I hit it on something."

"You don't have a weapon? A can of mace? Nothing?"

"Not exactly bright, is it?" Rachel managed a half smile. "I knew the homeless were here, but they're harmless enough." Wanting to stand, but not sure she could manage it, she put her arms about her knees and hugged them to her.

"Your legs got scraped up. This is not exactly a great place to jog."

The woman was wearing what looked like Sports Chalet's latest in running apparel. The shoes alone would cost well over a hundred dollars. She read Rachel's look. "But I am armed."

She bent over to slip the small gun into the leg warmer on her right ankle. "And I have a reason for running here. It reminds me daily of what has been done to this state's rivers." A frown sharpened her delicate features.

She straightened and held out her hand. "Alexandra Miller. With Protectors of the Earth."

"Rachel Chavez. I own the Park-Rite garage."

"Across from InterUrban? Don't you love the rest of their name, *Water Authority*. Nice touch. Makes it sounds like a God-given right."

Rachel struggled to her feet, wincing at a sharp pain in her ankle.

"You okay to walk?"

"I guess. Haven't been up for two hours yet but I can tell you I'd like to cancel this day and cut to tomorrow. Thanks. I sure appreciate what you did." Rachel turned to hobble back the way she had come.

Alexandra matched Rachel's limping pace. "My past few days have been awful too. Terrible, the way we live these days, all tied up in knots."

"I can't think of any good alternatives." It seemed to Rachel that every halting step she took carried her further into a cave.

Alexandra said, "My grandmother knew some alternatives. She was a full-blooded Mojave."

A headache broke through the fog in Rachel's brain. "Communing with nature is nice, but I have to make a living." She wished the woman would go away. She didn't want to make inane conversation.

"Don't we all." Alexandra glanced at Rachel. "You don't look so good. Are you dizzy again? Maybe you've got a concussion. You should sit down."

Rachel grimaced. "No, no. My ankle hurts a little, but I'm fine."

Alexandra looked up at the skyscrapers. "We were never meant to live this way." She halted, frowned, eyes seeming to see something else.

Rachel tried putting weight on her injured ankle and made a face at the pain.

"Have you ever flown?" Alexandra asked. "I mean in a small plane."

More interested in her ankle than anything else, Rachel grunted, "Nope. Can't say I have."

"Suddenly you're lighter than air. It's wonderful. You come down a new person."

Rachel forced a polite smile. Maybe it was fun, but she didn't have time to spend aimlessly cruising about the sky. She couldn't remember the last time she'd had any fun. For some reason, she was suddenly close to tears.

They were nearing the garage. A car honked, and a hand waved from a green Mustang.

Alexandra pointed down the cross street. "My office is over there. If you're sure you're okay, I'll turn off here."

"I'm fine. Really." Rachel realized she was using the same words Lonnie had used earlier, and the same tone of voice.

Not wanting anyone to see her scraped up and looking like some derelict, Rachel went up the side stairs to her apartment, stripped and scrubbed herself in a warm shower, then dabbed at the lacerations on her arms and legs with a cotton ball and peroxide.

Freshly dressed, hair still damp and curling on her forehead, she got into the elevator to go down to work. Her hand hovered over the button marked C. Was the car with the dented fender still there? She pressed the button.

The garage was full. A lone latecomer was circling, looking for a space. Rachel walked along the bumpers, counting the spaces; she could see there were no empty slots, but the car could have been moved and another parked in its place. Her arms began to tingle as she approached space C-19. She hoped the Caddy would be gone. Then the matter would be out of her hands.

Afraid she might be seen as unduly interested in that particular car, she only slowed her pace as she approached. It was still there. She flicked her eyes toward the dented fender as she passed. Someone was coming toward her down the line of cars on the other side. Rachel pursed her lips, frowned, and turned back the way she had come as though she had forgotten something.

She had almost reached her office when a voice called out, "Dear girl, dear girl!" Irene, the woman who had tried to foist a tarot reading on her, was just outside the main entrance, waving her arms.

Rachel waved back and turned again toward her booth.

But Irene was not to be shrugged off. "Come, come, dear girl. Come out in the sun. It's bad for the eyes and the complexion, to say nothing of the heart, to be always shut up in such a gloomy place. Come. I must introduce you to someone."

Irene's companion was impeccably dressed in a suit the color of yellow pansies. A rather odd couple, Rachel thought. Looking down at her own faded blue tee shirt, dirty sneakers, and the knee of her jeans where the denim was wearing thin, she decided she would fit right in.

Unable to think of a polite alternative, she joined the two women on the sidewalk.

Irene took Rachel's arm and patted it, her eyes almost disappearing behind the round red cheeks. "This is Charlotte, dear girl."

Rachel nodded distractedly, realizing that Charlotte was one of the executives from the water authority to whom she had handed keys.

"A very important personage, I'll have you know," Irene was saying. "Chairman of the biggest board of directors in the state, and not a whit less. I have just done her horoscope and she has even greater things in her future."

Charlotte, Rachel saw, was not as young as she first thought. The hair was white, not blonde, and she was one of those women who were never quite as beautiful in youth as they became in older age.

"Yes, I think we've talked on the phone. Irene did your horoscope?" Rachel was unable to disguise her surprise.

"She did indeed. I'm not sure I'm a true believer, but I like to hedge my bets." Charlotte had the easy geniality of those born to public office. There was a suggestion of a wink from her clear, pale blue eyes as she nodded again to Rachel and departed.

Irene beamed. "Chairman of the board of directors. Imagine that, imagine that." She waddled off.

The rest of the day Rachel did what she hated most: bookkeeping. She wished she were more orderly and often tried to make up for weeks of tossing invoices and receipts into a cardboard box with a penance involving a day or two of intensive ledger posting. She was stunned to see it was already dusk by the time she finished. She had worked right through the dinner hour.

She was giving the ledger a final examination when a voice at her shoulder said, "So now you're fraternizing with the enemy."

Rachel jumped, startled. "Beg pardon?" Hank Sullivan's broad, pleasant face was grinning down at her. "How long have you been standing there?"

"Only half an hour."

"I don't believe it." She closed the ledger. "What do you mean, fraternizing with the enemy?"

"You were jogging this morning with Alexandra Miller."

She remembered the Mustang, the waving hand. "We hadn't been jogging together. She—" Rachel stopped. Why mention the mugging? "We just happened to meet. She seems nice."

Rachel swiveled the stool to face him, but he suddenly seemed too close. Standing, she turned her back to him, and put the ledger away. "So what's that got to do with some enemy?"

"Alexandra has made it her goal in life to bring down Inter-Urban. According to her, our one abiding desire is to rape and pillage Mother Nature."

"Seems a little dramatic, doesn't it? Raping, pillaging, enemies?"

"Maybe."

"Got to close up," Rachel said, moving toward the door of the booth, leaving Hank no choice but to step back.

His eyes seemed to laugh at her. "Then we're going to have some hot dogs and lemonade."

She stared at him. "Excuse me?"

"And maybe some cotton candy...."

She gave him a disconcerted glance and briskly began her closing ritual.

Hank followed her to the first gate. "You're working too hard."

"Now there's a seriously black pot calling a kettle dirty names."

"Both of us could use an evening off."

"But...." She tried to wave him away.

He grabbed the hand she was waving at him and looked straight into her face. "There's a carnival in the empty lot over on Sunset. You can decide whether we walk or drive, but *no* is not an option. You owe me."

"For what?"

"For not filing assault charges."

"But carnivals are for kids," she said. "I haven't been to one in years."

Hank gave her an amused look. "Way too long a lapse. You need to work on that."

Something in his voice reminded her of her father.

Chapter Ten

Colored lights flitted over faces of bikers, priests, Koreans, Nicaraguans, gawking four-year-olds, cranky infants, and gnarled seniors. Near the fence three teens labored at nonchalance. The smell of taffy apples and popcorn blended into something salty-sweet. A gawking toddler was trying to lick cotton candy from his cheek.

Rachel stopped to watch the chipped and faded merry-go-round horses glide by. "I didn't know carnivals came this far downtown," she said over her shoulder to Hank.

Turning when she got no response, she saw him loping toward her, his business suit seeming slightly out of place as he wedged his way between a nurse still in uniform and a probable hooker examining a tear in a fishnet stocking.

"What I have here are two tickets for the Ferris wheel," he announced.

"Oh, no. I don't do rides."

"They make you sick?"

"No."

"Then come on, it's good for the soul."

"My soul is fine as it is, thanks."

Hank caught her hand and looked into her face. "I know there's a little kid in there somewhere. She's way too busy being a grown-up."

Inexplicable anger welled inside her. Looking down, she extricated her hand. "I guess you prefer childish behavior."

He folded his arms across his chest. "Life's a little grim without a little of it."

"So now my life is grim." She turned, intending to stalk off, but there were too many people to walk quickly. He followed in awkward silence.

A woman wearing leather and chrome knocked over a Coke bottle with a rubber ball and gleefully clapped her hands when she won a pint-size stuffed panda.

Rachel stopped. The stream of fun-seekers made its way around them. She tilted her chin at Hank. "Okay. Okay. I'm sorry."

Hank's puzzled look faded to an uncertain grin.

"I'm out of sorts. I was rude. I apologize. Let's do the Ferris wheel."

He followed her to the gate and they watched the huge wheel bring a seat to the platform.

When the attendant raised the bar, Rachel hesitated. "I haven't been on one of those things since I was a kid. I threw up."

"I thought you said they didn't make you sick."

"I forgot," she said, but got in anyway.

He settled onto the seat beside her. "If it happens, promise you'll lean over the side. This is a new suit."

She laughed. "Count on it."

Cool air rushed softly across her face as the wheel slung them slowly skyward. It halted, teetering at the top. Feeling somehow vulnerable, she drew her shoulders up. Peering over the rooftops, she was surprised to see all the way to the garage. "I think I can see the lights in my apartment."

"Where?"

The seat swung dizzily as she leaned forward to point. Her hand brushed his as she grabbed the cross bar.

"It won't fall," he said.

The wheel began its downward slide.

"What makes you so sure?" she shouted.

"Odds are against it." he touched the back of her shoulder, then put both hands in front of him on the bar.

When they bounced to a final stop at the bottom Rachel declared, "I'm starving,"

He offered his hand to steady her exit from the seat. "I thought Ferris wheels made you throw up."

She took it. "Not any more, I guess. I want a hot dog."

They doused their buns with everything available, although in the dim light at the side of the concession stand they were hard-pressed to identify the contents of the condiment bowls.

Hank downed his in four bites.

"Your eyes are watering," Rachel said, handing him her cup of lemonade.

"Jalapeños." He wheezed and drank some lemonade. "So what's next?"

"A teddy bear. Or a panda will do."

He spent eight dollars missing the row of dingy mechanical ducks at the next game booth.

He handed her the gun. "You try. I think it's rigged to miss."

She nodded solemnly and shot down five ducks before pausing.

Hank whistled.

"My father taught me," she said when the man handed her a small brown bear.

"A dead-eye with a rifle and a trigger-happy knee. Not your average *femme fatale*." He laid an arm lightly on her shoulder. Laughing and from time to time pointing at some oddity, they toured the remaining tents and booths.

An old woman with stringy black hair thrust a long-stemmed rose into Hank's hand. *"Para la señorita, señor,"* she lisped, her mouth showing places where teeth should have been. "Take it," she said to Rachel. "You'll get precious few pretties when you're old." The woman bowed her head in studied supplication. Her scalp showed blue-white through the thinning hair.

Hank took the rose and shoved a five-dollar bill into the woman's gnarled hand.

When the woman departed Rachel said, "You paid her too much."

"She seemed so…pathetic."

"She's probably got fifty thousand dollars in the bank."

"You always believe the worst case scenario?"

"And I'm usually right."

Rachel caught sight of a clock behind a man hawking fresh-pulled taffy. "It's almost eleven and we've got nine blocks to walk," she said and quickened her pace.

Darting around a broad Mexican woman, Rachel almost knocked over a short, thin man with a cane at the woman's side. Hank had to jog to catch up.

When they reached the side door of the garage she already had the key in her hand. "Thanks. I'm glad you insisted," she murmured, more to the key than to Hank.

"Me, too."

"Go get your car. I'll open the gate."

He pulled up to the exit and lowered the window. "I trust you'll give it a good home. Be careful of the thorns. It bites." He thrust the rose at her and was gone.

The flower, its ruby red made black by the streetlights, was beginning to droop. Rachel told herself she should just toss it out. But in her apartment she filled an empty Coke bottle with water and slid the stem into it.

⌐⌐⌐

By morning, the rose had lifted its head. She carried it down to the glass booth with her.

Lonnie wasn't there. She called, his name echoing through the garage. No response.

Thinking he might have overslept, she phoned his home, and when his machine answered, shouted into the mouthpiece, hoping to wake him up, until the final beep cut her off.

Rachel performed the opening chores herself. How could she have been so gullible? No one knew better than she the intricate patterns of the addict's lies and denials.

Of course Lonnie was using again. She should have packed him off to some inpatient program. But she hadn't wanted to deal with it. So she had played the game, listened to his lies. She was as angry with herself as she was with him.

When the flurry of noon traffic had subsided, Rachel headed for her apartment to grab a sandwich. Gazing dully at the elevator's panel of buttons, it occurred to her that she was playing the same sort of game with that damn car, knowing full well that it was responsible for Jason's death and doing nothing.

The decision came like a pinball finally slipping into the slot it has been avoiding: She would call the cops now. Right now. What harm could there be in an anonymous phone call? Why had she let her father and Bruno frighten her about it?

She got off the elevator at level C and walked briskly toward the water agency's row of cars. She hadn't taken more than a dozen steps when she saw the gaping space, like a missing tooth, where the DeVille had been.

Chapter Eleven

The helicopter arrived mid-afternoon with a package for the water quality lab. Rachel locked up her little office, hoisted the box to her shoulder, and crossed the street to the InterUrban Headquarters, thinking she hadn't hired Lonnie as a favor to him. She definitely needed another pair of hands and feet.

Still, she had been curious about the laboratory, had wondered just how much science there could be in a glass of clear water. So here was her chance to see it.

When she opened the door to the lab, a shaft of sunlight was slanting through the windows and bouncing across row upon row of shiny steel cabinets. She stepped inside, taking in computerized equipment that seemed to belong more to science fiction than to something as ordinary as water.

A man strolled toward Rachel, hands in pockets, the broad shoulders of a weightlifter straining at the seams of his immaculate lab coat. He gave her a wide, well-practiced smile, stuck out his hand and announced his name like an emcee introducing an entertainment act. "Harry Hunsinger. What can I do for you?"

"Just making a delivery." She had seen him before. He drove a ruby-colored Maserati. She'd figured he must make pretty good money to afford it and wondered why anyone needed a car that went two hundred miles an hour.

"Hey, that looks too heavy for a lady." He reached for the box, bringing his body close enough for her nose to fill with the scent of a designer cologne. The face that looked down on her was the sort that seemed calculated to make a teenager swoon.

Rachel slid the box to a counter, thinking he probably had great abs, probably took off work to go surfing.

He stepped toward her again. "Why have they got you delivering packages? Where's the guy who usually brings this stuff?"

Rachel leaned away. "He's sick."

"Ah," he sighed as if she had told him the secret of the universe. A look passed over his handsome face and was gone. "But I thought the garage ran the deliveries."

"I do. I own the garage."

"That right?" Harry Hunsinger leveled an intent gaze on her. It didn't seem to go with the rest of him. "Mind telling him I need to see him when he gets back?"

"Sure. What about?"

"One of the boxes he brought over was damaged."

"I remember it. But it wasn't Lonnie's fault. The package arrived like that."

"I'm sure you're right. Say, since this is your first visit, how about a tour?"

"Thanks, but I—" Rachel wiped her hands on her jeans, feeling tacky and somewhat soiled in the pristine laboratory.

Harry's grin was almost like a rubbing together of hands in anticipation. "Biggest and best laboratory of its type anywhere. Come on," he said boyishly, flashing another glimpse of very white, very perfect teeth.

Rachel wondered what he had paid for an entire mouthful of caps. "I've only got five minutes."

He looked at his watch, clearly an expensive one. "Okay, we'll make it quick." Putting a hand at the small of her back, he guided her down the aisle between cabinets, pointing, pronouncing eight-syllable words, and sounding as though he did all the work single-handed.

"What's this used for?" Rachel asked when he began to wind down. She was pointing at the package she had delivered.

Harry picked it up, stared at it a moment, and frowned. "A special project." He set the box down, turned back and folded his arms. "Just a little something we're doing for someone else. We like to help out anyone, even competitors, if there's a water quality problem."

"Like what sort of problem?"

He shrugged. "This one's a trace element. By itself, it's not poisonous, but some of its compounds are toxic." He put his hand on her elbow and moved her toward the door. "Water is about the closest thing there is to a universal solvent. You could call it the world's best thief." He chuckled at his own joke. "Picks up a little of everything it touches."

"Thanks. I didn't know there was so much to water quality."

"Next time, we'll do the full Cook's tour—chromatograph, centrifuge, electron microscope, the works. Water's a hot topic. I get a lot of TV cameras in here." He preened as if about to face CNN and flashed another glorious smile.

So that was it. He was camera-ready. Rachel wondered what had become of all the owlish chemists with the thick glasses.

⌒⌒⌒

Andrew Greer set down his leather briefcase on the escalator long enough to poke at the cuff of his white shirt so he could see his watch. Gold-rimmed glasses gave his rosy, squarish face the look of a well-scrubbed, energetic scholar.

It was eight-oh-five. He'd left home at six-fifteen. He pulled the starched white cuff back down again. Other men at Inter-Urban wore striped, no-iron Oxford-cloth shirts. Every shirt in Andrew's closet was very white. And very starched.

His wife Jackie's deep brown eyes had narrowed slightly when he'd told her not to hold dinner, that he would be home late. They had already had all the arguments about his hours.

He examined the crowd milling in the foyer below the escalator. No matter how great his hurry, he always had the same thought when he entered headquarters: *If there are three black faces in these exalted halls, I don't see two of them. How'd you get here, black boy?*

The shiny steel ridges on the escalator began to flatten. Andrew picked up his briefcase, stepped off, turned right, straightened his shoulders, and strode toward his corner office.

He had not only managed to get himself into this lily white crowd, he had made his way up near the very tip of the pyramid. So what if he was a token? Had he sold out?

He could almost see his marching, demonstrating sister Polly's piercing eyes as she asked him that question every year at the Christmas family gathering. No. He always said no.

But lately Andrew wasn't so sure. He'd made it a habit to be agreeable. He called it courtesy, he called it good manners. But Polly probably would call it selling out.

Jason was a hard man to work for. He had destroyed careers as if it were a hobby. When Andrew became Director of Human Resources, he had made it a studied habit to ignore the casualties of Jason's games.

But now, in the power vacuum after Jason's death, Andrew would begin doing things differently. He would be less agreeable. He would make that clear to whoever was Jason's successor.

〜〜〜

All day, Rachel had studiously refused to think about the missing Cadillac. But the moment she had closed garage gate number four, thoughts swarmed into her head like a Marine platoon taking a stronghold. She would have to make up her mind what to do, and she would have to do it soon.

If she talked to the police now, there was only her word, no hard evidence. Still, was that a reason to do nothing? The other side of herself fought back: *What's so bad about doing nothing? You just happened to find something. Suppose you hadn't found it?* The battle ended in a draw. She flung herself onto the sofa and opened a book.

After reading the same page four times, she threw the book across the room, went to the chest of drawers in her bedroom and opened the old wooden cigar box where she kept what little jewelry she owned.

The tie tack lay in a corner of the box beside a string of wooden beads. The etched tortoise did not look likely to sing. It seemed to gaze at her accusingly.

Chapter Twelve

The next morning, Rachel got down to work early. As the old brass clock she kept in the booth edged toward six, a frown etched itself into her face.

Lonnie was always at work by six. He might be late returning from lunch or drag his feet while running deliveries and doing errands, but he knew she relied on him to open the garage. Something might have kept him away for one day without telephoning, but not two.

She opened the gates herself, and the drivers who came early to beat the rush hour began streaming in. At nine she decided to drive over to Lonnie's apartment. Maybe he just had the flu.

But he would have called in. No, he'd had a bad trip and crashed. She would have to find a good dry-out clinic and drag him to it.

With entrances controlled by key cards, the garage could practically run unattended during the day. She climbed into her old Honda, hoping the scene she anticipated with Lonnie would at least take her mind off Jason and the dented DeVille.

The apartment was the end unit in a bank of neat two-story stucco condos. Some relative paid the rent on the condition that Lonnie never darken the family's door.

Japanese pines and purple-leaf plums were arrayed in front of the white walls. Pots of geraniums stood near each entrance.

Rachel banged on Lonnie's door till her knuckles began to hurt, and a woman from the adjoining condo came out to see what was going on. She was short and plump with wisps of blond hair escaping from curlers, and small puffy blue eyes.

"Hey, cut the racket for God's sake. I work nights, y'know."

"I'm looking for Lonnie. Any idea where he is?"

"Ain't seen him since last...." The woman rolled her eyes toward her curlers. "Couple days ago," she said finally.

Rachel hammered on the door again.

"How long you gonna do that?"

Rachel threw up her hands in exasperation. "I really need to see him."

"Well, if he ain't there, he ain't there. Banging on that door ain't gonna make him be there."

"You have any other ideas?"

The woman narrowed her eyes. Rachel could see the pale hair on her cheeks. "You a friend of his?"

"He works for me."

The woman studied her for a moment, then the curlers bobbed as the round head nodded. "Can I see some ID?"

"All I have is a drivers license." Rachel flipped open her wallet.

The woman peered at it a moment and the plump shoulders shrugged. "He keeps a spare key in that pot." She pointed to the geranium. "Sometimes I water his plants for him. Go on in, see for yourself and quit the damn racket."

Rachel tipped the flowerpot. "Thanks."

"*In* the pot, not under it." The woman waddled back into her own apartment and pulled the door shut loudly behind her.

The soil was dry and the geranium roots lifted out easily. At the bottom of the pot was the key. Rachel wiped off the soil, carefully replaced the plant, and inserted the key in the lock.

The living room was furnished with beanbag chairs and strewn with empty soda cans. A half-eaten bag of pretzels had spilled on the red-and-black-striped carpet. Tightly closed blinds blocked most of the sunlight.

The door swung shut behind her and the room went dim.

"Lonnie? Are you home? It's me, Rachel."

She stepped carefully over the soda cans. The kitchen was just beyond the living room. Dirty dishes were jumbled every which way in the sink. At the edge of the counter, a dainty, lidless porcelain teapot looked self-conscious among the lidless canisters and dirty glasses. Without thinking, Rachel picked it up to move it a safer place.

Inside was a Ziploc bag.

Her shoulders sagged. She blew a stream of air between her lips and held the bag up to the light. The contents looked like sugar, but there was sugar in one of the canisters. She opened the bag and sniffed, couldn't identify the odor, sealed it again and, knowing what it had to be, stuffed it into her purse.

Lonnie was probably passed out somewhere. She herself had once slept forty-seven hours after a three-day binge. She'd have to get him on his feet and to a clinic. Maybe the rent-paying relative could be coerced into footing the bill.

From the living room, she followed a narrow hall past a bathroom to a closed door. She knocked on it and called out. No response. She turned the knob. The door opened easily.

He lay like a bundle of dirty laundry on the bed, his face turned away toward a window darkened by a heavy shade. A pale blue carpet had pulled loose from its tacks and was curling in from the wall.

"Lonnie," she called loudly, feeling remotely embarrassed. Ambling into a man's bedroom and shaking him awake seemed a little crude.

This was a job for his AA sponsor, but she didn't know the guy's phone number. She would have to do it herself.

"Lonnie!" she called again. A tiny fear licked at her insides. He didn't stir.

She crossed the blue carpet. His elbow stuck out toward her. A faint odor of garlic rose from the sheets. She shook his arm.

The flesh was cold, the arm rigid.

Rachel's stomach pitched. "Oh, God," she breathed. If only she had come sooner. She moved her hand to his shoulder. His head tilted stiffly toward her. There was no need to search for a pulse.

Hand covering her mouth, she slowly backed away as though fearful of disturbing him. The doorway was right behind her. If she could get to that, she thought stupidly, she would be okay.

When she reached the door, she closed it carefully and quietly behind her, as if once she could no longer see the body, it would cease to be there.

The world began a slow spin. She staggered down the hall, breath coming in small, ragged puffs.

In the kitchen, she took the receiver from the wall phone and dialed nine-one-one.

There was little reason to wait for the medics. Nothing she could do would help.

She didn't bother to lock the door of the condo. Forcing limbs that seemed made of lead to move, Rachel climbed into her car.

She had just entered the Pasadena Freeway when a red light began flashing behind her. Heart racing irrationally, she hit the brake and guided the car to the shoulder. Had she been speeding? She wasn't sure. She reached for her purse, opened it and stared, mouth open.

The Ziploc bag was crammed between her wallet and sunglasses.

She drew out the wallet, rolled down the window, and tried to smile as the cop approached.

He was built like a rocket and looked about seven feet tall.

Hand trembling, she held out her license. "What did I do, officer?"

He bent nearly double to look in the window, eyes darting about the car's interior. "Mind getting out of the car, ma'am?" The voice was low, but nothing about it was friendly.

"Why?" The scene was all too familiar, all too much like another. "Was I speeding?" The words had a plaintive squeak. She cleared her throat. "Officer?" The throat-clearing hadn't helped.

He backed a step or two from the car, hand hovering over his holstered gun. "Just do as I say, ma'am. Keep your hands in sight. Open the door slowly and get out."

Rachel's sweaty fingers could hardly work the latch. Still clutching her handbag, she managed to get her feet on the ground and body into a standing position.

The cop's eyes swept her up and down, looking, she knew, for the hint of a hidden weapon.

Her tongue moved across dry lips. "What's going on?"

He moved slightly behind her and took her upper arm in a light clasp that she knew could instantly tighten like a vice.

"Mind coming with me?"

In lock step, they moved toward the squad car. When they reached the passenger side he said, "Please hand me your purse. Slowly. Just hand it to me." The letters on the silver tag on the breast-pocket of his blue shirt spelled HAMILTON.

"But why? What have I done?" Her arms went weak and she almost dropped the purse as she handed it over.

So much for her new start in life. The lush plants along the freeway looked bright and green, as though they were part of some other, happier scene.

"Lay your hands across the hood and keep them there. You can lean on your elbows if you like."

He walked to the driver's side of the squad car, set the purse, unopened, on the front seat, then moved sideways, to her car, which he circled slowly, his eyes leaving her only long enough to dart quick glances into the interior.

"Mind if I look inside?" he shouted. Somewhere in a passing cars a boom box was going full blast.

Refusing would only convince him she was guilty of something. He could easily haul her into the station where legal technicalities would be dealt with and they would search anyway.

Despising the awful feeling of helplessness that overwhelmed her, she drew herself up and with what she hoped was some dignity said, "Suit yourself."

He opened the Honda's door, all but his feet disappearing as he searched beneath the seats.

"The glove compartment is open," she called, praying for a way to distract him from searching her purse. "The lever for the trunk is on the floor next to the driver's seat."

He extracted his tall frame from the Honda, nodded, bent over again and popped the trunk lid, keeping his eyes on her until he reached the back of the car.

Rachel tried to remember what was in there. Not much, she thought, beyond jumper cables, an old umbrella, a box of Band-Aids, and a tire iron.

A driver, obviously speeding, whizzed past on the freeway, jammed on his brakes, and slowed to an innocent crawl.

Officer Hamilton removed the spare tire, examined it, went back to rummaging in the trunk, and emerged with the device she used to open car doors. Holding this out, his eyebrows aiming for his hairline, he strode toward her, looking like Wyatt Earp closing in on Billy the Kid.

She explained what the device was and why it was in her trunk.

He returned to the squad car and reached inside.

Rachel almost stopped breathing. Now he would bring out the purse.

His hand emerged holding instead the receiver of a phone.

She wilted with a relief she knew could be only temporary.

He turned slightly away from her. His words were lost to the traffic noise.

After a long wait, he spoke into the receiver again, then put it back into the squad car and brought out her purse.

A silent scream rose in her throat as she struggled to keep her face impassive. Her knowledge of the law was limited to television shows and one personal incident so ghastly she remembered almost nothing about it.

She decided to ask him for a search warrant, which might only prolong things, but at least she would have more time to think.

Could he claim probable cause and open the handbag anyway? If so, she would be taken to the station and life as she knew it, tenuous as it was, would be over.

They might even charge her with selling Lonnie the drugs that had killed him. Certainly they wouldn't believe she didn't know what was in that packet in her purse.

Officer Hamilton handed her the purse.

She gazed at him blankly, waiting for the demand, disguised as a request, to open it.

"Sorry," he said. "The car we're looking for is a dead ringer for yours."

Chapter Thirteen

Her apartment had seemed airless and dismal, so in the false light of Los Angeles' night, Rachel sat on the bench in front of the garage eating an orange. Carefully, as though she had never done it before, she dug her fingers into the peel and tore away a small chunk. It was nearly midnight and this was the first food she had eaten since her hasty slice of morning toast. Before Lonnie.

The flood of relief when the highway patrolman handed back her purse had made her light-headed, but relief was now fading to dull despair. If only she had gone to Lonnie's apartment yesterday, as soon as he failed to show up for work, he might still be alive.

She was still chewing the last bit of fruit when a woman appeared on the steps at InterUrban's entrance, waved, circled the Merry Maids van parked in the horseshoe in front of the building, and strolled toward Rachel. Despite Goldie's rumpled tee shirt and khaki pants rolled up at the cuff, there was something about the way she held her head that was almost regal.

She leaned over to peer into Rachel's face. "You sleeping on the street again, sweet pea?"

"No, no. Just getting a breath of air."

"I figured you'd be feeling fine since we solved all those problems of yours the other night, but here you are looking peaked as a rooster on an egg farm. You been working yourself too hard?"

"No, I'm fine."

Goldie swung her hips down on the bench. "You call the cops about that car?"

Rachel swung her face away. "Nope. I'm not going to, either."

"The kids aren't finished over there yet." Goldie nodded at the InterUrban offices. "You might as well tell me why."

Rachel picked up a pebble from the ground. "I really can't talk about it."

Goldie turned, leveled a gaze at her, then dipped her head. "Okay. Sorry I asked." She got to her feet and sauntered toward the curb.

For reasons she couldn't account for, Rachel blurted, "A friend of mine is dead and it's probably my fault, and I came within a gnat's eyebrow of getting myself arrested." She kicked at an imaginary stone on the pavement.

Goldie turned back. "You sound like that guy in the Bible, Job. Next thing, you'll be getting yourself a case of hives."

"Boils," Rachel said. "Job got boils."

"Whatever. The preachers all say he didn't have much fun." She sank again onto the bench, leaned back, crossed her ankles and her arms. "So this friend of yours—what happened to her?"

"Him," Rachel's voice choked and a tear dribbled its way toward her chin. Slowly, the words began tumbling out.

A Chevy Blazer passed and minutes later, a Volvo, tires hissing along the pavement. This area, like the office buildings that flanked it, was almost deserted at night.

"Don't see how you think you're responsible," Goldie said when Rachel finished. "Everything that happens in the universe ain't your say so. This Lonnie was a grown adult person. Why d'you think you were his keeper?"

Rachel was staring at her feet. The heels of her loafers were worn, she'd have to remember to get them to the shoe shop. "A couple of years ago, he pretty much saved my life. I should have gone over there sooner. I shouldn't have waited."

"Lord, girl, if people did all the should-haves, my Mama wouldn't be going to church on Sundays 'cause we would all be in Heaven."

"If I ever find out who sold him that stuff, I swear I'll kill him."

"Guess it wouldn't do much good to tell you to lighten up." Goldie leaned forward as a boy from the cleaning crew crossed the street. "What you doing out here by yourself, Peter?" she called. "You got all that work done?"

Peter grinned widely as he got to the curb and waved something that looked like a piece of dark paper. "Those others are slow. But they be done soon." He seemed to chop his sentences to a manageable length.

"What you got there?" Goldie frowned at the envelope. "You didn't take anything from the offices did you?"

"No." Peter looked pleased with himself. "Not from an office. I don't do that. You know I don't." Rachel noted a dimple in his left cheek that made his face winsome.

"Then where did that come from?" Goldie pointed at the dark rectangle in his hand.

"Bathroom."

"Give it here." She held out her hand.

Peter held it above his head and Rachel could see it was a brown envelope, about five by seven inches. Abruptly, his resistance evaporated and he held it out. "Didn't steal it. Found it."

"Not a lot of difference between stealing and finding," Goldie said, taking the envelope from his outstretched hand. "Depends on whether the owner lost it before you found it."

Peter hung his head.

Goldie ruffled his hair, fondly. "I know you didn't mean anything by it, but I sure don't want anyone getting the idea you stole it."

"Looks like it's just an empty envelope," Rachel said.

"It's an envelope, all right." Goldie was opening the flap. "But not quite empty." She shook some of the contents into her palm. The little mound glowed purple in the streetlight. "What the hell is this?"

Rachel stared at the small sand-like heap in Goldie's hand. "Let me see." She shook the envelope into her own hand, got up and moved to the yellow light over the garage's pedestrian exit, where the color became whitish. "Peter!" she called. "Where did you find this?"

He had started back across the street. "Bathroom," he called. "Like I said."

"They doing H over there or what?" Goldie muttered. "I'm not sure I ever seen any myself, but I expect that stuff ain't sugar."

Peter stood on the sidewalk on the other side of the street, his shoulders slumping dejectedly.

Rachel gazed at him a moment, then strode across the street, squatted down at his side and looked up into his cherub's face. "Can you show me where you found that envelope?"

Goldie, moving as deliberately as ever, arrived at Rachel's elbow. "You know what it is?"

"All I know is it looks exactly like the stuff that was in the teapot in Lonnie's kitchen."

"The stuff that did him in?"

"Far as I know, yeah," Rachel said. "Peter, show us where."

The office, almost as big as a conference room, was paneled with a dark wood that showed red in the grain. On the gray plush carpet, a blue-and-white-print Victorian sofa and two pale blue, velvety wingback chairs sat across from a huge, highly polished teak desk. The top was barren of papers.

"This is where you found it?" Rachel asked Peter.

He shook his head. "Not here." He pointed to a door on the other side of the sofa. "In the bathroom, like I tell you." Nervously, he chewed on a fingernail.

Goldie gave the room an appraising gaze. "This guy don't like cheap bric-a-brac does he?"

"What makes you think this is a guy's office? The chairman of the board is a woman."

"No joke?"

"Nope." Rachel moved across the thick, plushy carpet, opened the door Peter had pointed and flipped on the light. On the shelf over the sink sat a marble mug and two onyx-handled brushes, one obviously for shaving.

"If this belongs to a woman, she's got a beard," Goldie drawled.

"Might be Jason's office," Rachel muttered distractedly. "He was the only exec high enough to rate an office like this, except the chairman." She picked up the mug. Something inside it rattled. Goldie frowned. "The guy who got himself killed?"

"He was general manager of this place." Rachel was peering into the mug. There was no soap inside. Instead there was something small and shiny. She tipped the cup over her palm and a cuff link rolled out. On its silvery face was the etched form of a tortoise.

She motioned to Peter. "Show me exactly where you found this envelope."

"Over there." He pointed.

"In the toilet?"

"No," he giggled. "Behind it. I was doing the mop. I bump it." Peter pointed to the lid of the tank. "That envelope, it fell down behind."

Rachel examined the envelope. The rim of the flap was damp. "Look," she said, as much to herself as to Goldie, "he fit the flap over the edge of the tank and the lid held it there. But why?"

Goldie was still staring at the tank. "Because if he was a coke freak or something, he couldn't exactly leave the stuff laying around."

"But in a regular office envelope? Not wrapped up or anything? Any user knows you have to keep the stuff clean and dry."

"You're making a big mistake if you think folks always do things sensible."

Rachel's gaze was fixed on the envelope's contents. "No," she said softly, running her tongue over dry lips. Her eyes, huge and dark, found Goldie's. "I don't think Jason was a user. But I think I might be looking at why he was killed."

Chapter Fourteen

"You telling me he was a dealer?" Goldie's voice cracked with shock.

"No."

"Then what are you getting at?"

Rachel didn't answer. She moved to Jason's desk.

Peter was shifting his weight from one ragged tennis shoe to another and flicking anxious glances from one woman to the other.

"It's okay," Rachel said to him. "It's nothing to do with you."

Goldie patted him on the shoulder. "The others are gonna be finished by now. You go on out to the van and tell them to get in and wait for me."

He nodded, clearly glad to be done with it. The door sighed on its hinges as it closed behind him.

Rachel opened the desk drawers and began pawing through the contents.

Goldie peered over her shoulder. "What the devil you doing now?"

"They haven't packed up his shaving mug. I thought there might be a schedule book in here. One of those things where executives write down every thing they do. But I don't see one."

"You think he wrote down 'Thursday, ten a.m., meet with Colombian drug dealer'?"

"Not exactly."

"Well, seeing as how you think he got himself killed because of something we just found, if it's all the same to you, I'm gonna get the hell out of here."

Rachel closed the drawers. They both headed for the corridor. Goldie was pulling the door closed when a sharp voice behind them split the silence.

"Who are you?"

Rachel jerked upright and dropped the cuff link, which skittered across the floor tiles and landed at the feet of the woman who had spoken.

Pale hair gleamed in the bright light of the hall as Charlotte Emerson, in a cobalt-blue cloak, bent over and picked it up. She looked tense when she straightened and, despite her size, formidable. "Where did this come from?" She eyed them both, then recognized Rachel. "Good heavens. What are you doing here?"

Eyes meeting Charlotte's, Rachel said with as much aplomb as she could muster, "This is Goldie—she's in charge of the office-cleaning crew. Goldie, Charlotte."

"I lost something," Goldie said.

Rachel nodded. "While she was working here tonight. I came over to help her look for it."

"I see. Is this what she lost?" Charlotte held up the cuff link.

Rachel paused on the edge of saying yes, but Charlotte probably had seen Jason wearing the cuff link. "No, that's something we found on the floor while we were looking. We should've just put it on the desk. I didn't realize I still had it."

Charlotte turned to Goldie. "What did you lose?"

"A…ring."

"Well, it wasn't just any old ring," Rachel added. "It belonged to her mother, and to her grandmother before that. Goldie lost weight and the ring was loose. The last time she remembered having it was when she was cleaning the bathroom in there." Rachel tapped the door to Jason's office with one hand and smoothed her shirtfront with the other.

The stiffness in Charlotte's shoulder relaxed. "What does it look like, in case someone turns it in?"

"Gold, with a…a red stone," Goldie said carefully.

"A garnet," Rachel added smoothly. "Is there someone we could call to report it?"

Charlotte smiled. "I'll report it myself in the morning. When I turn this in." She held up the cuff link.

"Sorry to have disturbed you," Rachel said.

"Quite all right. I was just a bit startled to find someone here so late."

It wasn't until later that Rachel began wondering what Charlotte was doing at the office at that hour.

Outside, tiny drops of mist hung in the air and the pavement was damp.

Goldie let out a low whistle. "You just may be the best liar I ever heard, and I have heard me some genuine champions."

"You weren't so bad yourself."

"We are real lucky she didn't come in when you were going through that desk. We would've been in shit so deep we would've been drawing flies for the rest of our very short lives."

"Funny," Rachel mused, "I wasn't even thinking about that. All I was trying to do was get out of there without her seeing this." She reached under her shirt tail and drew out the envelope.

A car passed, its taillights making red holes in the mist.

"Christ almighty, girl. I forgot about that friggin' envelope."

Rachel tapped a corner of it against her forehead. Her hair was damp, and not from the weather. "If what's in this envelope is the same as what I found in Lonnie's apartment, I think they got it from the same place.

"Oh, my God," Rachel said softly.

"What?"

"Lonnie hates garlic."

"You are making about as much sense as a valley girl on LSD."

"He couldn't eat garlic. Said it tore up his stomach."

"So what?"

"When I found him, he smelled of garlic."

Goldie frowned. "Don't make sense. Nobody went in there and forced him to eat Italian sausage."

Thicker Than Blood 71

"But the whole bed smelled of it."

"So maybe he was doing an Italian hooker."

Rachel shook her head, trying to make sense of it.

"You thought the stuff you found in his kitchen and what we found in that envelope came from the same place," Goldie said.

"They sure look alike. It's possible they came from the same place."

"And where might that be?"

"The water quality lab."

Goldie's mouth dropped open. "You gotta be joking."

"Lonnie delivered a lot of packages to them. Come to think of it, the guy I talked to in the lab asked about him. Maybe Lonnie found out they were making some kind of drug and stole a couple of fixes."

Goldie's right eyebrow and shoulder rose in unison. "Must be pretty potent stuff to just up and kill him like that. Mmm-mmm. A drug factory, right here in River City." She looked back at the InterUrban building.

"But that don't explain the garlic," Goldie went on. "And it sure don't explain Mr. High-and-Mighty Jason getting himself offed by some maniac driving a car."

The crew had spotted Goldie and was beginning to pile out of the van. "It's raining," one of them called.

"So what are you doing standing there? Waiting to drown?" Goldie called. "Get back inside. I'll be there right quick."

Rachel was staring at nothing, hardly aware that the mist had become fat drops of rain. "Maybe it does explain about Jason. What if he found out his own water quality lab is making street drugs?"

Chapter Fifteen

Goldie said it under her breath: "We gotta call the cops." Raindrops were beginning to collect on her eyelashes.

Rachel shoved the envelope under her shirt again to keep it dry, her eyes locked on Goldie's. "I can't. At least not yet."

Goldie cocked her head. "I guess that's nobody's business but yours." As though defying the rivulets of rain that ran down her cheek to her chin, she crossed the street to the van.

"Hey!" Rachel called. "Thanks for your help."

A hand waved as the van pulled away from the curb, the wipers sweeping across the windshield.

When Rachel reached her apartment, she locked the door, stopping only to grab a towel for her dripping hair before taking a dinner plate from the cabinet and pouring out two tiny piles of granules, one from the plastic bag she had found in Lonnie's teapot, the other from the brown envelope.

"Bingo," she said softly to Clancy, who was watching her intently from a bookcase shelf.

The two samples looked identical.

Oh, Lonnie, how could you do this to yourself?

She drew a deep breath, let it out slowly and decided it probably wasn't wise to leave this stuff lying about.

Standing on a stool, she unfastened one of the two light fixtures on the bedroom ceiling, removed the bulb, and inserted the packets. The room would be a little dim with only one light, but it would have to do.

Exhausted, she shucked her damp clothing, left it in an untidy muddle on the floor, and got into bed.

The first rays of sunlight on the bare windows woke her. Rachel rolled over and tried to go back to sleep, but her mind began to chatter about the tie tack she had found in the Caddy's dented fender.

Finally she rose, took the small piece of silvery, coin-shaped metal from the cigar box and gazed at it. The tortoise gazed back. Too bad she'd had to give Charlotte the cuff link.

There couldn't be many pieces of jewelry with that design. Perhaps she could find out where it was from. Hadn't Jason said it was Indian? But there were dozens of Indian groups in the Southwest alone.

Should she just go to Charlotte, tell her the truth? But she'd have to explain why she hadn't called the cops, and that might risk her contract with InterUrban. She'd have to think it through.

In the meantime, the old cigar box on her dresser would not be missed by a burglar. A few days ago, the notion that someone might ransack her apartment would have struck Rachel as silly. Now, she almost expected it.

Opening her handbag, she tossed the tie tack in among the jumbled contents. Since she could never find anything in that purse, she doubted anyone else would either.

After she opened the garage gates, and the cars had begun streaming in, Rachel sat in her glass booth, her thoughts as jumbled as the contents of her handbag.

Jason's murderer no longer seemed anonymous. It was as if he had done her some monstrous personal harm. Perhaps he had. Maybe he had sold that stuff to Lonnie.

She knew little about Jason, but she was sure that behind his death was the lust for drug money. She understood too well the destruction bred by that lust. Lonnie would be only one of many casualties.

Tears pooled in her eyes and leaked across her cheek. Angrily she brushed them away, ran long fingers through hair still damp from the shower, then reached for a pad of paper and began to fill it with scrawls.

First, she would find someone to help out with the garage and locate a laboratory to analyze those packets.

Then she would canvas nearby auto-body shops. What if the Cadillac was run off a cliff or something? But it was a company car, she thought. That might be a little hard to explain. Most likely it was being repaired, and whoever moved it wouldn't have driven it far. The E plates used by the water authority, coupled with the huge dent, might invite attention.

Then there was the water quality lab. She would have to find a way to search it. Her eyes fixed on a scratch on the booth's glass.

A chill prickled up from her toes until the top of her head tingled as it dawned on her she had something in her possession that could unleash treacherous forces. All of them aimed at her.

She covered her mouth as if afraid she might say something reckless.

Before, if she screwed up, she might have landed in jail. Now, it could be the cemetery.

If only she could go to the cops…but she couldn't. Unless.…

She reached for the phone book, looked up the number for Merry Maids, dialed, and asked if she could leave a message for Goldie. Then she sat, almost frozen in place, until the sound of knuckles on the booth's glass startled her.

Between a shock of pale hair and a cleft chin, a mouth grinned at her. "Up late last night?"

She tried to smile, but her face seemed stiff.

Hank's features melted into a look of concern. "Something wrong?"

"No, I'm fine. Just a lot on my mind."

"It so happens, I know how to fix that."

"I bought a lifetime supply of snake oil years ago."

"No snakes, no oil, just a lake, a clear sky, the scent of pine trees, and a couple of fresh trout—prepared by a master chef—for dinner."

Rachel's eyes skidded away. "I can't be away from the garage. Especially right now."

"Not now, Sunday. I know you're closed Sundays because I've had to park in the street." He crossed his arms over his chest, and lowered his head as though peering at her over invisible eyeglasses. "Or do you swab the place on Sundays—maybe scrub it with a toothbrush?"

The phone began beeping. She turned her back to him and reached for the receiver.

"You going to the cops?" The voice crackled on the line like the squawking of a wet hen.

"Goldie," Rachel interrupted, "I need your help."

"No way. If somebody's making drugs right there in that building where I take my kids every night, I am not going to get involved. You know how dangerous people like that are? You can't do nothing on your own, girl. Maybe I'll be calling the cops myself."

"What would you tell them?"

The line went silent.

Rachel bit her lower lip. "Can we have lunch?"

"Why?"

A hand touched Rachel's arm and she almost dropped the phone.

"I'll pick you up Sunday, five-thirty. That's a.m. If you aren't down here, I'll start yelling. Wake the neighbors." Hank gave her a crooked grin and left the booth.

"Five-thirty," he called over his shoulder. "We have to catch the trout first, then cook them."

She frowned at his receding back until the voice on the phone began sputtering.

"You know the Plum Tree, in Chinatown?" Rachel said into the receiver. "Please, Goldie, meet me there at two."

"This better be good." Goldie hung up.

⌐⌐⌐

Rachel hurried past a store where large, rubbery sea creatures were splayed over crushed ice, past a dingy window with a poster taped to the glass lauding the merits of ginseng, and across the street to the yellow brick walls and blue awning of the Plum Tree.

Inside, a few late diners still dawdled, but most of the tables, draped in forest green then topped with a square of white linen, were empty. A tiny woman in very high heels greeted her.

"I'm meeting someone here," Rachel said.

The woman led her to an adjoining room where Goldie sat at a corner table drumming her fingers on a menu.

Another woman, delicate and wispy as a feather, took their orders.

"You said your brother is a cop," Rachel began. "He might believe me if you told him...."

Across from her, the dark face of her friend was troubled. Slowly, as though she had missed a no-trespassing sign, Rachel said, "Maybe I shouldn't have asked."

"He got shot," Goldie said. "In the gut. A domestic dispute. The guy that killed Marcus was defending his right to beat his wife."

"Jesus. I'm sorry."

"He had friends on the force, I could call one of them."

Rachel shook her head. "Thanks anyway."

"What are you going to do?"

"Wish I knew."

When they finished their meal, the waitress brought almond cookies.

"Ask her for fortune cookies, instead," Goldie muttered dryly. "We could use a little fortune." She dug a ten out of her wallet and put it on the table.

Rachel picked up the money and handed it back. "Don't even think about arguing."

Goldie's laughter came out like a snort. "Honey, if I was going to argue with you I would have done it when you asked me to meet you here. You ever take a hard look at what they sell in Chinese grocery stores? Those huge whatever you call 'em, naked clams, those black mushrooms, and seaweed, for God's sake."

Back at the garage, Rachel anxiously surveyed each parking level. Although she didn't guarantee someone would always be on duty, she hated to leave the place unattended.

As she was leaving level B, a slender woman emerged from the stairwell and, with the grace of a dancer, moved toward a car on the opposite side. She looked familiar, so when the car had backed into the driveway, Rachel raised her hand in a small wave.

The woman rolled down the window. "Rachel Chavez."

Rachel tried to connect a name with the pale, heart-shaped face.

The woman read her look. "Alexandra Miller. I probably look a little different in my jogging shorts."

"Of course." Rachel put her hand on the car door. "Good to see you again. You probably saved my life. I don't think I thanked you properly."

"Don't be silly. Anyone would have run off those thugs and dusted you off. But as a matter of fact, I was looking for you."

"Yes?"

"I mentioned my plane that day."

Rachel looked puzzled.

"Flying?" Alexandra added.

"Oh, right. But your plane? You have your own plane?"

"I do. I fly every Thursday. Come with me. Day after tomorrow."

"Thanks." Rachel straightened, a little surprised. "Thanks a lot. It sounds wonderful. But it's really hard for me to get away."

"You'd be doing me a favor. Truly."

"I'd like to, but I've had some problems...."

"All the more reason to get away for a bit."

"I just don't see how I can." Rachel was beginning to feel guilty. The woman had certainly helped her out.

"I've had some problems lately, too. I'd really welcome the company."

Two parallel lines appeared over Rachel's nose as it occurred to her she not only couldn't remember the last time she had any fun, she couldn't remember the last time she'd spent any time just enjoying herself with a friend. A woman friend.

"It'll be fun. I promise."

Alexandra's smile seemed so friendly and wistful that Rachel found herself agreeing.

Chapter Sixteen

As Alexandra drove off, Rachel stared after her, half annoyed with herself for giving in.

A voice rang out on the level below: "Dear girl! Are you there, dear girl?"

Rachel hurried down the ramp. "I'm here."

"Ah, good, good." Irene's stout body was planted at the main entrance to the garage, her foot propped against the wheel of the supermarket cart to keep it from rolling.

"You know Rosetta?"

"Should I?"

"She's a Gypsy, dear girl. A true Gypsy from Romania or Estonia or some such. But that don't matter." Irene was so full of news she sputtered. "She is teaching me to read palms. And I thought perhaps I could practice with you."

"No." Rachel jammed her hands into her pockets as if Irene might suddenly grab one and blurt out what she saw in the palm.

"But I assure you it is quite simple and quite accurate. Just yesterday I read Herbert's palm. He works in the butcher shop at the farmers market. His palm said he was going to come into a good deal of money. And do you know, that very afternoon, he won five hundred dollars from the lottery. I didn't mean that I would charge, you know, although Herbert did give me twenty-five dollars from his windfall. For you it would be free, of course."

"Thank you, no. But I do have a money-making proposition for you."

The woman beamed. "Ah, yes?"

"Could you baby-sit the garage for me a few hours here and there? Ten dollars an hour."

"Of course, dear girl. Anytime."

~~~

Thursday morning Alexandra Miller woke with a monster headache. Stress always brought this awful hammering just above her left ear. She called her office and took the day off.

This afternoon, she would fly. That would help. And she had invited that woman from the garage. The company would be nice.

In the meantime she would finish the yard work, migraine or no. She could have hired someone to pull the weeds, but somehow that seemed like shirking. She should like gardening. Her grandmother had loved the digging and planting, and Alexandra was, after all, executive director of Protectors of the Earth. Rooting around in earth was supposed to soothe the soul.

But today it seemed such grubby labor. Perhaps it was the headache.

She stood to survey her progress. Her white shirt was little the worse for wear, but her khaki slacks had muddy ovals at the knees. Strands of dark hair had escaped the red bandana she had used to tie it back and perspiration was trickling down her neck.

Irked, she wiped the back of her hand across her brow. Only one job left to do.

Bending over the anemones, she uprooted the weeds that were encroaching on the White Queen. There would be no buds until autumn. When most of the flower world was preparing to die, the White Queen bloomed. And what wonderful blooms they would be: tall, stately, with yellow stamens, and stems clothed in vine-like leaves. They reminded Alexandra of her grandmother. And why she herself had become an environmentalist.

At sixteen, Alexandra had discovered ecologist Aldo Leopold's essays on the dire need for a land ethic.

When her grandmother died, Alexandra spent a little of her huge inheritance on herself—a small but elegant house, an ARV Super 2 lightweight plane, a helicopter, and, finally, a hot-air balloon.

With the rest of her grandparents' legacy, she had founded Protectors of the Earth and dedicated herself to helping the people of farms and cities to live in harmony with each other and with nature.

POE banners read "No privilege without obligation." Alexandra believed the slogan.

In the years since, she had learned a very great deal. For one thing, far too much privilege had been taken. Discovering that environmental concerns were a business, much like any other, she hardened into a shrewd businesswoman. And she learned to rule out nothing, to negotiate with anyone who could provide something she wanted.

Plucking the last weeds from the bed of White Queens, she tossed her hair from her eyes and stood up, relieved to be finished, but above all, proud of her job.

⌒⌒⌒

The plane banked and smoothly turned east.

Alexandra's face lit with pure, sensual enjoyment. "Your first time?" she asked Rachel.

"In a small plane, yes," Rachel nodded nervously, willing herself to relax. The cockpit was compact, but not at all cramped, and her companion was clearly a skilled pilot.

They quickly left the Burbank airport behind. The ocean of toy houses below seemed to stretch all the way to the horizon as they flew along the Angeles mountains.

A persistent breeze had scoured the smog from the Los Angeles basin, and the sky was the color of violets—the sort of day that made Southern Californians smug.

Rachel was eyeing the small bank of instruments feeling somehow cheated. She had supposed that a plane would require more dials than this to get off the ground and stay in the air.

Alexandra swung her gaze toward the mountains and made a slight adjustment with the lever in her right hand. "No more thugs leaping at you while you're jogging, I trust."

"Haven't had much time to jog. Maybe that's why I'm sort of stressed out."

"Ever notice that?" Alexandra pointed ahead. "When you enter the desert, the land changes from the green of money to the color of poverty."

Rachel peered out the window of the plane as the lush landscapes around homes gave way to desert scrub.

"But that's natural, isn't it? I mean it isn't poverty, it's just the difference between where people water the landscape and where they don't."

Alexandra's laugh pealed through the small cabin. "The point is, where do they get that water? Most of our great state is desert—every square inch of the southern third certainly is." Little spots of color had lit her cheeks. "Every morning, we get out of bed in a desert. Sixteen, seventeen million of us."

"Is that bad?"

"Bit of a strain on the water resources, don't you think?"

"Guess I haven't thought much about it."

"I think of nothing else."

Rachel considered the annoyed look on Alexandra's face. Or was it anger? "Not likely to change, is it? I mean seventeen million people aren't likely to get up one morning and decide to move to Pennsylvania."

"Pity Pennsylvania if they did," Alexandra said. "You have no idea the devastation, the destruction of our birthright. Rivers once wild and free now shackled by dams, diverted into canals, and turned into sewers."

Alexandra leaned forward to look over the plane's silvery wing. "The salmon are disappearing. Ducks, geese, herons won't be far behind. If nothing is done, humanity will strangle on its own pollution."

Not one to get excited about abstract concepts, Rachel wondered at her companion's fervor.

"I don't mean to argue, but didn't there used to be too much water? I mean the Colorado jumped its banks every spring and drowned everything in its path. The delta was saltwater marshland. Nothing grew there but tules."

"Where did you hear that?"

"My grandfather." Rachel started to say her family had been delta farmers, but thought better of it. "I used to live up north."

Alexandra flicked a glance at her. "They grow rice up there. Sucks up more water than any crop in the world. And you know what they do with the stubble when they've slashed what they want from the plant?"

"They burn it," Rachel said, feeling somehow responsible.

"And for days the smoke hangs like a filthy shroud over the water. What do you think that does to the birds, the fish?" Alexandra's eyes were bitter.

Rachel squirmed in her seat, relieved that her family hadn't been rice growers.

She recalled her grandfather, Bruno and even her father spending entire evenings bemoaning the onslaught of environmentalism. Rachel had never paid much attention to the other side.

"I guess it's a good thing we just have yards to water here," she said weakly.

Alexandra's laugh was like the breaking of a branch. "The cities pay more for their water," she said. "And city people care more, at least superficially. But agribusiness and the water developers—they're like mountains. Protectors of the Earth, even the entire environmental movement, we're like ants trying to move those mountains."

"I was under the impression that nobody even thinks of building dams these days."

"Oh, they think about it, all right. But they don't try it. Not since we trussed up the water developers like Thanksgiving turkeys. The sad thing is, so much damage is already done."

"I thought a lot was being done to help the environment."

"You think San Francisco will give back Hetch Hetchy Valley? They say it was as beautiful as Yosemite before it was turned into a reservoir. You think the farmers will just clear out of the delta?"

"Not real likely," Rachel said uneasily.

Alexandra's mouth curved into a smile as enigmatic as an angel's. "Actually, they just might."

Rachel gave her a puzzled look.

"I have a plan," Alexandra said with a soft chuckle. "I call it Operation Jack-and-the-Beanstalk. Jack accomplished quite a lot just by dropping a few pebbles on a couple of giants. My grandmother used to tell a similar story about a small boy and two huge brutes from a marauding tribe."

"I'd forgotten. Your grandmother was a Mojave, wasn't she?"

Alexandra nodded. "A shaman."

"A healer?"

"Shamans are only part healer. They're also part artist, part politician. They are the mediators between the profane and sacred worlds."

"And your grandfather. Was he a chief?"

"Not exactly," Alexandra said. "He was a bootlegger during Prohibition. In the thirties, he bought up poor people's housing. By the end of the Depression he owned a sizeable chunk of New Jersey."

Rachel almost squealed with surprise. "And he married a shaman?"

"Don't ask me how they did it, but apparently they were quite happy."

"How did they even meet?" Rachel asked.

"He came to Southern California to acquire land for orange orchards. My grandmother was in Anaheim for some meeting. The hotel clerk assigned them both the same room."

"What a story!" Rachel said. "Did you see them often?"

"I barely remember my grandfather. He died the same year my parents went down on a ferry that sank in the Mediterranean. I was only four. My grandmother took me and returned to her own people."

"So you were brought up as a Mojave?"

"It was wonderful. The Mojave believe dreams are the source of all special powers. When I was twelve, another shaman had a dream about my future. He told my grandmother I would bring the people of a great region the harmony of the Mojave heritage."

Without warning, the plane lurched and seemed to Rachel to fall away beneath her. She grabbed for the handhold, knocking her handbag from her lap. "What was that?"

"Just an air pocket. You get used to them."

Alexandra frowned at the odds and ends that had spewed from Rachel's handbag across the cockpit floor. "Better get those picked up, they can take on a life of their own up here, leap right up and bite you in the face if you're not careful."

Rachel brushed the hodgepodge of items together, scooped them back into her purse, and reached for the tie tack, which had landed near the fire wall.

"That looks Native American," Alexandra said, following Rachel's gaze.

"It may be," Rachel said, straining, but still unable to reach it. She released her seat belt and swept up the tortoise.

"My father gave it to me." She smiled at Alexandra. "He used to say there was nothing so beautiful as the song of a tortoise."

"What a sweet story." Alexandra squinted at it. "I'd like to take a closer look."

Rachel started to show it to her, but another air pocket jostled the plane and the tie tack fell into her purse. She rummaged through the contents, gave up, and refastened her seat belt. "It's in there somewhere. One of these days, I've got to clean this out."

"What happened to the guy who worked for you?" Alexandra asked. "Mid-twenties, short, thin. He used to deliver packages."

A pair of lines appeared over Rachel's nose. "Lonnie."

"Haven't seen him lately."

"He…didn't show up for work for a couple of days. He was found in his apartment. Dead."

"Good heavens! He was just a kid."

Rachel shrugged. Her arms were so tense the motion made them ache. She waited until she could get the words past the lump in her throat. "I'm afraid it may have been drugs. They're doing an autopsy."

"So that's what has been bothering you."

"It was a horrible shock." Rachel examined the horizon.

Alexandra expertly moved some levers and the plane began a graceful turn. As the right wing sank lower, she pointed over it. "There's the reason for Southern California's population overload."

Rachel watched the long straight streak in the desert as they flew along it. "Looks like a river, but it's too straight."

"One of InterUrban's rivers, not one of God's. That aqueduct has more ugly power than you would ever imagine. It has killed fish, deprived Native Americans, robbed Mexicans. Even as we speak it is slowly destroying the Grand Canyon and helping us gorge ourselves."

Alexandra looked at Rachel. "I should pack up the soapbox. We came up here to relax. My work has been so tense lately that I have aches where I never knew I had nerves."

Alexandra's smile was so plaintive and ingenuous that Rachel grinned back. "I know the feeling."

Chapter Seventeen

The scene through the window of Charlotte Emerson's ten-year-old Volvo was not a pretty one. Brush fires had left the Verdugo Hills charred and bare in spots, like mange on the coat of a once-handsome dog.

The sign for Forest Lawn swung into view, and beyond it she steered the Volvo up the hill to a huge rock where she brought the car to a stop and got out.

Her dress was a very dark pink with wide lapels that made her shoulders seem broad, her waist small. She smoothed the skirt and opened the back door of the sedan. On the back seat was a mound of amaryllis, their stamens long and curved, their long petal trumpets a vibrant pink much paler than her dress. There were three dozen flowers but not a single leaf.

Carrying the flowers as one carries an infant, Charlotte made her way up the hill.

The grave was very green. Most of the flowers from the funeral had already wilted and been removed. She stood for several minutes, her eyes fixed on the mound that covered the place where she had last seen the casket.

Then she bent down to slip the amaryllis into one of the brass vases near the headstone. It was difficult to rise again, an irksome reminder of her age. A breeze fanned her cheeks.

"We were never friends," Charlotte nodded to the mound of earth behind the proud pink flowers, "but I have come to say goodbye." She stopped.

She could almost hear him laughing derisively at her as he had sometimes done, but only in private. He had brutalized others in public, but never her, not even when he could have gotten away with it. She had to give him that.

"Twenty-two years ago, when you were a hot-shot attorney and I was running Riverside Water, and we both still had a sense of humor, you told me a dozen naked ladies would dance on your grave before you'd let me have my way. Well, here are three dozen. Not quite the sort you had in mind, I suppose. The florist says they're also called Belladonna lilies, which seems rather appropriate. Belladonna is a deadly poison. "

Charlotte closed her eyes, as if in prayer. *I admit I'm not sorry it turned out the way it did. Some things just have to be. And soon I am going to do something that would have vexed you even more, Jason. But I trust you are beyond that now. I am going to appoint a black man as your successor. And then I'm going to step down and retire. Without telling anyone about our little conflict.*

She opened her eyes and raised her chin. "You were my most worthy opponent, Jason, you were indeed."

~~~~

"Lovely flower," Rachel said to Charlotte, nodding at the graceful amaryllis in a cobalt blue vase on Charlotte's desk.

"Yes, isn't it. It's called a naked lady," Charlotte said in a conspiratorial tone, and they both laughed.

Spread out on the gleaming desktop were the remains of hamburgers from Tommy's. The two had met standing in the long, hot, noontime line for what many regarded as Los Angeles' best burger. Rachel had waved; the other woman had waited for her. They had strolled back along the sidewalk together until Charlotte had invited Rachel into her office to share the air conditioning.

Now, Rachel leaned back in the chrome-legged, black-leather chair. She was pleased at the bonanza, the easy opportunity to ask her question. "How would I find out who was driving one of InterUrban's cars on a certain day?"

Charlotte's eyes examined Rachel's face. "Why would you need to know?"

One of Rachel's shoulders lifted a few inches and dropped. "I found something in the space where one of the cars was parked. A…watch with a broken band. I figure it must belong to whoever was driving that car that day and thought there must be some system for checking the cars out."

Charlotte was carefully folding the hamburger wrappers. "You know which car it was?"

"License number E147G62."

"I'll see what I can do." Charlotte slid the folded wrappers neatly into the bag, picked it up, and placed it carefully in the wastebasket behind her desk.

Chapter Eighteen

Jolted from a sound sleep, Rachel jerked upright in the dark, adrenaline charging, unsure of what had wakened her. The bedroom windows were just beginning to brighten with dawn.

Three sharp raps came at the door.

But the garage was locked. No one could get to her apartment unless he had been in the parking lot when she locked up.

Reaching under the bed, she brought out the telephone book and drew out the old thirty-eight.

The raps came again, steady this time and loud.

Heart hammering, she planted her feet just left of the door, lifted the gun and cocked it. The knocking ceased and in the silence that rushed in to take its place, her pulse drummed in her ears. "I have a gun pointed straight at you. It will easily penetrate that door."

"Rachel, for God's sake!"

She threw the latch and opened the door. Hank poked his head inside. She glared at him. "Are you crazy?"

"Is it safe to come in?"

"How did you get in here?"

"The side pedestrian door was open. Put that gun away. I've seen what you can do with it."

"What the hell are you doing here?"

"Don't tell me, let me guess. You forgot we were going fishing."

The lake seemed to pulse with the reds and yellows of the rising sun. A breeze filled the water with ripples, tossing Rachel's hair back from her face, which was studious with concentration as she added one more weight to her fishing line.

Her Honda was perched on the road above them like a white bird. They had left the Mustang in the garage when Hank had discovered its spare tire was flat.

"You look like you're examining the findings in a project that could win you a Nobel. No self-respecting trout is going to dive that far for his dinner."

"Who wants trout?" She rubbed her nose with the back of her hand. "Water's too warm for good trout."

Hank's line snagged on something just beneath the water. It whiplashed when he yanked it free, sending the hook sailing toward shore where it imbedded itself in the cuff of his pants. Reddening a little, he began the process again.

Rachel took a chunk of cheese from her pocket, molded a wad of it to her hook, then sent her line gracefully snaking across the water until it slipped beneath the surface with hardly a sound beyond the purr of the reel.

"This isn't your first fishing trip," Hank said.

"Not exactly." A lizard scurried across her foot and disappeared into the coarse grass.

He gave her a quizzical grin. "Hey, this is a day of escape. Why so solemn?"

"I really shouldn't have come. Too much to do. And I'm getting careless. I could have sworn I locked that door last night."

Rachel picked her way across a dozen feet of scrubby plants and sat down on a rock thinking she wasn't organized enough to make time for this sort of thing, she didn't need it, and she'd rather be at the laundromat so at least she'd have clean clothes for the week ahead.

Hank was surveying the lake, which lay like a glowing gem beneath the luminous sky. "Isn't this gorgeous?" he called.

She held up a hand to block the sun. "You come here often?"

"Not lately. Too busy."

"What's it called?"

"The reservoir? Coyote." He traipsed through the scrub and sat on the rock next to hers.

"Busy doing what?" she asked.

"Figuring out how to squeeze a little more water out of thin air."

She watched a fish break the surface, snatch an insect and disappear, leaving a ring of ripples. "Why do we need more water?"

"Guess you weren't here fifteen, sixteen years ago."

"Nope."

"Real serious drought. Landscapers went broke. Santa Barbara had ships in the harbor desalinating water. San Diego was panicky. Half of what InterUrban does is guard against drought, find more water before someone else snaps it up."

An insect buzzed at Rachel's ear. She swatted it away. "Like who would grab it?"

"Environmentalists, for one. They want to turn half the state into wetlands. We'd have real happy birds, but the people wouldn't fare too well."

"And other cities?"

"San Francisco gets all holier than thou about *their* rivers, and ecology, and Nature. But a hundred years ago they dammed up a valley in the Sierra. If they hadn't, there wouldn't *be* any San Francisco. Nobody talks about that."

Rachel's line jiggled. She stood, peering at it intently, but it had gone still. She sat down again. "So who's the bad guy?"

"No one, I guess. Just not enough water."

A large bird dropped onto the water, sending ripples radiating in every direction. Rachel thought it was a heron.

"Farmers get their water cheap because the Feds wanted to jump-start agriculture in the thirties," Hank said. "If ag water dried up now, the farmers would be looking at instant bankruptcy. Mostly they're on our side because we've got the population, meaning the votes."

She gave him a crooked grin. "I grew up on a farm in the delta. All we worried about was too much water taking out the levees."

Hank watched her lean back on the rock and raise her face to the sun. "So you're a farm kid?"

She caught his glance. "I don't get much sun. The garage is pretty dark. Yes, a farm kid."

"Then you must know about the snarls in the delta."

"Not a lot. Farmers don't talk business to kids."

Hank scratched his nose. "Nasty stuff brewing up there. The delta's a mess. Terrible water quality for one, an earthquake could turn the whole thing to jelly, for another. And most of the water for us beggars in the bottom third of the state—where most of the population lives, I might point out—comes through the delta."

She closed her eyes. The sun felt warm on her eyelids. "Guess I knew that. Just never bothered to string it all together."

"More political intrigue over water than anything else you could name. Eighty percent of people in the state never think about it. For the other twenty percent, it's like a religion. Fire, brimstone, the works."

A fish flipped out of the water and splashed back in.

Rachel said, "I've missed that sound, fish plunking around in water."

"When did you leave the farm?"

"Oh, years ago."

"Family still there?"

"Nope." She sat up, unable to be still for too long.

"Miss it?"

A frown skipped across her face. "Like childhood, I guess. You miss the smallness of that world."

Something about her posture warned him not to ask more.

A dog began to bark—a big dog, from its sound. Rachel's gaze swung toward the sound. In the distance, a big flat-roofed building crouched against an equally flat mesa. The sun exploded off the roof in little bursts that hurt the eyes. She gave a self-conscious sigh. "I never knew the water business was so complicated."

Hank moved his eyes to the water, folded his arms over his knees and rested his chin on his hand. "That's exactly why I love it. Ask Charlotte, sometime. Her father was a power behind building that aqueduct." He poked his chin toward a broad concrete ditch that seemed to run clear to the eastern horizon. "I've heard he knew both Roosevelts and was in on some sort of skullduggery."

"Skullduggery?"

"Hardly a day goes by that someone isn't hatching another plot about water, and I don't know about half of them." Hank shuffled a foot clad in a scuffed rubber lace-up boot against the dry earth.

The heron, if that's what it was, rose, splashed clumsily on long legs for a few feet across the water, and took off.

"What do you know about Charlotte Emerson?" Rachel asked. "Interesting that a woman chairs a utility where most everybody else who's anybody is a good ol' boy."

Hank glanced at her.

"Present company excluded, of course. But I know who drives those cars in the fleet."

"In this business, water may be at least as thick as blood," Hank said. "But blood matters. Don't ask me why, but it does."

Rachel gave a wry smile. "Come to think of it, with good old boys it usually does." An insect buzzed at her cheek. She slapped at it. "Charlotte's family was in the water business?"

"I guess you could say the Emersons are the Kennedys of the California water industry. Big thinkers, big plans. Big roles in state politics, especially when it came to water." Hank dug around in the red canvas shopping bag he had packed, took out a thermos, poured some lemonade into a paper cup, and held it out. Rachel had to move to his side to take the cup.

"Came?" she asked, settling back on her rock.

Hank looked puzzled.

"You said came. Past tense."

"Most of them died pretty young. Her father was killed in the wreck of a private plane. Her husband drowned while rafting on the American River. About a dozen years ago, her son was shot while hunting."

"Good God! So she was the only one left to carry out their plans."

"Not exactly. Charlotte never much subscribed to their plans. But she wasn't above using the Emerson name."

"How does her thinking differ?"

"She seems to think this urban sprawl will suck us into a black hole if something isn't done to curb it."

"The men thought urban sprawl was good?"

"Well, it wasn't as bad then," Hank said. "And you can't exactly say that business and development and a good economy are terrible."

Despite the sun that blunted the desert's features as it heated the rock where she sat, Rachel wrapped her arms around herself.

Hank walked over, put the back of his hand against her arm. "You cold?"

"Of course not."

His finger lightly traced a line down her arm.

She drew away and gave him a long look. "You aren't going to go squishy on me, are you?"

"Squishy?"

"You know, waking up in the middle of the night. Cold showers. I don't want that." She hugged her arms to her chest. "I don't need it."

His eyes narrowed a little, seeming to appraise her statement, but not answering it.

"Look," she said, "I don't mean to be crass or anything, but I've run through enough men to know the romance thing ain't for me." She rummaged through the canvas bag, withdrew two sandwiches, and tossed one to Hank.

He caught it and shrugged. "My word on it. No squish."

Sitting in sun so bright it hurt her eyes, eating a limp sandwich that didn't taste that great, Rachel had a powerful urge to leave and wished she weren't stuck here with no polite exit. The silence began to sink under its own weight.

She cast about for something meaningless to say. "Did you like Jason?"

Hank stared at her a moment. "Can't say I liked him," he said finally. "But things have been ragged without him. There was an air of absolute certainty about Jason. Like even God wouldn't argue with him."

"But God did." And God had won. She took another bite of sandwich. She wasn't sure why she blurted the question, "You think his death was accidental?"

The sandwich paused halfway to Hank's mouth. "That's what they say."

"Suppose I told you I found something that...." She was looking past him toward the pond. "Your bobber went under!"

Hank turned and charged toward the rock where he had propped his fishing pole.

Rachel could hear the reel unwinding. She watched him grab up the rod and her mind fixed on whether to tell him about the tie tack.

She didn't notice the noise until it seemed to explode around her, bearing down on her like a runaway truck. She spun around, but nothing moved among the scraggly shrubs and rocks; then she saw it. And the noise stopped abruptly, as if her eyes had silenced it.

The small plane was very low. For a moment it seemed to aim straight at Rachel.

Hurling herself into a patch of coarse brown grass, she hunched against a rock and shaded her eyes to peer at it.

The plane, wiped clean of most of its markings by the direct sun, crossed over the road on a long downward diagonal. It tilted, then seemed to right itself and rise a little before it disappeared behind a scattering of boulders.

A sharp crack was followed by a second crunch, like an axe through metal. Then nothing.

"The pilot!" Rachel sprinted across the empty road toward the rocks. She skirted a Joshua tree and topped a rise.

Just the other side of a steep, brush-filled arroyo, the plane lay like a dead bird, its mouth open to the sky. She jumped to the bottom of the cleft, clambered across, and dug her toes into the clay walls to climb the other side.

The plane's bubble-type canopy had been thrown back as though some giant child had been playing with it. One of the broad wings—surely too big for the relatively small body—had bent, forming a knee on which the rest of the plane leaned in sideways supplication.

Where was the pilot? Was he hurt? Had he jumped? Been thrown free?

A sudden gust of hot wind pushed Rachel toward this flotsam that had fallen from the sky. Her foot landed on a protruding stone and she teetered, ignoring the pain that shot to her knee. No smoke. No sign of fire. The air was eerily still. No birds, no insects, no sound at all.

She grasped one of the rungs welded to the body near the crippled wing and pulled herself up. The cockpit was empty. *Where's the pilot?*

Hank emerged from the arroyo shouting, "Is he hurt?"

"Not here," she called.

None of the nearby rocks or brush were tall enough to conceal a body.

Hank pulled himself up on the wing. "Must've been thrown clear," he grunted.

Rachel's eyes skimmed over the desert to the road, but nothing between the plane and the glassy glare of the pond moved.

"Hello!" Hank shouted. "Pilot?"

"Maybe he was thrown behind the seat." Rachel scrambled into the cockpit.

Something icy trilled its way up her right arm. The cargo that had slewed into a jumble. Dark brown shards of broken glass were strewn everywhere. And there was no mistaking what had spewed from some of the garishly colored broken cartons.

"Not likely to be a shipment of cornstarch headed for a bake-off," Rachel muttered.

Nor were the bricks that had tumbled out of red, yellow, and black boxes labeled *Double UO Global* likely to be building material.

"Jesus," Hank whistled softly behind her. "What a payload."

Chapter Nineteen

A small carton with no markings had rolled toward the cockpit, spilling tiny white crystals through a triangular puncture. Rachel picked it up, screwed her sun-dazzled eyes shut, then opened them again to stare at the box.

Hank said, "Looks like sugar."

"Right." Rachel lifted her eyes to Hank's. "And the pilot's Mother Teresa. No wonder he didn't stick around."

"And we're tramping around like ducks in hobnail boots begging to be shot," Hank said. "Get out of there."

The carton in her hand forgotten for the moment, Rachel backed hastily out of the cockpit.

In almost perfect unison, she and Hank leaped to the ground, stirring a jackrabbit that broke cover and raced with them toward the arroyo.

They scrambled down one wall and up the other, still running, the soft sand sucking at their feet until, air harsh with heat drying their lips and whipping their lungs, they reached harder earth near the road. A few yards away their fishing poles still rested undisturbed where they had left them. In the distance, the dog was still barking.

Hank ran toward the poles.

"What if he's watching us?" Rachel's words tumbled out so fast they slurred together. "Leave the rods. Let's get out of here."

Picnic leftovers spilled from the canvas bag as Hank yanked it up and in unison they ran toward the white Honda, which huddled forlorn and unprotected a quarter-mile away.

She dug the keys from her jeans pocket and jammed one into the trunk lock.

Hank stowed their gear and started to close it.

"Wait." She dropped the carton inside and slammed the lid shut.

With a spray of gravel, the little Honda squealed into action. Rachel whipped the car around to double back toward the hard road and didn't let up on the gas till a spine-jarring jolt nearly sent both their heads through the roof and three thumps came from the trunk.

She glanced at Hank. "First time I've wished I had a cell phone."

"Left mine at home. Peace and quiet and all that."

"So where's the nearest public phone?"

"Haven't the foggiest." His face was the color of putty. "You often drive like this?"

"Only when I have to." Rachel down-shifted as the road turned to caked dirt and passed through an arroyo, then sped up again. "That plane was chock-jam full. We need to call the sheriff," she said over the engine roar.

"Might be nice to be alive when we find a phone."

"Funny they use such gaudy boxes," Rachel said. "Red and yellow, with black cats yet."

"I guess they figure no one will look for contraband in such a blatant package."

The road widened and met the main highway. Rachel sped right. A small sign said *Wilson's Summit*, a large one said *Texaco*. The gas station was white stucco gone dull with dust.

An attendant stood in the doorway watching. Hank opened his window and shouted, "Phone?"

Eyes between the shaved head and dust-colored coveralls glared. The man's face was sunburned the color of ripe tangerines above a neck as thick as a bulldog's. He jerked his chin toward the other side of the building, then winced. The sunburn must have hurt.

Rachel bolted from the car, ran to the booth at the side of the building, and dialed 9-1-1, but the number didn't ring. She dug a solitary quarter from a nest of pennies in her coin purse, dialed 0, and the operator patched her through to the local sheriff's office. "I need to report a plane crash," she told the deputy who answered.

"Mmmm?" The voice on the other end sounded sleepy.

"Can you take the report?"

"Mmmm."

She described the downed plane, the spilled boxes, but not the contents. They could find that out for themselves. "We looked for the pilot, but never found him."

The voice, more awake now, wanted to know, "Where, exactly, did this happen?"

"Across the road from a reservoir....Hang on a minute." She slid open the door of the phone booth and called to Hank, "What's the name of that lake?"

"Coyote Reservoir."

She repeated the words into the phone.

"That all?" The deputy sounded like he was losing interest.

"Guess so."

"Name?"

She told him, spelling it out.

"We'll look into it," the deputy drawled as though desert plane crashes were reported six times a day.

"That was comforting," Rachel muttered as she hung up the phone.

Back at the car, she told Hank, "I think I woke him up."

Hank moved toward the driver's door. "Want me to drive?"

"I'm fine." She climbed back behind the wheel and waited for him to get in on the passenger side. The Honda jounced back to the highway, causing more thumps from the trunk.

Hank groaned. "What the hell is loose back there?"

"The box from the plane." She caught his look. "Forgot I had it."

Hank unlocked his door.

"What are you doing?"

"So I can throw myself into a ditch if you get stopped by a cop."

She bit her lower lip and hit the brakes. "Didn't think of that. You want to drive?"

"Not on your life."

The Honda crept back to LA in heavy Sunday traffic.

She parked next to the Mustang, which looked like a lost puppy in the concrete desert of the garage.

Hank said a weary goodbye and climbed into his car.

Not until she was in the elevator, digging through her purse, did she remember putting the apartment key in her shirt pocket to keep it separate and easy to find.

A search of all pockets yielded nothing but her car keys, a used Kleenex, and a Tootsie Roll wrapper. She screwed her eyes shut in frustration, pushed the elevator's stop button, and sent it back down to level A where she kept a spare key in the booth.

Finally home, she closed and locked the apartment door and realized she was hungry.

As she slapped together a turkey sandwich, a realization shook itself loose from all the other thoughts cluttering her brain: she had lost the key at the plane, either when she was wriggling into the cockpit or sliding down from the wing.

No ID on the key, no name or address, she reassured herself. Nonetheless, she made a mental note to get the lock changed.

Another thought percolated to the surface: the box from the plane was still in her trunk. Reluctantly, she left the food on the counter and headed back to the elevator.

The smell didn't hit her until she opened the trunk. She fanned the air in front of her face. A pale, lopsided circle had appeared on the floor of the trunk. In one corner, next to a faded blue first-aid kit, was a quart bottle of Clorox. Under Hank's forgotten canvas bag was the bright yellow cap that must have popped loose when she bounced over the chuckholes.

The box had fled to a far corner. It was lined with plastic but the bleach had seeped through the puncture. The carton was sodden and reeking. She found a trash bag, scooped the mess into it, and left the trunk open to air out.

Back in the apartment, turkey sandwich and cottage cheese in hand, Rachel sagged onto the sofa and clicked the TV's remote.

"...some biologists say the dying birds at wetlands surrounding Farwell ponds near Salinas are...."

She flipped through the channels and took another bite of the turkey sandwich.

Chapter Twenty

Twenty-four hours later, Rachel looked up from posting invoices to find men in uniform peering at her through the booth's glass wall.

One looked about sixteen, with red hair that stood up in irregular little spikes despite the fact that it had been shorn within a quarter inch of the scalp.

The other officer was shorter, thirty years older, with the face of a disappointed basset hound. "Rachel Chavez?" The words had to work their way past some ardent gum chewing.

"Yes." She wanted to ask if they had found the plane, but she had learned painfully and well not to anticipate a cop's questions.

The basset's eyes sneaked a glance at a piece of paper in his hand as if it held notes for a speech he should have memorized. "Lonnie B. Saltillo." He pronounced the silent L's almost belligerently. "He worked for you?"

She stared at him in astonishment, then nodded slowly.

"He a vitamin freak?" This from the baby-faced redhead.

"A what?"

"Vitamins." The word made its way around the older cop's gum. "He do a lot of health shop stuff?" Across his nose was a tiny red web of blood vessels.

"Not that I knew of." Both men seemed to be watching her closely. She stared at the older one's jaw as it worked away at the gum, wondering how vitamins could be sinister.

The older man pointed at his mouth. "Just quit smoking."

"Good for you." She gave him a stiff smile, thinking he looked like he could use some vitamins himself.

Long-suffering brown eyes peered at her from beneath brows that slid down at the edges. "Nothing good about it. It's lousy." The redhead gave an ill-concealed smirk. "You say this Lonnie Saltillo was not a vitamin popper?"

"He never mentioned it."

"You are, of course, aware he is deceased?" the gum-chewer asked.

"Yes."

He glanced again at the paper in his right hand. "According to the autopsy, the death was caused by ingesting a toxic substance."

Rachel shifted her gaze to her desk. "Is that a politically correct term for drugs?"

He shrugged. "More like poison, I think."

She gaped at him. "Poison?"

The younger man was fidgeting with a pencil. "Selenium something or other."

"What's that?"

"Sold in health food shops. Supposed to stop skin itching, and I don't know what all." The gum popped.

The redhead glanced at his partner, then back at her. "He have itchy skin?"

"I have no idea." *Why would Lonnie take selenium at all, much less an overdose? Could it be snorted? Did it deliver a rush, a high of some sort?* But Rachel asked none of these questions.

Instead, she looked at one man, then the other. "Did he, uh…take the poison himself?"

"Far as we know. We do have to rule out homicide, though," the young officer said stiffly. "You know any of his friends?"

"No. Lonnie was pretty much a loner."

"You ever been to his apartment?"

"Yes," she gulped, realizing her fingerprints would be everywhere. *Did they run prints in a case like this?* "You have any suspects?"

"Not really," the older cop said in a bored voice.

The younger one asked, "He have a locker or anything? Leave any personal belongings here?"

"No." She ran nervous fingers through her hair and willed herself to composure.

The older man handed her a card. "If you happen to find anything…unusual, give us a call."

"Right." She looked at the card, then calmly back at the officers and nodded goodbye.

In the after-hours darkness of the garage, Rachel's face glowed bluish as her eyes peered at the computer monitor. There was more information on the Internet about selenium than she would be able to sift through in a week.

It was a trace element that had "a close interrelationship with vitamin E." It was supposed to "aid in body growth." Among sundry nonmedical items was the diverse news that selenium was responsible for the color in red lights, as well as for the "loco" in locoweed, which caused cattle to go berserk.

She paused when she came to the comment that a "large dose gives the breath a faint odor of garlic."

Was Lonnie telling the truth? Was he so bent on improving his health that mega doses of vitamins had actually killed him?

Rachel supposed that was not impossible. Addicts were famous for overkill on just about anything.

But if that was the case, what was the powder in the plastic bag she had removed from Lonnie's teapot? And what about the envelope in Jason's bathroom?

Goldie looked at Rachel as if she were babbling in Farsi. "They said *what* killed your friend?"

Rachel leaned her head back against the vinyl-covered headrest in the cab of the Merry Maids van. "Selenium. It's a mineral they put in vitamin pills."

One of Goldie's eyebrows rose over a disbelieving brown eye. "You saying he OD'd himself on vitamins?"

"I guess large doses are lethal."

"Must've chowed down enough to choke a friggin' horse."

"Maybe it wouldn't take a whole lot if it entered the bloodstream all at once."

Goldie cast her eyes to the roof of the van. "Some of those health freaks are pretty weird. It's a wonder more of them don't keel right over into their alfalfa sprouts."

Rachel could see the windows on InterUrban's second floor going dark one at a time. She glanced back at Goldie. "First Jason and the powder in that envelope, then Lonnie and the bag of powder in his teapot, then that plane...."

Goldie stared at her. "What plane?"

"Sunday." Rachel leaned back in the seat, propped her feet on the dash and explained. "I keep wondering if there's some connection."

A car sped past the van and jerked a fast turn at the corner, tires squealing.

"SOBs who drive like that oughta be shot," Goldie muttered, then leaned her elbow on the steering wheel. "You sure got a way of getting yourself smack in the middle of a lot of things that smell to high heaven of dope."

Rachel didn't answer. Something was nibbling at the edge of her mind like a skittish fish.

⌐⌐⌐

The phone was ringing when she got back to her apartment.

"You Rachel Chavez?" The voice was male, and stern.

The back of her neck prickled. "Yes." In a knee-jerk reaction to the sternness she added, "Sir."

"This is Deputy Sheriff Moran. You reported the crash of a small plane on Sunday near Coyote Reservoir, on County Road one-nine-four?"

"Yes." She drew the word out but gave it no tone.

"Are you aware that it is a criminal offense to make a false report?"

"Ex—excuse me?"

"There was no debris from a plane crash."

"But of course there was!"

The voice on the other end grew icicles. "I assure you there was not. We made a thorough search. Are you aware you could be billed for the expense caused by your little prank?"

"But that's impossible." She said it twice before she realized she was talking to a dial tone.

Chapter Twenty-one

Rachel hung up the phone and called Hank, whose husky mumbles spoke of sleep. Her words tripped over each other as she repeated what the sheriff had said.

"That's crazy," he sputtered. "They must have looked in the wrong place."

"But he said 'near Coyote Reservoir.' You think someone could have moved that plane?"

"Sure didn't look to me like it would be off the ground anytime soon. Those cops must be blind. Maybe one of us should drive out there, show them exactly where it is."

"Not me," she said quickly. "Can't you think of some business reason to go to the reservoir? It belongs to InterUrban." She could hear Hank breathing into the phone in the pause that followed.

"Too many real things to do. My desk is breeding paperwork like fleas."

Annoyance rose in her like heartburn. Was his work more important than hers?

But it wasn't because of her work that she didn't want to go. She didn't want to talk to cops. "If they can't find something that big, I guess that's their problem," she said irritably.

"You okay?" he asked.

"I'm tired of all this. Why is it happening to me?"

"It didn't just happen to you. I was there."

"I don't mean only that damn plane." Her voice shot over the line before she realized that Hank didn't know about Lonnie or the envelope from Jason's office, and certainly not why she was so peevish about talking with the sheriff. Maybe it was time to tell him, if not everything, something.

One thing she knew for sure. It was time to do *something*. She had made plans, had even made a list. But she had done *nothing*.

"Sorry," she said. "I didn't mean to snap. Can we talk sometime soon?"

Hank hesitated. "I've got a terrible week coming up."

"Never mind." Knowing she shouldn't, doing it anyway, she hung up. She was getting into bed when the phone rang. She turned out the light and pulled the covers over her. *Let him talk to the tape.*

"Rachel. Pick up," squawked Hank's voice from the answering machine.

She reached for the phone, clicked it on. "I said, never mind."

"Okay, let's talk. Just tell me where. And when."

Something silenced the angry retort before it spilled from her mouth. She asked him to meet her the following night at the Pig's Whistle.

The next morning, Rachel stopped at level C just in case the Cadillac had been returned. The space was still empty. It had been gone a week now.

While the cars streamed in, she sat in her booth with the Yellow Pages and a Thomas Brothers map, cross-checking body shop locations. As soon as traffic thinned, she drove over to Wilshire.

The BJ Body Shop was in a short stubby building sandwiched between two high-rises on the rim of the inner city, miles below the chic addresses the Wilshire Boulevard was known for.

A man looked up from his paperwork at the jingle of a bell when Rachel opened the door. His white shirt was so full of starch the fold marks stood out. The name *Jeff* was embroidered in a white oval above the pocket. "Yeah?" He threw his pencil down but didn't get up. "Tax audit," he growled. "Three hundred million liars out there and they have to pick me."

"Sorry for interrupting. I'm not even sure I'm in the right place. I'm looking for a late-model Caddy that had a dented—"

"You a fuzz?"

Rachel almost laughed. "No. It's my father, you see. He used to be very sharp and everything, but now he's sort of…forgetful. He took the car to a body shop in this area because of a dented right front fender, and now he can't remember where he took it."

Jeff stared at her a moment, then nodded. "Yeah. Happens, don't it? We're living longer these days, but we can't even remember who we are. Piece of crap, you know? Then we arrive at the pearly gates, and they audit your goddam life."

She examined her thumbnail. "I don't suppose you've got a Caddy like that in here for repair? It's a late-model. Black." She hoped that if the car was there, Jeff wouldn't remember that it bore an E plate and couldn't have belonged to an absentminded old man.

He thought a moment. "Not that I remember, but already I'm losing it. Have a look for yourself." He pointed at a door to the right of his desk.

"Just go look?"

"You need an escort? No one here but me. Can't get a good body man to come in before eight-thirty."

"Thanks," she said moving to the door. Engrossed in his paperwork, he didn't look up.

Nine cars sat in various states of disarray like women in a department store dressing room. The only black car was a Chrysler.

"Thanks anyway," she told Jeff, who grunted as she exited to the street.

⌒⌒⌒

An overhead light gleamed on the balding forehead of the round-shouldered, round-faced man behind the counter at Benchmark Analytic as Rachel handed him a Ziploc bag.

Wordless, he tipped his chin up to peer at it through bifocals. Wiping perfectly clean fingers on the front of his short-sleeve white shirt, he plucked at his necktie, then held the bag up to gaze at it again. He put it down as carefully as if it were an egg, picked up the brown envelope, folded back the flap, and examined the contents.

Rachel shifted her weight from one foot to the other. She had given her name as Wanda Feiner. "They look the same, don't they?"

His round shoulders rose and fell noncommittally. "Many substances look alike."

"Can you tell me what they are?"

He was peering into the brown envelope again. "Expect we can."

"How long will it take?"

He fixed her with an owlish gaze that declared that the first mark of civilization was patience. "You have no idea what it is?"

She shook her head. "None. Could be sugar for all I know."

His watery blue eyes looked at her sadly. "I'm afraid we're a bit backed up. At least a week, possibly two."

Rachel rubbed a thumb over her forehead. "What if they turn out to be a…?"

He cleared his throat and then supplied, "Pharmaceutical?" His round face grew a shade pinker.

"All right, yes, a drug. Suppose it's even an illegal drug?"

"I expect we could not return it to you."

"You'd just confiscate it?"

"We would have to let the police know. I hope it's nothing of that sort. The paperwork is terrible." He held the paper she had filled out between two fingers, then laid it on the counter. "You forgot to fill in your phone number."

"I'm not in much. I'll call next week."

"Cell phone?"

"I've never needed one."

"We do need a number."

She wrote the garage number down, reversing the last two digits.

Chapter Twenty-two

Charlotte Emerson closed the door of her office and took a zippered packet from her purse. It was embroidered in bright greens and blues and contained her makeup. In the adjoining restroom, she stood before a mirror framed with blue stained glass, feeling as if she were primping for a date. In a way, she told herself, she was. Perhaps the most important date of her life.

This was why she had done it. This was why she had wanted to become chairman. This would set the stage for the renaissance of this wild, throbbing, gasping, choking, astonishing place called the Southland by those who knew and loved it best.

Why, she wondered, does water howl in the Emerson veins like a werewolf?

She ran a tissue over her face. "Not a bad complexion for an old lady," she said aloud, well aware that her warm ivory skin was the envy of women far younger. She brushed blusher onto her cheeks and darkened her eyebrows with a little mascara.

They hadn't wanted to meet in either of their offices, settling instead on neutral territory. And Charlotte would be just a little late. Seven minutes would be about right.

She blotted the rose lipstick, put the cosmetics in her desk, took her navy blue leather purse, and told her secretary Janet she would be late returning from lunch. It was only six blocks. She would walk. Parking was a nightmare and she needed the exercise.

The streets were crowded with Asian youngsters. Scrubbed and groomed within an inch of their lives, they toted book bags, looking more like Valley girls and boys than kids who lived in the San Fernando Valley.

An Anglo man was trudging toward her. His beard was gray and shabby, his shirt filthy, but his eyes were clear. He held out his hand in a silent plea. Charlotte opened her purse and took out a dollar. No, she would make it a twenty, in honor of the day. He was still blinking at it when she glanced back a block later.

The old man and the shiny kids would have better lives because of what she had agreed to.

Eventually. Ultimately.

She reminded herself that for a while, things might get worse. At first she had been uneasy. But the greater good, as her father used to say, demands sacrifices from time to time.

She covered the few blocks briskly. Already she could see the silly drawing on the green enamel sign. Charlotte slowed, brushed a shred of lint from her navy gabardine skirt, lifted her chin, crossed the street, and opened the door.

On the fourth floor of Everly Laboratories, Alfred Lieberman pressed the toe of his well-worn loafer against the bottom drawer of his desk and pushed. His swivel chair rolled across the white linoleum to another desk.

Susan Stankowski turned an ankle trying to follow him in her new high-heeled shoes. "Of course I'm sure the figures are right," she said.

Alfred checked the figures again, absently running his fingers through his thick thatch of dark hair, sprinkling dandruff on his thick glasses. Without taking his eyes off the figures, he removed the glasses, wiped them with a rumpled handkerchief, replaced them on the long nose, and tapped the end of a ballpoint pen on a cheek scarred by acne during an adolescence he could hardly remember. "Interesting," he muttered.

Susan smoothed her newly styled, highlighted, and moussed hair. After nearly twenty years of preferring research to men, Susan had fallen in love.

Alfred liked her work okay, he just never seemed to *see* her. After appraising her thin face and angular body in the ladies' room mirror, Susan had spent a week of her vacation and a month's pay at a spa being "made over." She was still struggling to master her new persona. Not that it mattered. Alfred hadn't noticed.

Now, however, she had his attention. With a perfectly ordinary job of spectrochemical analysis. "Would you…," she began, then rehearsed the rest of the sentence in her head and started over. "Would you like to come over for dinner Friday?"

Alfred hadn't caught the interruption in her speech. He was still examining the figures. "This is going to excite a few people," he said to no one in particular.

"Why?" Susan dropped her hand to the desktop.

"If that's what's ailing those ducks, it had to come from the soil. My guess is irrigation water leached it out and washed it into those ponds. Exactly what happened at Kessler. Except this is much, much worse. The environmentalists will be hopping mad. Good thing we're not farmers."

He moved his eyes to Susan and stared. "Did you do something to your hair?"

Carole Steigholtz was mad. She hardly ever got angry, but this time she was really mad.

It was bad enough that as Assistant Director of Water Quality she had to run the whole shop while Harry schmoozed with reporters and visiting dignitaries. This was too much.

Eyes flashed in the squarish face that had never been contaminated by makeup. Short stubby fingers around the pen showed white at the tips as Carole jotted down numbers from the gas chromatograph printout. For the fourth time, her sensible shoes marched across the tile floor to Harry's office. A little cowlick of short-cropped brown hair bobbed as she marched.

She'd left him a note. She'd called him at home and left a message on his blankety-blank machine. She was still itching to tell him face-to-face her opinion of his behavior.

Last time, he'd been shacked up with the little bar kitten whose peroxided bangs did nothing to cover the lack of a brain. Carole had covered for Harry then, and the time before. But this was one time too many.

Chapter Twenty-three

The Pig's Whistle, for all its seediness, was a much-loved watering hole for blue- and white-collar crowds alike. Some of the clientele had something to celebrate, others a rotten day to forget, and there were always those with something at home they couldn't face without a drink.

"Soda on ice," Rachel told the short, swarthy bartender, who was chewing on a toothpick as though his life depended on turning it to pulp. He eyed her stolidly, then stabbed a glass into the ice bin as she sat down at the bar.

"Got a piece of lemon?" she asked as he unceremoniously set the drink before her. He slid a small plate of lemon slices down the bar; it came to a stop directly in front of her.

Five televisions suspended on various shelves were set on mute, the talking heads working their mouths earnestly. Someone was playing an old Beatles tune on an even older jukebox.

Would Hank come? Or would he forget the time, like her father did when his poker game was on a roll?

The bartender nodded at her club soda. "Just quit drinking myself." He spit out the ruined toothpick and replaced it with another.

"Hey, good for you. The first couple months are tough, but it gets easier."

"Piece of cake."

She had downed her drink and was asking for another when the door opened, admitting a short, stocky man in a yellow sweater that did little to mask a barrel-like midsection.

"Bruno!" she waved.

"Hey, kid." He hoisted himself onto the stool next to hers.

She caught his long look at her drink. "Soda, Bruno, only soda. Smell it." She held out the glass, feeling like a twelve-year-old, but doing it anyway. "Want a taste?"

"Since when is it any of my business?" He wagged a finger at the bartender. "J and B and water, easy on the water."

"I didn't know you were in town."

"Emergency Farm Bureau meeting. We got trouble, kid. Big time trouble." He took a gulp of his scotch and sagged over the bar.

She put her hand on his arm. "Like what?"

"Those ponds."

"What ponds?" Rachel squeezed some lemon into her soda and took a sip.

"Up by Salinas. It was me talked the guys into donating the land. I got newspaper clippings of me shaking hands with Tony Holland. You know Tony? Environmental Defense Fund. The mealy-mouth bastard. Now he's blaming us like we were doing it on purpose."

"Blaming you for what?" Rachel knew that to Bruno, farming was the next thing to a religious calling.

His face turned even more dour. "Those damn enviro nuts think we'd kill anything for a buck. They say we're poisoning wildlife."

"I don't understand."

"We built those ponds to take irrigation water that runs off the farms and evaporate it. Then these enviros said we should plant some weeds, make it some kind of paradise for birds, and give the whole kit and caboodle to them. I think okay, why not make some points, maybe the nuts stop snapping at our backsides for a while. So I talk the guys into it. Now they say the runoff is full of poison, like we planned it that way. Sure. Why not? Don't everybody like to hurt ducks?"

"What does that mean? Is it a pesticide?"

Bruno ordered himself another Scotch and her another "whatever." Then he removed his glasses and pinched the bridge of his nose with two fingers. "Wish I knew, kid. Wish I knew. They just might be able to ruin us this time. They been trying for a lot of years. They may go after the water folks, too."

"Why?"

The bar had filled up. Someone played "Only the Good Die Young" on the jukebox. No new music had been added in at least ten years, but the crowds never seemed to mind.

"Farmers get cheap water, you know that," Bruno said.

"We took ours out of the delta, for free," she said. "We had to keep an eye on the levees or we got flooded. That's about all I know."

"We get delta water in the valley, too, but it comes in an aqueduct. Thank God that pipe got built before the green nuts were hatched. The water's pretty cheap. If it wasn't, we'd have to charge five bucks a melon."

Rachel tried to look attentive, but her eyes kept darting back to the entrance. Where was Hank?

Bruno didn't notice. He was staring into his glass. "Inter-Urban wants more water for the people down here. That's their job. The enviros have just about managed to cut them off."

Billy Joel's voice from the old jukebox came to an end.

Bruno's had not. Rachel had never seen him so dejected.

"Lots of voters down here," he said, examining the ice cubes in his glass, as if they were tea leaves. "But none of them knows beans about water, so the city water guys—that's mostly Inter-Urban—line up with us because ag has a good lobby and we sure as hell know about water. Between us, we've had enough votes in the legislature to keep the duck-lovers from cutting our throats and eating our gizzards."

The door opened, ushering in a breeze from the street. Hank stepped inside and scanned the crowd. Rachel caught his eye and waved.

Hank threaded his way through the throng of drinkers bent on making the most of happy hour.

Bruno looked him over as he approached as if he were an overgrown melon.

Rachel squirmed on her bar stool and introduced them.

Hank's hand brushed her back, leaving a tiny shiver in its wake.

"Well, I see you got other business." Bruno buttoned his sweater. "I got to meet some guys for supper." Slumped shoulders giving him a desolate look, he pushed his way out to the street. A twinge of guilt pricked at Rachel's innards.

The bartender stopped in front of Hank, who had taken Bruno's vacated stool. Hank ordered a Mexican beer. Someone was playing the Billy Joel number again. It reminded Rachel of Lonnie.

She frowned into the mirror that covered the wall behind the bar. Lonnie was so young. He should have lived another sixty years. Her fingers around the soda glass whitened.

Hank was examining the label on his beer bottle. "Any more from the sheriff about that plane?" he asked.

"Nope." She inspected the ring her glass had made on the bar.

Hank shoved the straw-colored hair away from his eyes and exhaled as if he were blowing out candles. "So what's on your mind?"

"What do you know about Jason Karl's death?"

Puzzled eyes sought hers before he gave an almost invisible shrug. "What's there to know? He was apparently taking a pee by the side of the road and some crazy driver, probably going way too fast, lost control of his vehicle, veered off the road, smacked Jason, then got away without being seen. Fairly typical hit and run."

"Any witnesses?"

"Happened out in the desert. Nobody around."

Rachel opened her handbag, dug to the bottom of it and extracted the tie tack. "Ever seen this?" She tossed it on the bar. The etched tortoise seemed to turn its head to watch her.

Hank squinted at it. "What's it supposed to be?"

"Hello there!"

The smooth female voice came from behind Rachel. She covered the tie tack with her hand and turned to meet the almost-black eyes of Alexandra Miller. The three of them danced the prescribed steps of small talk, then Alexandra excused herself and made her way past the bar toward the booths.

Rachel caught sight of a white-haired woman in a bright yellow jacket. "Isn't that Charlotte?" she asked Hank. "In the booth where Alexandra sat down."

"Not likely," he said. "They hate each other."

Rachel opened her hand. The metal caught the light.

Hank swiveled on the bar stool and peered intently at the tie tack. "Could swear I've seen it somewhere, but I can't think where."

"It belonged to Jason."

"Where'd you find it?"

"Wedged under the hood of that car in the garage. The one with the crinkled fender." She plucked at the limp napkin under her soda glass and plunged on: "Did you know that the guy who worked for me also died unexpectedly?"

Two lines appeared over Hank's nose. He loosened his red-and-blue striped tie. "When?"

She told him and added, in slow, measured words: "I don't think either one was an accident. I have some pretty persuasive reasons."

"And the cops? They think these reasons are persuasive?"

"They haven't heard them." She ran her finger back and forth on the grain of the oak bar top.

He glanced over the rim of his beer mug at her. "Why not?"

"I'm not sure they'd believe me." Rachel mopped up the little puddle around her glass with the frayed napkin.

His eyebrows climbed into the shock of sandy hair. "That's their problem, isn't it?"

A truck lumbered by on the street, shaking the entire building. The urge for a drink swept over Rachel, bringing an overwhelming sense of loss. The jukebox was playing "A Whiter

Shade of Pale." She banged a fist on the bar. "They need to get some new music here." She tossed her head, relinquished the bar stool, and moved toward the exit.

"What's wrong?" Hank stepped down from the stool, left some bills for the bartender, and caught up with her at the door. "How about dinner?"

"No thanks. Don't you have to get back to work?"

He turned her toward him, looked into her face. "Whatever I said, I apologize."

For a long moment she glared at him, but slowly her scowl wilted. "My fault. I've been uptight lately. I know I'm not exactly the playgirl of the month."

"Let's grab a hamburger at least."

She dropped her eyes, wanting to tell him she was an alcoholic, knowing she wouldn't, but nodding to dinner anyway.

Chapter Twenty-four

The burgers and fries they picked up from Tommy's filled the car with a rich, salty smell. The evening was dimming toward full dusk when Hank turned the Mustang onto a narrow road that twisted uphill.

"This goes to a park?" Rachel asked.

"Sort of. I live up here."

She opened her mouth to say this wasn't a good idea, but he quickly added, "Beyond my house, the road goes into the Angeles."

Hank parked the car and held the burgers while she climbed over the chain to a trail that led toward national forest land.

She eyed the mountain looming ahead. "Are we trespassing?"

"If we are, I do it all the time."

Keeping an awkward foot between them, they hiked between California oaks and scrub.

Rachel turned and was stunned by the view of city lights, like drops of water spilling out of the mountains and pooling into a burst of brilliance before paling again in the distance.

"Not bad." She kicked at a pine cone, sat down and put her arms around her knees. "You bring a lot of women up here?"

"One or two. The last was my cleaning lady—she had trouble making it the last few yards. She'd never seen the lights. Can you imagine living in LA and never seeing the lights?"

"So the only woman in your life is your cleaning lady?"

Hank studied his shoelaces for a moment, then returned her gaze. "You don't leave people a place to hide, do you?"

She shrugged, still looking at the lights. "I guess I want to save all the hiding places for myself. You don't have to answer."

He handed her a burger. The wrapping paper crackled in the stillness. "There have been a few women in my life."

"None of them important, though, right?"

"Actually, a couple were fairly important, and one was earth-shaking."

She cocked her head at him, but said nothing.

He leaned back against a rock and looked at the sky. A breeze churned the air. "I flunked out of college in my freshman year, joined the Peace Corps, went to Brazil to teach the natives how to farm. Without pesticides, of course. But the bugs there were the size of frying chickens. The kids used to hitch beetles to little cardboard carts and have races."

"You're kidding."

Hank scratched his cheek. "No joke. Wound up teaching them to dust their crops with as many pesticides as we could lay our hands on."

"You taught them? You mean you flew?"

"Had to learn how so I could teach them." He glanced at Rachel, then unwrapped a hamburger and began to eat. "I married a Brazilian girl, had a daughter."

Rachel congratulated herself for predicting that something would be wrong. She was losing the struggle to keep her face blank and glad for the darkness. Instead of the question she wanted to ask, she said, "You speak Portuguese?"

"The Peace Corps gave us four weeks of intensive training."

Rachel was careful not to look at him. "So if you were having such a good time, why did you come back?"

Hank said nothing for a moment, then, "I got tired of the bugs, the humidity, of so many people barely able to feed themselves. The few rich were very rich, the rest were dirt poor. Corruption was so bad that postal employees stole the mail, and you had to pay bribes to get anything from canned goods to an education. People were routinely accused of imaginary crimes and had to bribe their way out of jail."

An insect buzzed at Hank's ear. He slapped at it and went on. "At first, you think you can make a difference. But soon you realize you have to play the game. And the name of the game is eat or be eaten."

Rachel looked down at her hands, which were busy shredding a napkin. She rolled the paper into a ball. "Your wife doesn't fish?" She stared levelly into Hank's puzzled frown. "What were your wife and daughter doing that Sunday when we went fishing? What are they doing now?"

Hank made a sound, more a bark than a laugh. "Haven't the foggiest, they're in Brazil. I haven't seen them in over a year."

"You left them there?"

"My wife couldn't bring herself to leave papa and all the servants. Eventually, I came home alone."

"So you're divorced?"

"No. She's Catholic and won't. I never bothered to file here. I give her a chunk of my paycheck. She doesn't need the money, but it makes me feel better. I've been back three times to visit my daughter."

"Funny," Rachel said huskily, "how you can think you've got the world by the ying-yang and you wake up one day and it's all gone sour."

"Yeah, isn't it."

They watched the city lights the way people look into a fire, seeking something unknowable.

Hank shifted his gaze to her face. "What about you?"

She studied the sky for a moment. "I was a farm kid. My mother died and Pop, well, he couldn't deal with things without her. He lost the farm, along with just about everything else. I inherited the garage, what there was of it, from my grandfather."

"Where was the farm?"

"Up in the delta. Hot, humid, lots of mosquitoes, but terrific farmland. More vegetables to the acre than anywhere in the state, maybe the country. My grandfather used to say with land like that we could almost feed the world."

"Big tug of war, the delta," Hank said. "A real pressure cooker. Farmers want the land, cities want the water, the greens want it for ducks and fish. One of these days, something will blow."

"You'll never get the farmers out of the delta. They're all like my grandfather. You'd have to shoot them first."

Hank gave a dry chuckle. "You don't know how determined the others can be." A sudden breeze plucked at the empty bag. He grabbed it as it began to dance away. "I've been thinking about what you said. About Jason."

She took the bag from him, shoved the empty wrappers into it, jammed it under her heel, and turned to look at him. His long legs looked awkward sitting on the sloping ground.

"It's sure a weird string of incidents, last but not least being a plane that falls out of the sky and then disappears," she said.

His features knit themselves into a frown. He turned toward the lights. "Why didn't you call the cops when you found that tie tack?"

She wavered, wishing she hadn't begun this. "It's not that simple."

"What's hard about it? You pick up a phone." The moon was becoming bright as daylight faded.

She started to get up. "Hey, I'm probably an idiot. Never mind."

He put his hand on her arm, but she rose to her feet anyway, then looked down into his face, studying the expression there. A cloud floated across the moon, darkening the landscape. The silence drew out and grew leaden.

Hank reached for her hand, but she pulled it away. "I'm fine." She got to her feet. "Let's go." She started down the trail toward the car.

"Hey!" he shouted.

She didn't turn until something struck her lightly, first in the shoulder, then in the calf. She swung around. He was pelting her with pine cones. "Cut that out!"

"Lighten up," he called. "We need to get a life. Both of us."

"Sorry. I'll try to be more entertaining." She turned back to the trail, wanting only to get away from him.

Thorns caught at her shirt. She stumbled over a rock, sat down hard, and skidded down a small hill, landing with a splash at the bottom. The water wasn't so cold as it was surprising. She tried to stand, but the rock under her foot rolled, pitching her again. This time even her shirt got soaked. "Shit."

"If this is your siren act, it needs a little work." Hank's voice came from her left, but she couldn't see him.

A hand snaked out of the shadows, grabbed one of her flailing arms, and hauled her out of the water.

"Good God, you're soaking wet." He took her face between his hands and raised it to his.

The kiss was slow and deliberate and when he ran his tongue lightly over her lips, she stopped struggling.

Then he began to unbutton her blouse.

Chapter Twenty-five

In an earlier life, Andy's Bodyworks had been a tire store. The letters spelling *Firestone* were still visible under the whitewash that covered the cement block walls.

Rachel couldn't find a place to park, so she drove around the block to the city lot, turned off the car and propped her elbows on the steering wheel, thinking of the night before.

Hank had wrapped her in his own shirt, taken her back to his house, an A-frame on the rim of the canyon, and loaned her a pair of jeans and a rope to use for a belt. "As a matter of fact," she had told him earnestly, "I have something in common with your cleaning lady. I had never seen the lights, either."

The door to the body shop was heavy and as soon as she pushed against it, a buzzer sounded, the door gave way, and Rachel almost fell against a burly chest.

"Excuse me." She shouted the words into a broad black face atop a massive neck.

Thick fingers jammed a cap onto a nearly hairless head. Rachel gaped after him, taking in the uniform and the badge as he stepped past her to the sidewalk.

A second man, this one short and wiry, followed his partner to the parking lot.

Rachel swallowed a little gulp of air as they got into a beat-up car with more primer showing than paint and roared off with the sound of a jet plane.

"Close the damn door," came a surly voice from inside the shop. "You're lettin' it all out! You got any idea what air conditioning costs?"

"Sorry." She pushed the door shut. "What were the police doing here?"

"If that was any of yer business, I'da sent you a special delivery letter." The man behind the counter was fortyish with a round face beneath red hair; his lips were thick, his fingers looked permanently grease-stained. The sleeves of his once-white shirt were rolled up and the name of the shop, *Andy's* was tattooed on one forearm. His belly bulged over his belt like a poisonous mushroom.

Rachel launched into her story about an absentminded father who had left a black Cadillac DeVille for repairs, but couldn't remember which body shop.

"Naw." The man shook his head.

"You sure? I think it almost has to be here. I've checked just about every other shop in this area." She moved toward a grey door that obviously led into the business end of the shop. "Mind if I take a look?"

The man moved out from behind the counter. "Yeah, I do mind." For a big man, he was fast on his feet. He put a shoulder against the door, blocking her way.

"I just thought I might recognize the car."

"Look, I got cops up my ass for a couple hours, I got two guys off sick, and the one left, I gotta give him directions even on how to pick his nose. The day's half over and we ain't got any work done. I ain't about to let you monkey around in there askin' questions and screwing up the other half." His small eyes had turned mean and pig-like.

Rachel dropped her hand from the door's steel handle and shrugged. "Mind if I come back tomorrow?"

"Matter of fact, I do. I don't let customers back there. Ever. 'Count of the insurance. You know what liability insurance costs? And you ain't even a customer."

"But I think my father left a car here. A black—"

He cut her off. "Don't bother comin' back till you know for damn certain sure." He heaved himself back into his chair behind the counter.

Rachel was careful to close the door behind her, hoping this episode wasn't a harbinger of how the rest of her day would go. Her mind wandered back to Hank, wondering if last night was bogus or maybe—just maybe—the real thing,

Halfway up the block, a slender man who reminded her of Lonnie looked up from a clipboard of papers and asked, "Andy's Bodyworks down this way?"

Rachel nodded. "Be careful, though. He's in a seriously foul mood."

The man gave a dry laugh. "Figures. After a robbery, they're either whiney or macho."

"Robbery?"

"Guess somebody broke in last night. Don't know what they took, but they cut all the wires on his burglar alarm. He's not going to be happy when I tell him it'll be a couple days before we can get the alarm fixed."

Peter's round face furrowed with concentration as he slipped the Visa credit card between Rachel's apartment door and the molding and carefully drew it down toward the lock.

Goldie snorted. "If that don't beat all. I am standing here watching a child show you how to crack a lock."

"Ssh," Rachel hissed. "Let him concentrate."

The lock gave a muffled click. Peter's eyes danced. "See? Easy." He opened the door. "Good?" He handed the plastic card to Rachel. "You do."

"Ever hear of contributing to the delinquency of a minor?" Goldie clucked.

"I'm not teaching him, he's teaching me." Rachel slipped the card into the slot and slid it down the side of the door, but when it reached the tongue of the lock, it would go no farther. She tried twice more without success. "Damn."

Peter took the card from her and opened the lock on the first try.

Goldie grunted, "I am not going to feel safe in my bed ever again. Where'd you learn that, boy?"

"Danny," Peter said.

Goldie looked at the ceiling and muttered something under her breath.

Rachel made another try with the card and failed again. "Who's Danny?"

"His brother. Now I know why he did time in Chino."

Peter beamed. "Danny does it real good. He say it's a gift of the touch."

"Well, I sure don't have the gift." Rachel looked at Peter. "When do you get off work?"

He shrugged and looked at Goldie, who said, "When we finish and not until." Peter scampered back down the garage ramp.

Goldie swung back to Rachel. "You cannot be thinking of making a criminal of that child."

"I have to get into that body shop. If the car is there, it won't be there long. You were the one saying I shouldn't let someone get away with murder."

"I didn't say you should do it yourself."

"I need some solid evidence. Not just a tie tack I can't even prove was Jason's."

Goldie pursed her lips, stared at some spot in space, then held out her hand. "Give me the card." When Rachel did, Goldie fed the gold plastic into the slot between the jamb and the door, drew it down, and the lock clicked open.

~~~

Arriving at Benchmark Analytic, Rachel was so nervous she knocked against the door jamb, ripped her jeans and gouged her knee on a small, barely protruding nail. She looked over her shoulder almost expecting to find a cop behind her.

The chubby, bald man behind the counter, oblivious to her less than graceful entrance, was studying a piece of paper, the tip of his tongue protruding between his lips.

Somewhere in the bowels of the lab, someone turned on a faucet.

"Excuse me," she said.

"Eh?" He blinked as though he had just emerged from a cave into bright sun.

"I left some stuff here a couple weeks ago. To be analyzed." Her mind blanked when she tried to remember the phony name she had given. Fumbling among the contents of her handbag, she found the receipt and held it out. "Is the report ready?"

The bald man took the receipt, studied it, then disappeared, leaving Rachel to shift her weight nervously from one foot to the other. Minute after minute passed with no further sound save the running water. Something in the air hinted of damp metal.

Had they been instructed to call the police when she returned? Was the delay a ruse to keep her there till they arrived?

The walls of the lab reception area were a bright lime green. Who on earth chooses such colors, she wondered, pacing skittishly between the counter and the exit. Her knee hurt. She bent to pull up her pants leg. A trickle of blood was running down her shin.

"Gracious." The man was peering over the counter.

Rachel pulled her pants leg down.

"You'd best put some ice on that." He set a tray on the counter and disappeared again.

In the tray was the plastic packet, the brown envelope, and a piece of paper. She was craning her neck to read the paper when he returned with a plastic bag of ice cubes.

"To stop the bleeding," he said, unperturbed, as though people bled there daily.

A trickle of blood found its way to the floor. "Sorry about the carpet."

"Peroxide," he said. "Blood comes right out."

"I didn't know that." She took the ice from him and applied it to her knee. "Thanks."

"Everything is chemistry. Everything. Just chemistry."

"Did you find out what they are?" she asked, hopping on one foot to point at the tray.

"Of course, yes. That's what we do." He began reading the paper, glanced at her, then went back to reading. *Was there a suspicious look in his eye?*

He tipped his head back and peered at her through his bifocals. The fluorescent light overhead made his chin look pale purple. He nodded. "Sodium selenate."

Rachel gaped at him. "What is that?"

He seemed to be trying to decide how much she knew about chemistry. "Selenium salt. A form of selenium."

Why would Lonnie have a batch of selenium lying about in his kitchen? Why would he have swallowed enough to kill him?

"What does it taste like?"

He looked at her as if she had asked him to take his pants off. "This is a laboratory, not a kitchen."

"What about the envelope? What was in that?"

"The two are, I believe, quite the same."

Rachel forgot about her knee. *Jason stashed selenium in his john?* "But they can't be."

He glanced at the paper again. "I assure you, they are."

"Selenium isn't a drug, is it? I mean, I heard it was a sort of vitamin…?"

He shrugged. "People will call anything a health food. It is an element, of course, just a trace element, quite common."

"But how would it get— Where does it come from?"

He lowered his chin and looked over his small round glasses the way her third grade teacher used to look at her when she had asked something silly. "From the earth, of course. It's not a gas, is it?"

She ignored his look. "Is it poisonous?"

"Most of its compounds are highly toxic. Pure selenium, in small amounts, no. Large amounts, yes."

"How large an amount?"

He scratched his left ear. "Of pure selenium? I wouldn't recommend ingesting more than a few hundred micrograms. Your samples aren't pure, of course." He looked down at her knee. "I'm afraid you are bleeding again."

Chapter Twenty-six

Rachel swallowed the last of her tea, banged the cup into the saucer, and said to Goldie, "It just isn't logical."

Goldie was staring at the ceiling of Rachel's apartment. "Nope, honey. It don't make a lot of sense to me, either."

"Why would Jason put an ounce or two of an ordinary trace element in an envelope and put the envelope behind his toilet tank?"

"There's nothing illegal about it?"

"At Walgreen's it's sitting right there on the shelf with the vitamins and minerals. That's pills, of course, not powder."

"That stuff of Jason's was the same as your friend was keeping in an old teapot in his kitchen? And they didn't know each other?"

"Lonnie and Jason didn't live on the same planet. They had zero in common."

"How do you know?"

Rachel stared at her a moment. "I guess I don't know for certain."

Goldie got to her feet. "It's dark. You ready to go? I got to be back by midnight."

Pain twinged in her knee when Rachel stood. "It's nothing," she said to Goldie's look. "I walked into a door."

"Right."

Rachel locked the apartment. "It isn't far. We should walk."

"With you on that leg? Why?"

"Because if the alarm goes off and the police come, we're better off on foot." Rachel's voice was high and sharp with nerves.

"I thought the burglar alarm wasn't working."

"It isn't."

A soft, high-pitched sound came from the bottom of the stair well near the side exit from the garage. Rachel jerked around. "What was that?"

"I don't think anything else goes *meow* but a cat." Goldie scratched her nose. "I can't believe you talked me into this. I am just gonna walk down the street and commit a felony."

Rachel opened the door and they stepped out onto the side-walk. "Had to be you or Peter." She checked her watch. It was straight up eleven o'clock. Across the street, the Merry Maids van sat in front of the water agency headquarters.

The whitewashed cement-block building that was Andy's Bodyworks glowed pale purple in the huge light that shone down on it.

Goldie stopped on the sidewalk, gaping at the front door. "Jesus, Mary, and Joseph. If we're going to break into that place, we might as well hire a marching band."

"Maybe there's a back door."

A passing car made the storefront even brighter.

"Maybe we don't really need to get in there," Goldie muttered.

But Rachel was already rounding the corner of the building toward the back. She was studying the door's lock when Goldie reached her. "Give me the credit card."

Goldie, eyes so big they seemed to take up half her face, nodded. Darting glances over each shoulder, she brought the card from a pocket.

Eyeing Goldie, Rachel said, "You look guilty as hell."

"I *am* guilty as hell."

"We're not going to steal anything," Rachel hissed.

"Try explaining that if the burglar alarm got fixed."

"The guy said it would be a couple days."

Goldie slipped the card between the door and the jamb. "Don't watch me, watch the street."

A glowing curtain of light suddenly swept over them; they both gasped and froze.

Rachel's heart pounded so loud in her ears it was a few seconds before she heard the throb in the air above them and looked up. A helicopter was moving slowly toward Chinatown, sweeping a path beneath it with a huge cone of light.

Goldie's eyes filled with fright.

"Give me the card and go on back," Rachel said in a hoarse whisper. "I can't ask you to do this."

The black woman stared after the helicopter. "I'm no quitter." Her trembling fingers were clumsy, but on the fourth try, the card nudged the door free.

Rachel breathed her relief. "No alarm."

Goldie was less sanguine. "Don't just stand there with your feet all over the floor, get inside."

Patches of light from various windows mottled the linoleum. "What if the burglar alarm is a silent one that just dials the cops?" Rachel whispered.

Goldie hissed in the dark: "*Now* you think of that?"

They moved through the front office to the shop, where the ghostly glow from a skylight gave the row of cars a crouching, sinister look. Rachel pulled a mini Maglite from her pocket, but in her rush stumbled over something. The resulting loud clank spooked both of them again.

Regaining her balance, she moved on down the line of dented fenders, bumpers, hoods. Next to the last on the left was a dark Cadillac. "Yes!" she whispered loudly, motioning to Goldie.

The Caddy's back bumper was crowding the wall, making it impossible to see the license plate, but the right front fender was missing. The Maglite's narrow beam halted on the rearview mirror. The misspelled message was there: OBJECTS IN MIRROR ARE CLOSE THAN THEY APPEAR.

"This is it." The passenger door creaked as she opened it. The overhead light flashed on.

"What do you think you're going to find?" Goldie was at her elbow.

"Don't know." Rachel ran her hand over the dash. The glove compartment was locked. "Shit."

"Since you already made me an accomplice, you might as well let me take a look."

Rachel stood aside while Goldie reached under the seat for the lever, slid the seat back and ran her hands along the floor. "It's a filthy mess under here," she said, bringing out, one at a time, a crushed tissue box, a comb, three quarters, and a small slip of paper.

"What's that?"

"Says Texaco on it. Looks like one of them receipts you get when you pay for your gas in person with a credit card." Goldie handed it to Rachel.

"I thought all gas stations were set up so you pay at the pump."

"I guess some aren't," Goldie said.

"Then it'll have a date and a name." Rachel shone the light on it. "Damn. The part with the name is torn off and the signature looks like it was written by a baboon."

"Nothing else under there but lots of dust," Goldie grumbled.

Back out on the sidewalk, they walked steadily to the corner, then broke into a run. "If they're putting on a new fender, what do you think they did with the old one?" Rachel gasped, her knee reducing her gait to a hobble.

"I not only don't know, I don't want to know," Goldie grunted.

They were still out of breath when they reached the parking garage. Giggling like schoolgirls, they threw themselves onto the bench in front.

"Good thing we both have jobs," Rachel said, clutching at her knee.

"Might have trouble making it in a life of crime," Goldie tittered with glee. "But by Jehovah, we did it, didn't we!"

Drawing from her pocket the slip of paper Goldie had found, Rachel examined it with the Maglite. "The date is the day Jason was killed," she said, all trace of humor gone from her voice. "It's from a Texaco station in Riverside and there's a ticket number. Somewhere, there's also a full copy of this bill. With the name."

Slowly, Goldie nodded. "And I'll bet whoever signed it killed Jason."

Chapter Twenty-seven

Two mornings later, Rachel woke up in a fretful mood. Why hadn't she heard from Hank? Well, it was only a few days since.... *Yes, but....*

And what the hell had happened to that Caddy?

When most of the cars had parked, the warm, yeasty smell of Dunkin' Donuts lured her down the street from the garage. Sliding onto a stool in the corner behind the register, she ordered two glazed and a large coffee. By the time the cup arrived, one doughnut was history. Rachel was wiping the crumbs of the second from her mouth when a pair of male voices rose above the usual buzz of break-time snackers.

"Gimme a man to deal with any day."

"At least men understand why you can't pick a fender off a tree and slap it on a car in fifteen minutes. Andy's already hot enough, after those tools got swiped."

"I still think there's something weird goin' on with that Caddy."

"I don't give a rat's ass. That's their problem. But what are they doin' putting a woman in charge of it? She sashays in acting like the Queen of England. And he chews us up and spits us out at her feet."

Rachel stared at the two men. One had a small potbelly and a serious need for a shave; the other had the pained look of someone who needed some Tums. Both wore short-sleeve blue work shirts.

"You talking about that DeVille the water agency sent over for a new fender?" she asked, keeping her face blank.

The big man stared at her with watery pale-blue eyes. "What if we are?"

"It's my job to keep track of where all the cars are. We've been wondering when that one would be ready."

"You're behind times," the darker man piped up. "It's already picked up. This morning."

Rachel dropped her napkin and stooped to retrieve it. "We were told it wouldn't be ready till next week. You know who picked it up?"

Both men shrugged.

"It sure would help me a lot to know who picked up the car. I spend all my time tracking down the jerks who make personal use of the fleet cars. You know how it is."

The younger man laid a five on the counter. "Some woman."

"White hair," said potbelly. "A little long in the tooth, if you know what I mean, but used to be a looker. You could tell that."

Rachel's napkin skittered from her lap again.

The younger man plucked it from the floor and handed it to her. "Check with Andy, he probably knows."

"Thanks."

As she paid the cashier, Rachel could hear Potbelly grunting, "I sure as hell hope the old dingbat is in a shitload of trouble."

∽∽∽

"Well? What do you think?" Rachel asked Goldie as she turned onto the Foothill Freeway toward Riverside.

"If this Charlotte rushed the fender job and picked up the car herself, we got a real live suspect."

They found the Texaco station just off the freeway in Riverside. The small whitewashed building was decked with pots of petunias in macramé hangers.

Inside, the woman standing behind the counter was well over six feet with bright auburn hair. She was dressed as impeccably as a Saks mannequin, right down to two broad gold bands on her wrist. "Mornin', ladies. What can we do for you?" The deep, rich voice delivered the words as if they were a line in a play.

Rachel held out the torn receipt. "The name is missing from this and we were wondering if you might have the original."

The woman studied the slip of paper. "That's weeks old, hon. The original is sent to the credit card company." She drawled the words in a campy rendition of a Southern accent.

Goldie peered over Rachel's shoulder. "Don't you have to keep a copy?"

"Well, of course, the bookkeeper takes care of that. I'm sure he has just reams of these things."

"Could we possibly talk to your bookkeeper?" Rachel asked.

"Well, now I suppose you could. But he's a very jittery type. Trust me on this, he does not take to being bothered. Gets him rattled, and then he can't find any papers at all."

"You on the stage?" Goldie asked. "I think I saw you somewhere."

The woman beamed. "Why I sure am, honey, I sure enough am. I sing, I dance. They call me Princess. As of right now, I'm at Tiny's. Maybe you heard of it? North Hollywood?"

Goldie was nodding. "Of course. We go there all the time. Maybe we could get together a party and come some night soon. How long you going to be there?"

"At least a month, honey." The woman was straightening her already perfect clothing. "We would love to see you."

"How many people does that place hold? We might just rent out the whole place."

"Oh, my, wouldn't that be nice. I do believe it seats at least eighty."

"That might not be quite big enough," Goldie said. "You ever do special shows?"

"We certainly do." The woman patted the back of her auburn hair. "Especially if the price is right."

"What's your agent's phone number?" Rachel kept her face a perfect blank.

Retrieving a gold mesh handbag from behind the counter, the redhead handed her a card.

"That receipt," Rachel purred. "It's real important. How can we get a copy?"

"Let me think a minute." The woman tilted her head and touched her cheek, then walked with a swaying gait brought on by four-inch platform heels to the far end of the counter. She looked at a list of numbers taped to the wall, then picked up the phone and began to dial.

"Angel, I need to talk to someone in customer service. Merchant customer service.... Hello, honey, this is Colleen at Ivy's Texaco. Riverside C-A. We have a silly little problem here and I wonder if you could help.... Well, you see, the boss has a little something on the side, if you know what I mean, and he gives her free gas.... Ummm, some of us hold out for diamonds and furs.... Apparently his wife caught him, so she knows who this little gal is. The boss tears the name off his sweetie's charge slips, so wifey won't see that she's still around. Problem is, he tore the name off two of those little slips, and we need to get in touch with the person who signed the second slip, but we don't know who it is.... Oh, honey, I do hate to put you to so much trouble.... Yes, I have the receipt number right here: 5417680. That's right. Ivy's Texaco." She gave Rachel and Goldie a dazzling smile.

"Well, I don't know. Could be I could find the time, but I cost a tiny bit more than a tank of gas.... Merchant number 2879320.... Well, yes, the ticket is a couple weeks old. We are runnin' just a tad behind. You can't read it?"

Colleen glanced at the two women. "The first name is maybe Carlotta? And the last name begins with E-M or E-R...."

Rachel took a deep breath and nodded.

"I guess that would be it, sweetie," Colleen said. "You be sure and call me now, you hear?" She hung up. "Most problems can be solved with wee little dab of deception."

Goldie burst into appreciative applause and Rachel thanked Colleen for her help.

The moment they were out the door, Goldie let out a whistle. "She should charge admission to that station!"

"You were pretty good yourself."

"Company I keep is making me a liar as well as a burglar."

"Obviously the signature was Charlotte Emerson's," Rachel said as they got into the car.

"Whe-ew. I hope to tell you. We got something to work on now. Pull into that Dairy Queen up there. We have earned us a sundae."

Goldie went to the walk-up window and came back with two little tubs of ice cream. "I hope hot fudge is okay because that's all they got."

A spoonful halfway to her mouth, Rachel began to laugh. "How did you know she was an actress?"

Goldie was scraping her remaining ice cream into a neat mound. "I take it they don't have drag queens near that farm where you grew up?"

"Oh, my God!"

"Hands, honey, hands. Lots of big, tall women out there, but they don't have hands as big as hams."

Halfway home, freeway traffic began to bog down. Rachel tapped her fingers on the steering wheel as a dirt-buggy passed them on the right.

"Aren't we forgetting that this Charlotte person had every right to be driving that car and putting gas in it?" Goldie asked.

"There was blood on that fender."

"You sure you could tell blood from catsup, or chocolate ice cream, for that matter?"

"Jason's tie tack was snagged under the hood." A motorcycle buzzed past on the shoulder and cut in, forcing Rachel to hit the brakes.

"Must be thousands of tie thingamabobs that look alike, right here in LA."

Rachel pulled out to pass the now dawdling motorcyclist. "Not like that one. You saw it. Or you saw the cuff link that matches it. We know that was Jason's. Or maybe you think someone else kept cuff links in Jason's bathroom."

"You downright certain in your head they matched? That Charlotte took it before you had a chance to put the two side by side. That don't smell quite right either."

"I hardly think she knows I have the matching tie tack. That was coincidence."

Goldie was unconvinced. "*Maybe* that was coincidence, and *maybe* they match."

Rachel took her eyes off the road long enough to flick a look at her friend. "Of course they match."

"Be nice to know for sure."

"Okay, so maybe we can get hold of that damn cuff link." A truck lumbered by, rocking the car and leaving the air reeking of diesel.

"We get caught again, she won't believe your story about a ring. We'll be up to our earlobes in deep, bad-smelling stuff." Goldie tilted her head and peered at Rachel. "I just thought of something real outlandish. It's you that connects all these weird happenings."

"Good God! Are you saying you think I had something to do with this?"

"Don't get your underwear in a bundle, honey. Course not. Not that you know about anyway. I'm just trying to string all this stuff together. But it keeps jumping around. You're the only part that stays put. What was it you said when we first found the envelope in that bathroom?"

"I said maybe Jason was killed because he found out they were making street drugs in the water quality lab." Rachel tapped the steering wheel. "But we both thought the stuff in that envelope was some kind of drug."

"And your guy Lonnie was a drug user. You don't think he had any connection with Jason, but how about that lab?"

"Not that I know of. Except he used to make deliveries over there."

Goldie's brown eyes grew thoughtful. "Deliveries of what?"

"Packages that came in by helicopter."

"Ever look inside one of those packages?"

"Of course not. Why should I?" Rachel stared at Goldie, who suggested that most drivers prefer to watch the road. They rode in silence for a time.

"Did I tell you the cops couldn't find the wreckage from that plane?" Rachel asked.

"Out there in the boonies? They get the Academy rejects. They probably need a compass to find their own butts."

"Maybe. But I think that planeload would be worth a couple mil on the street. Seems likely they were smuggling it in from Mexico. That kind of money could turn a whole sheriff's department blind."

Goldie thought for a moment. "I agree it sure looks like drugs, and quacks like drugs. But this damn vitamin keeps turning up, and it's not a drug."

"How much do you know about the drug scene?"

Goldie gave a guffaw. "I've *heard* plenty about coke and crack. Weed is the only thing I've ever *done*."

"So we wouldn't exactly be the first to hear if there was some new drug on the street. How many people heard of acid or angel before they got popular?"

"So?"

"What if the selenium is involved in making some designer drug like Ecstasy or China White?"

"Selenium?"

"Who would have thought they could use Sudafed, for God's sake?"

Goldie's smooth, dark face furrowed into a frown. "Don't seem real likely, if this selenium stuff is serious poison."

"All drugs are poison," Rachel said. "Maybe it's a terrific high."

"For what? Thirty seconds and then you're snuffed? Not too good for repeat business."

"But if the amount is small enough...."

"Right. Then it's just good, clean fun. Get yourself a dose of vitamins along with your fix?"

"If you've got a lab—or free use of one—must be kind of tempting to brew up a little pot of gold," Rachel pointed out.

"You'd need connections on both ends, like where do you get the starters?"

"Maybe you just order what you need from a chemical supplier."

Goldie chortled. "Hello. I'd like to place an order for fourteen kilos of opium. What for? Oh, I'm just stirring up a little batch of H."

"Okay. Narcotics might be a little tricky. Amphetamines would be easier."

"Right." Goldie made a droll face. "Piece of cake. Or maybe a brownie."

"Suppose you could easily get everything you need. When you're done, you probably don't want to take it out on the street yourself. Not if you're a nice, clean, college-educated Gen-X chemist."

"No problem," Goldie said. "You just go down to the nearest high school with a few fifty-dollar bills. In two minutes the dealers would be lining up. Might take a little longer to work your way back along the chain to the wholesaler."

Rachel thumped the steering wheel. "Maybe that plane load was the raw materials."

Goldie studied Rachel's profile for a moment. "Maybe you need to start being real extra careful. Whoever is calling the shots on this is not Mother Hubbard. No ma'am. This smells like real dirty business."

"We've got to get into that lab and look around."

"What's this *we*, white woman?"

Chapter Twenty-eight

When the helicopter took off the next afternoon, Rachel braced herself against the downdraft, looked at the package in her hands, and knew what she was going to do.

Grumbling inwardly about the smog and humidity, she put the package on the dresser in her bedroom, shucked her jeans and tee shirt, and wriggled into a pair of stockings that in the dampness kept sticking to her legs.

She took an electric blue miniskirt from her closet and topped it with a white knit shirt. She hadn't worn the shirt in years because the V-neck plunged almost to her knees, but now she nodded approvingly at her image in the mirror and reached for the big round earrings she hadn't worn lately either.

Maybe she should dress up more often, she thought. Hank had never seen her like this.

He had asked her out for dinner at a seafood place in Venice. Rachel had told him no. She needed some time to think before seeing him again.

She slid her feet into a pair of black high-heel pumps, groaned at the way they pinched her toes, picked up the package and wobbled to the door, thinking there was a lot to be said for running a parking garage.

The black pumps squeaked their own resentment with each step along the featureless, grey corridor that ran along the street side of the fifth floor of InterUrban headquarters. The pair of stainless steel doors to InterUrban's water quality lab gave Rachel a blurry image of herself. She pushed one open. Along the counters, four people were perched on identical chrome-legged, backless stools. All four studiously ignored her.

"Is Mr. Hunsinger here?" she asked the nearest, a stocky man who had parted his dozen or so remaining hairs just above his right ear.

Without looking up, he jerked his thumb toward a glass-enclosed office.

With as much cheery sexiness as she could muster, Rachel smiled spicily at Harry Hunsinger, who sat behind the desk in the office reading some papers. Feeling as though she were auditioning for an X-rated movie, she flounced toward his desk, bending over to give him a look at the V-neck and beyond, as she set down the package. "This just arrived and I decided to bring it over myself. I was hoping I could take you up on your offer of a tour…?"

Harry got to his feet flashing her a look at his perfect teeth. "How nice to see you again! Gretel is it?"

"Rachel." Oh, please, she wailed to herself even as she fluttered on: "I always wanted to be a chemist, but my family didn't have enough money to send me to college."

"We have the most sophisticated, most technologically advanced laboratory of its kind in the entire world. But I'll bet you didn't know that for detecting some impurities in water, no equipment is as good as the human nose and palate."

"Really?" She gushed, "What kinds of chemicals do you use to purify water? Like was that what was in that package I brought over?"

"That?" He banished the package to a file drawer, casually snagged a key ring from a hook behind his drapes and locked the cabinet. "That's totally unimportant."

Rachel wasn't so sure. But maybe it was something personal sent by helicopter at company expense and he didn't want it lying around.

Harry rubbed his thumb ever so slightly suggestively against her arm as he escorted her through the lab, explaining the difference between chlorine and chloramine and the enormous, patriotic task of protecting the quality of water.

Half an hour later, she had heard far more about water quality than she ever wanted to hear again, and her toes in the black pumps had gone numb.

She had noted three closed doors. None with special locks. And she'd been able to maneuver herself close enough to try the knobs of two of them. One was locked, but the other responded with an opening click and she had jerked her hand back guiltily, relieved that Harry's back was to her, his attention no doubt fixed on the sound of his own voice.

He handed her the paper full of squiggles that resulted from his demonstration of the spectrometer.

"What about security?" she asked, opening her eyes wide and looking into his, which were almost cobalt blue with flecks that verged on fluorescent. "Do you have special inventories and controls?"

Harry laughed. "You mean could someone make a bomb with the materials we have here?"

Rachel's chin swung up. She hadn't considered that possibility.

But Harry was shaking his head. "Terrorists would be more interested in fertilizer suppliers than in us."

She cocked her head and smiled. "So nothing is locked up?"

"Not much." He shot her another smile. "We're not open to the public. Except for reporters, we don't see many people who aren't wearing lab coats." He glanced at her legs.

She reminded herself that she had selected her shortest miniskirt for that very reason, thanked him for the tour, and departed.

Goldie burst out laughing when Rachel described how she had spent the afternoon. "Ooooeee. You get tired of running a parking garage, you can go work for James Bond."

Rachel was slouching against the entrance to InterUrban headquarters. In the hazy cone formed by the streetlights, the kids were piling out of the van and marching into the building toward the room where the cleaning equipment was kept.

Goldie watched the procession with pride. Peter gave them a big grin as he passed. "Better than most people," Goldie said as the last of the group disappeared into the hall. "Not one smart-ass in the bunch. Not a lazy one either. They don't play games, don't shoot off their mouths, they just get their jobs done."

"And they're always so cheerful." Rachel slid a fingernail between her teeth, but caught herself before she bit down. She dropped her hand. "Makes you wonder if they've figured out something we haven't."

"How can this laboratory guy be smart enough to be a chemist and dumb as a stump at the same time? He really think you stopped by just hoping he would come on to you?"

"You doubt I'm irresistible?"

"Somehow I got a hunch you haven't had a whole lot of practice batting those eyelashes of yours. I hope you got that streak of grease on your cheek later."

Rachel made a face and swiped at her cheek with her hand. "If I didn't need your help, I'd never speak to you again."

"Help with what?" Goldie asked suspiciously.

"Two things. One, I want to get into Charlotte Emerson's office. It's in that wing behind the reception area where that guard sits. Can you get me past him?"

Goldie's face went somber.

"You're the one who said I can't just ignore all this. You're the one who thinks I need proof the tie tack and cuff link match."

"Where is it written you got to listen to me?" The look on Goldie's face went from nervy to thoughtful. "You think she's got that cuff link just laying around?"

"I doubt she's wearing it. Why would she take it home? She just figured we didn't have any right to it. She's probably forgotten it by now."

"Maybe. I hope you aren't counting on me going with you. That was a whopping big chance we took last time. That old gal finds me messing around where I shouldn't be again and she's liable to call my boss and I'll be on the outside looking in. You said there were two things."

"The next night or so, I want to poke around in that lab. That will take a while. And I want to go late."

"Why?"

"Too many people around before midnight. Half the offices have somebody working late. Hank is here half the night, for one. Is there a door you can prop open?"

"Maybe." Goldie's eyes took on a cautious look. "Even if they are making Ecstasy or something, how can you tell? You think they got batches of the stuff just stacked in some closet?"

"I wish I knew what to look for. Have you seen any sign of someone working there at night?"

Goldie pressed her lips together and shook her head. "We aren't in there very long, though. They keep that place neat as an operating room. About all we do is dust the floors and dump the waste paper." She turned and walked to where the empty escalator was still churning out stairs.

Rachel followed, dropping her voice. "What about trash, chemical containers?"

"Nope. I guess they take care of that themselves. OSHA probably makes them handle that separately."

Rachel started to put her foot on the stair that was emerging at their feet. "Just walk me to the lobby. You don't have to say anything. Just let the security guy think I'm part of the crew."

Goldie let Rachel get halfway up before following. At the top, she waved at the guard who was gazing blankly in their direction and muttered, "If you get yourself caught, I've never laid eyes on you." Even the semi-whisper seemed to echo in the huge open space.

The security officer had a little whisk-broom of a mustache. Perhaps it tickled, because his cheeks gave little twitches. Scratching the fringe of hair above his right ear, he nodded a vacant greeting and went back to reading the sports page as Rachel crossed in front of him to the executive wing.

Inside the outer secretary's office, Rachel bypassed the light switch, snapped on her Maglite, and moved quickly to the inner office and Charlotte's desk.

Four of the drawers were unlocked and as tidy inside as the rest of the room. No cuff link rested among the paperclips or in the corners. The fifth drawer was the largest. Rachel pulled at the handle. It didn't budge.

A hurried riffling through the credenza behind the desk revealed only spare office supplies. She swept the flashlight beam along the walls where a sofa, as regal as it was spartan, was accompanied by a conference table and chairs, but saw no cabinet where a stray cuff link might have been placed and forgotten.

Part way down the inner wall was another door. It groaned only a little when Rachel pushed it open.

Identical to Jason's, this bathroom was complete with shower, sink, and toilet. A round brush with plastic teeth, a tube of pale pink lipstick, and a bottle of ibuprofen sat on the small shelf above the sink. She couldn't resist removing the lid of the toilet tank and checking behind it, but there was no brown envelope.

She turned off the flashlight and made her way back through the shadows to the secretary's office. Here, despite trays piled high with papers, a sense of neatness still prevailed. Four tall file cabinets along one wall were locked, but the desk was not.

It took Rachel several minutes to search through the disarray of rubber bands, colored paperclips, pens, pencils, and scissors in the wide middle drawer.

The right front drawer held a supply of envelopes and, in the tray above them, three tubes of lip balm, but no silvery cuff link etched with the image of a tortoise. She had closed that door and slid open the one on the right when she heard footsteps in the hall.

Dousing the flashlight, she moved quickly toward the door as if she could escape into the hall. The steps were still coming toward her, soft and steady. Rachel put her back against the door as if to bar an intruder's entrance. But of course she was the intruder.

She swallowed hard and told herself firmly that it was probably just one of the cleaning crew. The door pressed against her back and she stepped into the corner as it opened. Unseen fingers flipped on the light switch and closed the door. Rachel found herself blinking into the startled eyes of Charlotte Emerson.

"I...." Rachel's mind raced, searching for some way to reasonably explain her presence. Finding none, an icy coldness descended on her. She stepped away from the door and Charlotte shrank back as though she, too, felt the coldness.

"Sorry to startle you," Rachel began, "but I'm glad you're here. Perhaps you can help."

"Yes?" After many years on InterUrban's board of directors, the older woman was no stranger to confrontation. But in a print dress and Mexican sandals, she looked small now, and uncertain. Still, she drew herself up, as she often did in the board room, apparently struggling to gain control. "What are you doing here?"

"I was looking for something."

"Again? In my office? In the middle of the night?"

"I suppose I should have asked you about it, but I didn't want to disturb you."

"I see. And it shouldn't disturb me to find a prowler in my office?" Charlotte had found her foothold and now it was her voice that was growing cold. She moved toward her secretary's desk, picked up the phone and jabbed a dial button twice. "You can explain it to the police."

As if she had done it many times, Rachel reached out and pressed the button in the hollow that held the receiver. "I think I know something about Jason's death."

Charlotte's eyes had not panicked at finding someone in her office. But they did now. Her face went white and drawn and she dropped the phone into the cradle. Her voice cracked, making "Yes?" into two syllables. Eyes riveted on Rachel, she sank onto the secretary's chair.

"I think he was murdered. I think I may be close to proving it."

The tip of Charlotte's tongue moistened dry lips. "Please explain."

Rachel told her of the car, the fender, the dent, the spot that was apparently dried blood, the tie tack caught under the hood.

"That's why you were in Jason's office a few weeks ago."

"You took the cuff link I found there. Now I need it, to be certain it matches the tie tack."

Charlotte's face seemed to reflect some vague but gnawing pain. "But I gave that to Jason's wife."

Rachel sighed and closed her eyes for a moment. "What's her address?"

"Yes, of course." Charlotte's voice faltered again. She reached for the address book on her secretary's desk. "How sure are you of all this?"

"Very sure." Rachel wrote down the address on a slip of scratch paper. "Am I correct that you picked up the DeVille from the shop after the fender was repaired?"

Charlotte's eyes went hard. "I beg your pardon?"

"Did you pick up the Cadillac with the new fender from Andy's—"

"I heard the question," Charlotte fired back. Silence seemed to hum in the tiny office. Finally, Charlotte broke it: "I may have. I collected some car from a body shop. The entire fleet was in use, I needed a car, this one had been repaired, I picked it up. I didn't ask why it was at the body shop."

Something in her eyes convinced Rachel she was telling the truth, but maybe only part of it. "You were going to find out exactly who was driving that car the day Jason was killed, but you never did."

Charlotte's brow pulled into a hard line and the eyes beneath it seemed to be fixed on something in another dimension. "I've been busy." She looked far older than Rachel remembered, but perhaps it was the overhead light.

"Will you do it now?"

Charlotte's voice sounded small in the stillness of the empty building. "I suppose I should."

Chapter Twenty-nine

The next morning, Rachel again put on clothes dredged from the back of her closet—this time a pale, businesslike blouse and black skirt. When rush hour had subsided, she drove around the neighborhood until she saw Irene leaning on her supermarket cart, elbows splayed on the bars, frowning intently over a somewhat disheveled newspaper.

Rachel rolled down her car window and called, "Can you do me a favor?"

The woman squinted into the sun that shone behind Rachel. A small felt bird dangled from the hat that sat rakishly atop hair that seemed determined to escape it. "Ah, dear girl, Wall Street is in trouble now, it is."

Rachel's thoughts stopped, backed up. "Really?"

"Too many mergers," Irene said sagely. "Too much of anything is never good."

"Could you go over to the garage and keep an eye on things until I get back?" Rachel asked. "Shouldn't be more than a couple of hours."

"Of course, dear girl, of course. You go on, now. Don't you worry about a thing." Irene ambled in the direction of the parking garage, pushing the cart, still reading the paper.

Rachel took the first ramp to the Santa Monica Freeway. Last night she'd felt nothing but relief when Charlotte didn't call the police. But now, Charlotte's reaction seemed oddly accommodating.

Westbound traffic on Interstate 10 was always slow, even midmorning. Nervously, Rachel reached into her purse to reassure herself that the tie tack was still there.

Jason Karl's house was on a cul-de-sac on a side street in Santa Monica not far from the beach. The neighborhood was clearly upscale, but the house itself was a plain brown stucco, not the pretentious castle Rachel had expected. Getting out of her car, she heard a piano. Liszt, she guessed as she walked up the driveway.

When the door opened, a great crescendo burst through the gap as though it had been bottled up against its will. The woman who faced her was small and pretty and wearing a bikini top so brief it might have been a costume for a strip show. White-blond hair had been tied carelessly in two long pigtails framing a pouty face.

"Mrs. Karl?" Rachel shouted above the music, thinking that if this nymphet was Jason's wife, the reason for his murder might be quite different than she had supposed. But Liszt and Lolita?

"I have something I think belonged to your husband."

The music came to a sudden halt, its echo shimmering in the stillness. The blonde rolled her eyes, whether at her question or at the music, Rachel wasn't sure. "You must want my mother."

Not sure why she was relieved, Rachel nodded. "Is she home?"

"Obviously. Or did you think that was a player piano?" The blonde still blocked the door and Rachel did not really want her to turn around in those cut-offs.

"Who is it, Mellie?"

Soon a tiny woman, exquisitely painted and manicured from what looked like size three high heels to her perfectly highlighted hair, appeared beside the blonde. She tilted her head toward Rachel like a hummingbird seeking nectar.

"I have something I think belonged to your husband," Rachel said again. "I'm sorry. I should introduce myself. Rachel Chavez. I own the garage where he used to park and I think—"

With no warning, the woman's eyes flooded and tears gushed down her cheeks. "Oh, dear. I'm terribly sorry."

Rachel thought she caught a whiff of brandy. She well remembered what it smelled like. Well, the woman was in mourning and probably still in shock.

"Mother," Mellie said impatiently before turning to Rachel. "Now look what you've done. You've gone and upset her again. That piano will be going all night."

"Perhaps I should come back later," Rachel stammered. She had been so intent on her own thoughts she'd forgotten this would be a painful time for Jason's family.

"No," the woman said, drawing a carefully folded lace handkerchief from the pocket of her black linen dress and patting it at her eyes—an exquisite wind-up doll. She stepped aside. "Please, come in."

The wall facing Rachel was entirely glass with a view over mounds of African daisies and graceful Japanese pines to a glimpse of the ocean. Other walls were a parquet of polished hardwoods. Beyond a banister, open space plummeted a dozen feet to a handsome living room arranged to grant ample room to a grand piano.

"The music was magnificent. Was that you?" Rachel asked as they descended a suspended curving staircase.

The woman gave a quick nod as they reached the final stair. "Thank you. Please call me Lily."

"The view is…incredible," Rachel said. She hated that word, but couldn't think of one better.

Lily dabbed at her eyes again. She gestured Rachel to a seat on the nine-section sofa that curled through the room. "Excuse me," she said and exited, returning a few minutes later. This time the odor of alcohol was unmistakable.

"Now where were we?" the little woman asked.

"I was admiring your home," Rachel said honestly.

"Jason was so proud to be able to buy such a fine house." There was ever so slight a lisp to the woman's words, and Rachel wondered whether it was natural or the booze.

"He said it wasn't a bad place for a dumb Polak," Lily continued. "He always regretted that my parents were not alive to see it. He wanted to show them they were wrong. We were old Philadelphia. Jason was from Pittsburgh. His father made sausages and sold them in a shop on the riverfront."

Feeling huge and clumsy beside her hostess, Rachel was grateful the daughter had disappeared, sparing her the feeling she was old as well.

"The family name was Karlinski," Lily went on, to no one in particular, the way people in nursing homes sometimes do.

Rachel wondered if grief had unhinged her. Or maybe the woman just wasn't used to drinking.

"To this day, I can't imagine how we made it through those first years. Jason was at the university all day and tending bar half the night," Lily reminisced dreamily. "But he wouldn't hear of my working. He wouldn't even allow me to drive. He bought this house to show my parents." She was staring, seemingly unseeing, at the view.

"They never did speak to me again." She turned to Rachel on the sofa. "Mellie is right. I run on too much. You said you have something of Jason's?"

Digging into her handbag, Rachel produced the tie tack. Despite a few scratches, the face of the tortoise seemed proud.

Lily took it, held it at arm's length on her palm, and didn't speak for a full minute. "He never liked this, but he wore it to please me. I bought it for him in New Mexico. I hardly ever bought anything. Jason bought things before I even knew I wanted them."

Rachel wondered if Lily had been bored with her life as a hothouse plant. What would that life be like now, with the hothouse suddenly gone? "I think I saw him wearing cuff links like this, too. Was it a set?"

"Oh yes, the Indians wouldn't sell just the one piece."

"I suppose you still have the cuff links."

"I don't know. I haven't been able to bring myself to go through his things."

Rachel waited for the tears to start again, but they didn't. "That's such an interesting tortoise."

"Really? Is that a tortoise? I thought it was a turtle. But thank you so much for returning it. Perhaps I can have earrings made. Of the cuff links, I mean. I wouldn't need three earrings." Lily gave a weak little laugh and stood up.

Recognizing her dismissal, Rachel rose, too. Then, feeling loathsome and deceptive, she plunged into the reason for her visit. "I was wondering if you might loan it back to me. Just for a short time."

"Really? Whatever for?"

"I'd like to show it to my father." The words came as easily as if she had thought it all out.

"He likes Indian jewelry?"

"When I was a child, he used to read to me out of a book that had a story about a tortoise and the illustration looked very much like that. I realize you don't even know me, but...."

Lily gave a real smile for the first time. "You would hardly have bothered to return it if you were dishonest. Of course you can borrow it. Jason won't be needing it, will he? What a dear story. You must borrow the entire set. I'll find them for you." Before Rachel could reply, she was climbing the stairs.

Feeling wickedly pleased with herself, Rachel sank back onto the sofa and waited.

It didn't take long. "They were right there on his chest of drawers. I remember now. You aren't the first to return one of these. That woman he worked with found one in his office. I've been so addled, I paid little attention."

Rachel stared down at the silvery ovals in her hand. Three perfectly matched tortoises looked back at her. "I'll return these very soon."

"Of course you will. But keep them as long as you like. I'm glad you like them." Lily's lower lip began to quiver again. "I just know that Jason would be pleased, too."

Rachel rose. "I can't tell you how much I appreciate this. And I'm so sorry for your loss."

Lily's tears were flowing again. She moved toward the piano as if it were a magnet, drawing her.

"You play beautifully. Do you tour? "

"I did once," Lily faltered.

"Perhaps you would enjoy it again." Rachel felt she should somehow be encouraging, that life would go on.

"My parents never forgave me for giving up the concerts," Lily was saying. "Now, well, Jason would never forgive me." Gazing at Rachel almost apologetically, she raised her hands over the keys. Then it seemed to dawn on her she was forgetting something and she stood up again. "I'm sorry, I should see you out."

"Please, don't trouble yourself. I can find my way."

By the time she had climbed three steps, the rippling notes of Liszt had begun again. Relieved, and a little sad, she closed the door behind her.

〜〜〜

When Rachel got back to the parking garage, Irene was sitting in the glass booth, plump arms planted on the counter, gazing at the street like one of the stone lions that guard public buildings.

She blinked at Rachel. "Nothing to this job. Not a thing went on aside from four fools who got it into their thick heads this was a public lot. I told them where they could park for free down by the river."

Rachel handed her two twenty-dollar bills.

"For a couple hours just keeping a chair warm?" Irene tried to hand one back. "Best I don't price myself out of this market, dear girl."

Rachel pushed the bill away. "So you owe me a couple more hours."

Irene rescued her cart from where it sat, a lost toy in an automotive jungle. Just before she reached the street, she turned and called, "Almost forgot. Two phone calls. Both women. Such a boring life you lead, dear girl. Look on the steno pad."

Chapter Thirty

Rachel opened the pad of paper she kept by the phone. The first entry read only *Charlotte*, followed by *616-0001*. She leaned her chin on her hand. So she had gotten the information on the car. That should be interesting.

On the second line *Alexander Millhouse* was neatly printed. She didn't know anyone named Millhouse, either. A possible client? She had maybe thirty slots left in the garage, and filling half of them would pay the electric bill. With the end of her pen, she dialed the number.

"Friends of the Earth." The person who answered sang the name as if it were a psalm.

"Rachel Chavez," she said into the receiver. "I have message to call Alexander Millhouse at this number."

"You sure you don't mean Alexandra Miller?"

"That must be it," Rachel said, scratching her eyebrow with the end of the pen.

"Rachel!" Alexandra's voice was full of energy. "I have good news for you. We are holding a parade on Earth Day—it's a Saturday. How many can you park?"

"On a Saturday? Nine-fifty or so." A full house on a weekend could bring in ten thousand dollars. "Thanks for thinking of me."

"We must have lunch someday soon. I'll call you." Alexandra rang off.

Rachel pushed the button and dialed again.

"Rachel Chavez. I got a message to call you," she said when the secretary put her through.

"Yes."

"Did you find out who checked out that car?"

"Yes," Charlotte said again and paused. "I need to talk with you."

"All right. When?"

"I'm not sure just now." Was there a tightness to her voice?

"Can you tell me who it was?"

Charlotte hesitated again. "It was checked out to me that day. But I was not the one driving it that afternoon."

"Who was?" Jason was killed in the late afternoon.

"I can't say just now."

"When?" Rachel warned herself not to push too hard.

"I'll call you later," Charlotte said and rang off.

~~~

After work, Rachel sat at her kitchen counter, a fork suspended over a microwaved dinner, trying to sort out the bits and pieces that cluttered her head.

No question it was Jason's tie tack she had found wedged under the hood of the DeVille. Which seemed to make it obvious the Caddy—owned by the water agency—had killed Jason.

And Charlotte knew who was driving it.

Or did Charlotte only know that she, herself, *wasn't* driving it?

Maybe she had checked the car out, driven it that morning wherever she needed to go, put it back in the garage, and someone else had taken it. Maybe Charlotte wasn't sure who that someone was but was trying to find out.

Rachel reached for a bottle of soy sauce and applied it liberally.

The packet of selenium from Lonnie's apartment looked like drugs. Apparently it could kill like a drug overdose. The envelope of selenium behind Jason's executive toilet tank had looked like drugs. The broken packages in the downed airplane had looked like drugs. Two people were already dead, one from an overdose; the other, she was increasingly certain, was murdered.

Related? Coincidence?

If there were some new designer drug made with selenium, someone was manufacturing it, and probably not in a laundry tub. Probably in an existing laboratory, by a chemist who did some very lucrative moonlighting. Rachel left her tasteless bowl of vegetables and rice and went to the window.

Across the street, the InterUrban office complex rose in the waning glow of the sun—a sort of geometric insect, spreading its rectangular wings toward the bordering side streets.

Lonnie's connection to InterUrban was minimal, but he did keep an eye on the cars in their motor pool and deliver packages from time to time.

Jason's connection to the water agency was obvious.

As for the plane, well, it had crashed near an InterUrban reservoir. She couldn't connect the dots better than that. And the line they made was weak.

But Rachel was becoming more and more certain that under the guise of water quality, one of the best equipped laboratories in the world was producing designer street drugs.

It was well after midnight when for the third time that night Rachel stepped outside the side pedestrian exit from the garage and listened to the automatic lock click behind her. This outing would be riskier. Much riskier.

The first time, she had walked over to InterUrban when the cleaning crew arrived. Goldie had agreed that when the crew finished up and left the building, she would leave a matchbook cover wedged over the tongue of the latch at the water agency's north door.

At eleven-thirty, a tense phone call had come from Goldie: all the building's outside doors, except those that opened into the reception area, were fire exits. All were locked to anyone outside, but opened easily with a bar from the inside. A stenciled sign warned anyone leaving that an alarm would sound if the door was opened.

So Rachel had crossed the street again, and together the two women had canvassed the exits. At the door that led from the cafeteria kitchen to the parking lot, they found the alarm wire held in place by steel staples. But when they traced the wire's path, it came to an end just above their heads. "We've got to test it," Goldie said.

Rachel stared through the door's small diamond-shaped window at the Dumpster just outside, counted to three, and opened the door.

"Jesus!" Goldie hissed, just above a whisper.

But no alarm sounded.

Rachel said, "It was your idea to test it."

"I didn't know you were going to just up and do it without thinking about it."

"What's there to think about?" They stepped outside onto pavement covered with cigarette butts.

"Kitchen help copping a smoke," Goldie had concluded. "I'll bet they kept setting off the alarm, so someone cut the wire."

Now, with only a few windows still lit, the building's front offered an odd lopsided face to the street. The window washer's platform, a few stories above ground, cut across one cheek like a scar.

This time, instead of crossing in front of the garage, Rachel turned left, crossed at the corner, and followed Olympic Street until she could see the Dumpster.

A small cardboard square fluttered to the ground as she opened the door to the kitchen and stepped carefully inside.

Darkness, broken only by a weak glimmer through the window in the door, engulfed her.

She switched on her Maglite and moved through the kitchen, then the dining room. The escalator, motionless now, climbed toward a pale light glowing from somewhere above.

Something about the parallel steel treads on the stationary stairs made her a little queasy and she was glad to leave them behind on first floor, and take normal stairs, reached through a door next to the elevators.

On the fifth floor, Rachel's steps faltered when the beam of her flashlight bounced back eerily from the double steel doors that led to the lab. Did they lock those doors at night? She hadn't thought of that.

But the one on the right swung open when she pushed against it.

Inside, the lab was as serene and neat as a church, as if a little disarray might denote a sloppy soul.

Rachel glanced at her watch: seven minutes since she had crossed the street. This was going to be easy.

She traced her way along the center aisle, between the rows of counters, to the wall where the storerooms were. The first was unlocked but appeared to contain only two sinks and rows of glassware. The second was not a storeroom at all, but a sort of locker room for staff.

A rack held fresh lab coats. Most of the narrow metal doors stood ajar, and only one bore a lock. Flicking the flashlight beam along the shelves of the open lockers revealed little more than a worn pair of jogging shoes, a slim book of Shelley's poems, a dusty King James Bible, and in a far corner on a top shelf, an unopened box of condoms. Like people everywhere, she mused: fitness, sex, religion, and forgotten hope.

The third room was as it had been when Harry escorted her through the lab: locked. Was this the chemical storeroom?

But when she opened some of the cabinets above and below the counters, her flashlight revealed dozens of brown-glass bottles, jars, and jugs holding liquids and powders.

If they didn't lock up the chemicals, what did they keep under lock and key?

Rachel leaned against the wall in the dark to think. More than ten minutes gone. The guard probably made rounds, and she had no clue as to his timing.

Outside, a strong wind was whipping up and she started at the sound of something scraping against glass. It seemed to come from the bank of offices that lined the front of the lab.

Moonlight streamed through the windows, lending an eerie look to all the tidy desks. The scraping noise was loudest near the office where, a few days ago, she had begun her ridiculous performance for Harry Hunsinger.

The desk there was as bare of papers as a stage set before the play. Was such meticulousness a trait of chemists?

Whatever the noise was, it had stopped.

Only the sound of the air conditioning turning on broke the stillness. The rush of air from vents on the floor made the drapery sway. Her eye caught a glitter to the right of the window and her mind flashed an image of Harry reaching behind the drapes for the key to the filing cabinet.

She could hardly contain her excitement.

A solitary key hung on a brass cup hook screwed into the molding. She slid it into the lock on the filing cabinet. The lock popped out, the sound exploding the quiet.

She froze until the galloping of her heart slowed, then slid open a drawer: nothing but ordinary files with neatly typed labels, in hanging folders.

The second drawer was more of the same. The third held a coffee cup, a package of disposable razors, and a supply of rubber bands. This was the drawer where Harry had locked the package she delivered.

Returning to the second drawer, she thumbed the files there. Nothing seemed unusual. She went back to the first drawer.

This time when she opened it, something rattled. She flipped through the folders, then pushed them back and slid her hand beneath them.

Her fingertips struck a ring of keys.

She rolled the drawer closed and made her way back to the door that Harry had said led to yet another storage area.

The first eight keys she tried were either too big or too small.

The ninth wedged itself in the lock and the entire ring jangled to the floor when she pried it loose. "Damn." Her foot gave an impatient stamp.

She began again. This time, the fourth key she tried fit snugly; the lock yielded.

Her flashlight cast an uneasy, blotchy pattern of heavy shadows and brightness. The room was smaller than the others.

Looking somehow naked and unaccustomed to light were a couple of boxes of new glassware, a bottle of Dawn dishwashing soap, two packages of clean utility towels held by brown paper bands, a case of paper towels, and half a dozen cardboard boxes.

Two boxes were still sealed; *Niagara Laboratory Supply* was stamped on the side. The third held an unintelligible assortment of wires and equipment parts.

A block of Styrofoam, wedged inside the flaps of the fourth box, gave a shrill screech when she dislodged it. Gingerly, Rachel lifted it out, exposing perhaps a dozen brown bottles labeled with long names. Nothing more.

The box scraped softly on the floor as she pushed it back into place.

In the silence that followed came an odd echo. *Footsteps?* She froze, hand still on the lid.

Yes.

The security guard must be making his round.

She clicked off the Maglite and stood in the alien darkness, listening to her own heartbeat.

And the footsteps.

For the first time, the full impact of what she was doing flooded her mind, swamping her resolve. She could very likely go to jail.

Terrors grew in the darkness like poisonous berries. The tops of her arms and the back of her neck went cold.

The footsteps stopped.

Had the guard left, or only paused to listen? Two more endless minutes passed before she decided he was gone.

There were two more cartons, both plain cardboard, unmarked and unopened. She found a place under the flap of one and gently pulled upward.

Inside were brown jars. She lifted one and shined the light on the label. Acetic anhydride. The next was sodium carbonate. *Baking soda? No, that was bicarbonate.* A slender bottle with a rubber collar and pressure cap was only a third full with liquid. The label was bright red: *Ether.*

The second carton was heavier. The flap sliced her hand as it opened. Rachel squeezed her eyes shut against the sting and put the cut to her lips.

Inside was another box. She tried to lift it out, but the fit was too tight for her fingers. Turning the carton on its side, she tilted it. The inner box slipped from its sheath.

Raw excitement nearly choked her.

The last thing she had expected was that it would be so obvious.

Chapter Thirty-one

The inner carton was marked *DOUBLE UO GLOBAL*, the red logo flanked by two slender black cats like a coat of arms—the same gaudy logos Rachel saw in the cargo of the crashed plane.

Her hands fluttered over the box, in surprise. She tore open the flap. A dozen slightly shiny, rich brown blocks the size of bricks winked back at her flashlight.

She needed to see nothing more.

She locked the storeroom and, muscles screaming with tension, tiptoed back down the laboratory aisle to the office.

Something was slapping against the outside wall. A tree limb? But this was the fifth floor. Spooked, she moved the drape, peered out the window. Nothing there.

Swallowing a growing urge to flee, she turned back to the file cabinet, fumbled in the dimness for the lower drawer, and slowly slid it open.

A hand closed around her arm like a vise.

Panic exploded. She tried to turn, but another hand closed on her other arm.

She shot out a foot, but only grazed the attacker's ankle.

"Wha…." His word ended in a hiss as she rammed an elbow into his midsection.

The hand grasping her right arm loosened, but the vise-like fist on her left tightened and slammed her into the file cabinet. A heavy book, from the top of the cabinet, smacked into her face.

She grabbed the book, turned, and stared into the face of Harry Hunsinger.

A gagging sound erupted when she shoved the edge of the book hard into his Adam's apple.

He staggered and dropped his hand from her arm.

She dodged, trying to get the desk between them.

He lunged. Snatched at her shoulder. Missed.

Gulping air, she raced toward the laboratory's exit door. But the security cop downstairs might have heard something, might be making his way to the lab.

Harry Hunsinger had a right to be here. She did not.

Rachel veered right down a cabinet-lined aisle, trying to remember where it led.

Harry might lift weights, but he was no runner: His footsteps did not seem to gain on her.

Was there another exit from the lab? She couldn't remember.

The row of stainless steel cabinets seemed to go on forever. Her foot caught the base of a stool. Pain ripped into her ankle. She spun sideways and pitched headfirst into a cabinet door. Metal crashed against tile. The stool went down, striking Harry's racing feet. He thudded to the floor.

Closing her eyes against a sudden dizziness, Rachel tried to regain her feet. Pain sliced up her leg.

She dropped to her knees and crawled, knowing from the scuffle behind her that Harry was rising again. And that she would be an easy target now.

Ahead, another stool jutted into the aisle. She grabbed its legs, flung it toward Harry, and was rewarded with a grunt when he failed to sidestep in time.

A cabinet door next to her swung open. Something rolled out and shattered on the tile. A strong acid odor rose from the debris.

Rachel's eye caught on a square of blacker darkness between the cabinets—a place for the knees of the technician who perched on the stool.

Trap or hiding place?

Unable to run, she was trapped anyway. She crept in.

The space ran the full width of the cabinet. She crawled through into another aisle and again tried to stand. Her ankle would have none of it. She dropped to her knees and crawled toward the row of offices. From somewhere to her right came the sound of running footsteps.

She could move no faster.

Finding another stool in her path, she tugged it into the aisle, slipped into the knee hole behind it, and drew the stool toward her, clutching its legs as if it were a life raft.

With barely enough room to turn around, she ran her tongue across dry lips and tasted blood. Her fingers found the cut just beneath her eye. She wiped her hand on her jeans and closed her eyes to think.

Had the guard at the desk in the lobby heard the running feet, the crashing stool? Or was he too far away? Regardless, Harry would certainly seek his help.

How much time did she have?

In the air hung the harsh odor of the spilled acid, now mixed with dust.

Quick footsteps were moving toward her.

She opened her eyes to find a bluish glow had dawned at both sides of her cubbyhole. Harry had turned on the fluorescent lights overhead.

Hugging her knees, and the chrome stool legs to her chest, Rachel tried to make herself smaller, as if that would matter if he yanked away the stool and peered in.

She saw his shoes as he passed: wing tips, the color of ox blood. They made dry little gasps with each step.

A door opened, and she heard something scrape along the floor, then the door closed. Had he gone in search of the guard?

But the steps now retraced their way along her aisle.

Again, she watched the wing tips pass.

Then the steps were coming down the opposite aisle. Rachel bent as far as she could to gain a line of view. The wing tips avoided a large shard of thick brown glass; smaller bits crunched under the soles.

He must know she was in one of the cubbyholes, but he did not seem to be stopping long enough to peer behind any of the stools.

Eight more steps. Nine. Each with a little crackle of ground glass. Another door opened. If he went downstairs to call the guard, she might have enough time to escape.

But he would not have to leave. He could telephone.

The sound of water running.

She ran cold fingertips across her forehead. Had he cut himself? Was he washing off blood? If he was occupied for a moment, this might be her only chance.

She nudged the stool away, slipped into the aisle and pulled herself to her feet, wincing at the pain in her ankle, but standing.

The fluorescent light, unbearably bright, seemed to hone in on her like a headlight on a jackrabbit. Scanning the walls, she spotted a set of switches and limped as quickly as she could toward them.

The water was still running. Surely he would notice when she turned the lights off.

She threw all the switches and ran, hobbling, but still upright, almost blind now in the renewed darkness.

She would have to pass the offices to reach the exit. Darting a glance over her shoulder, she saw Harry, silhouetted in yellow light, at a sink in one of the storerooms. She hobbled on.

Almost immediately she heard his quick steps again behind her but could not run faster.

Dodging inside an office, she grabbed the chair near the desk. It was heavy and she staggered a little under its weight. She spun around and feinted the legs at him like an old-time lion tamer.

He kept coming, driving her back, toward the windows. She jabbed at him again. One of the chair legs hit him in the chest and air whooshed from his lungs.

Something thudded dully against the window at her shoulder and her eyes jerked from Harry to the window, but she saw nothing.

Harry grabbed the bottom of the chair, shoved it at her.

She veered, lunged off balance. A chair leg shattered the window, opening a gaping jagged hole and sprinkling her with bits of broken glass.

Rachel braced herself for his next lunge, but when it came, she crumpled under the force of it and the chair bulldozed her through the glass.

Her blood seemed to stop dead in her veins as her brain leapt ahead, imagining five floors of windows speeding past, her own body splayed and broken on the sidewalk below.

Chapter Thirty-two

But she didn't fall.

Or perhaps she had already fallen.

She was sprawled, prone.

Harry landed on her back, forcing out her breath and slamming her face-first against the rough, cold surface beneath her. Pain erupting in her cheek, she struggled to raise her head. A salty stream of blood ran into her mouth and dripped from her chin.

Wrenching sideways, she rammed the side of her fist into his Adam's apple. Despite the gurgling sound that came from his lips, he clutched at her still.

She twisted, drew her knees to her chest, and thrust her feet hard into his gut, spinning him backward.

Freed of his weight, her body seemed to rise by itself. The ground beneath her gave a dizzying lurch and she stared down at flat little knobs of metal.

Harry's foot smashed into the backs of her knees, knocking her legs from under her.

The world swayed sickeningly. She was on some sort of plank, gripping a thick metal rope.

Far below, Rachel glimpsed the sidewalk. Bile rose to her throat, almost choking her. All that protected her from plunging to the street nearly a hundred feet below was a flimsy window washer's platform.

Blood was leaking in slow drips from her right hand. She saw she was clutching a shard of glass. There was no pain, only the searing, choking taste of acid in her throat. A lone pair of headlights was moving down the deserted street. She forced herself to go limp and waited for the next blow. When it came, she didn't resist, but gave way.

Harry crashed past her shoulder, slamming into the waist-high railing that surrounded the platform on three sides.

With a giant shudder, cables groaning, the platform swung out, and seemed to hover endlessly in the air before smashing back against the wall.

Rachel landed on his chest, her knees pinning his arms.

His eyes were like the heads of nails. Blood trickled from his nose toward the side of his mouth. He jerked sideways, tried to roll away.

She moved the dagger of broken glass to the small space between the open buttons of his shirt collar. "Move again and you'll be blowing bubbles."

Malevolent eyes fixed on hers, but he stayed quiet.

"Jason found out about the drugs, didn't he?"

The eyes seemed to bulge from their sockets.

She pressed the edge of glass into his skin. The thin line of blood that appeared looked black in the pale streetlight. "He found out about your little after-hours bonus work, so you killed him."

Something like bewilderment passed across the eyes that stared up at her. A hand shot out, pinning her shoulder against the railing, but she kept the shard of glass steady, pressed against his throat. Blood dribbled onto his collar.

The hand against her shoulder retreated. "I saw the car, the blood on the fender." She ground the words out. "And I saw your stash in the storeroom."

Harry's head moved right, then left like a drunken metronome. She stared at the darkening place on his collar, steeled herself for another attack, but his eyes, still bulging slightly, just stared into her face.

Then his mouth curled. "People die in this city every week from the stuff made in washtubs." He spit the words into her face.

"Right. You're doing a good deed. You got quality control."

"If I don't make it for them, a thousand others will. And they won't be nearly as careful."

"Is that what you told Jason?"

A dry, harsh chuckle came from Harry's throat.

"Why did you kill him?"

"I didn't."

When it came, she was totally unprepared.

His fist landed in the center of her chest, spilling her backward against the building like a rag doll. Glass splintered and pain flashed up her arm as it fell back inside the building and her hand struck something like wool. Carpet. The floor of the office.

He was standing over her, legs straddling hers, black against a slightly paler sky. In the distance, a siren whooped.

With no more thought than a cornered dog, she shot both legs against his ankles. He toppled, flinging out an arm, sprawling against the right railing, sending the platform dancing.

The cable groaned. The floor beneath Rachel lurched and seemed to sink a little. She screamed: "Don't move! Your hand is on the control!"

But he didn't hear or didn't care because the cable screeched again and the platform began to slip lower.

Rachel dug her fingers into the carpeted floor of the office, but the sinking platform drew her with it. Her hand slipped, caught on the edge of the window frame where the glass had completely broken away.

Harry hadn't moved.

The platform shuddered.

With both hands, she clawed at the frame.

The window washer's platform sank, slowly at first. Then, with a sudden wrench and a shriek of metal, it was gone.

Rachel clutched at the window casing, legs dangling, arms shrilling with pain.

The crash, when it came from below, left a thick-aired deadness in its wake. She braced herself against the wall.

Something slapped against the toe of her sneaker. The platform cable. If she could use it to climb just a foot or so, she might get back through the window.

The cable trembled with a life of its own.

Her numb, blue-white fingers began slipping from the window frame and she barely had time to weave her legs about the steel rope.

She loosened one hand and moved it higher, then the other. The ridge of the window casing appeared, emptying the world of everything else. Higher. Once more. Now.

Beyond thought, she coiled herself like a snake and lunged.

Her body seemed to hang weightless in mid-air.

Then, as if she had left one life and entered another, she was lying on the office floor, gulping air, scarcely aware of the sirens throbbing on the street below.

Rachel wobbled to her feet. Breath like ground glass in her lungs, legs threatening to buckle, she ran as if a mouse in some dimly remembered maze through dark corridors, down stairs, more stairs. She lurched through the empty lobby and unsteadily made her way down the steps of the inert escalator. The stripes of steel made her dizzy.

At last, the cafeteria. She tried to weave her way among the tables but knocked some askew. The kitchen. The back door. A Dumpster looming in the darkness.

On the side street, in the building's shadow, Rachel waited until her heaving, sputtering breathing slowed.

As if returning from an evening stroll, she passed the three squad cars and an ambulance, clustered like a pack of dogs at the building's entrance, and crossed the street to the parking garage.

She was inserting the key into the lock when a blue-white light exploded, pinning her against the door like a butterfly on an exhibit board.

Chapter Thirty-three

"Stop where you are."

Rachel swayed on her feet, her exhausted brain unable to process.

"Do not turn around. Put your hands on top of your head."

Mute, blood pounding in her ears, she moved her shaking hands to her head. It was over. Everything. The life she had tried so desperately to build from the debris of mistakes was over.

"An officer is approaching behind you. Please do not move."

A hand touched her shoulder and a normal voice ordered her to turn around. Slowly she obeyed, squinting into the light that still held her like a spear. She could see a black face with cheeks like overripe plums appraising her.

"Officer Milton!" he said.

Was he introducing himself? It sounded like a command. Numbly she tried to think what she was supposed to do. Hands patted down her sides all the way to her ankles. He signaled to someone across the street and the awful light spun away, drowning her in equally blinding darkness.

"What are you doing here?"

Pulse pounding like the wings of a bird caught by a cat, her throat refused to produce a voice. Finally, shakily, "I live here."

"Right. You live in a parking lot."

"I…own it."

There was a pause as he absorbed this.

"You look all cut up."

"I fell. There was some broken glass."

"Mind coming down to the station for a few minutes?"

She fought down laughter that would have turned hysterical if it had reached her lips. "I...I guess not."

⌒⌒⌒

The room was a drab yellow with green linoleum that smelled of floor cleaner. Rachel sat at a small metal table. The noise her nervous fingers made on the Styrofoam cup that had held coffee seemed unbearably loud.

She couldn't remember drinking the coffee, but knew she must have. Her head tottered, unsteady on her neck as she struggled to straighten shoulders that betrayed defeat although there was no one else in the room to notice.

The clock on the otherwise blank wall made a whirring sound. The time was five twenty-six. They had stopped at an all-night clinic where she had collected six stitches in her forehead, eight in her arm. She was sure she had compounded any case against her by lying, by telling the not unkind Officer Milton that she had not been able to sleep, had been jogging, had stepped on something in the dark and fallen on some broken glass.

Eight times, in eight different ways, he had asked if she knew anything about what had happened at the office building across the street.

No.

Had she ever been inside?

Yes, many times, delivering packages, mostly for the laboratory. If they took prints, this might explain hers.

Half an hour ago, a woman had put her head in the door and summoned Officer Milton.

Rachel wondered if leaving her alone in this vacuum was a ploy to increase her weariness, wear her down. She was certain he hadn't believed her, certain he or someone else would soon appear, read her her rights, and lead her to the lock-up.

The need for a drink rolled over her, an imperative, a promise that all would be well if she could have just one shot of Jack.

Two sets of footsteps moved along the hallway outside. The door, its edge muted by many coats of paint, moved inward a few inches. The voices were low, but she caught, "All I know, there was enough M triple P and Adam and Eve up there to make winning the lottery look puny."

The door opened just enough for Officer Milton to nod in her direction. "Thanks for your time, Miss Chavez. I'll have someone drive you home."

Chapter Thirty-four

The after-work crowd had not yet begun to unwind at the Pig's Whistle when Hank and Goldie slid into the booth where Rachel had been sipping club soda and reading a newspaper article for the fifth time. The bandages on her arms showed their bulk beneath the sleeves of her blue chambray shirt.

The waiter put his tray on their table and retied his black apron. "Champagne," Hank told him.

Rachel touched his arm. "No...."

"But we're celeb—"

"No," she said again, this time sharply.

Hank lifted his hands toward the ceiling. "A saint, we have here. Okay. But the rest of us will toast her in style." He folded a new fifty-dollar bill with its odd play-money look and stuck it into the waiter's shirt pocket. "Best champagne you can find, even if you have to get it down the street. And for the lady...."

"Another soda," Rachel said. "And maybe you could hunt up a lime somewhere?" The waiter agreed to produce both and sped off much more quickly than he had arrived.

Hank pointed to the now dog-eared front page of the *Los Angeles Times* spread in front of Rachel. Just above the fold, the headline stretched all the way across the page: *Laboratory Head Dead; Drug Factory Discovered at Water Company.*

"What a mind blower," he said. "I hear half the lab staff, even a couple of techs and bottle washers, were getting a cut."

The waiter returned with three goblets, a tall green bottle, its sides misted with fog, and a bucket of ice, and with the flourish of a magician produced a white linen napkin to wrap it. The cork hit the ceiling when Hank released it, and everyone in the pub cheered. He poured two glasses, then reached for the third. "Come on, just a sip?"

Rachel shook her head and covered the glass with her hand. "Gives me a headache." He looked so crestfallen she reached for the goblet and held it out. "Okay, why not?"

Goldie shot her a look, snared the glass from Rachel's hand with strong brown fingers, and held it up to the light. "Look at that." She pointed to the rim. "Lipstick."

Hank squinted at it. "Looks okay to me."

"Lots of flu going around." Goldie spun the stem in her fingers. "She's already trussed up with two cracked ribs. Don't want her to start coughing. No, sir."

Hank raised his hand to signal, but the waiter was talking to someone at the bar. He slid from the booth. "I'll get another."

Goldie put her own glass in front of Rachel and poured what remained of the club soda into it. The bubbles rose to the top, not a bad imitation. "I got three brothers always falling off the wagon," she said. "You better tell that guy of yours or you'll be watching that wagon making tracks from where you fell off."

Rachel dipped her chin twice and pressed her fingers to her forehead where her dark bangs hid the stitches but not the blues and reds that were emerging on her cheeks.

"Bumpiest road in the world is paved with good intentions," Goldie muttered.

"What a piece of luck. Hello!"

Rachel looked up into eyes surrounded by an artistry of black lashes. They seemed to make the heart-shaped face all the more pale. Alexandra Miller flicked a hand at the champagne. "Looks like you're celebrating."

"Sure are." Goldie brought her index finger down on the newspaper headline. "You see that? Well this little gal sorta helped it happen."

Rachel kicked Goldie under the table and said to Alexandra, "Not really. Had to do with a couple boxes we delivered."

"You're joking." Alexandra laughed, but her black eyes went serious as they took in Rachel's face. "You look worse than after that mugging." Eyes never leaving Rachel, she sat down next to Goldie. "What happened?"

Rachel grimaced at the twinges of pain her effort to smile set off in her cheek. "Just a little wrong place, wrong time."

Goldie thumped the table. "I swear, girl, you would walk twenty miles looking for a basket to hide your light under."

People were streaming into the pub. Hank made his way back to the booth through the sea of shoulders.

Goldie took the proffered glass, pointing at the one in front of Rachel. "She had a powerful thirst. Couldn't wait to get that headache," she said to Hank.

Hank nodded at Alexandra. "Be right back with another."

"No, I can't stay." Alexandra glanced behind her. "I was supposed to meet someone, but it seems I've been stood up. And I've got a lot of work to do." She rose, giving Rachel a smile liquid with concern. "You must take better care of yourself," she said and disappeared into the crowd.

"Goldie," Rachel said, in a low voice. "Do not tell anyone else. I swore to the cops I was nowhere near that building when it happened."

Someone elbowed Hank as he poured, sloshing champagne over his shirt cuff. He mopped at it with a cocktail napkin, then held his goblet aloft. "To the woman who's got more nerve than anyone I've ever met."

"More like a lot less sense," Goldie said around the glass rim as she tipped the still fizzing champagne into her mouth.

Rachel tilted her chin like a prizefighter. "You were the one who said—"

"I said maybe check things out," Goldie cut in. "I never said you should trade that glass brain of yours for brass balls."

"Sure did set fire to the board of directors," Hank said, obviously enjoying that fact.

"What will they do?" Goldie wanted to know.

"Have a king-size brawl over who to blame and how to duck the press. Probably name someone to replace Jason and dump the problem in his lap."

"They must be glad to be rid of that dirtbag in the lab," Goldie said.

Hank chuckled, relishing the notion of his superiors' discomfort. "If it could be kept off the evening news, most of them wouldn't care if he was barbecuing babies over Bunsen burners."

Rachel squeezed some lime into her soda, remembered it was supposed to be champagne and tossed the green wedge onto a napkin. "Jason stumbled onto something, so Harry killed him."

"And the boxes you found were the same as on that plane?" Goldie asked.

"Same as thousands of others being sneaked in from Mexico," Hank put in.

Half-listening, Rachel stared at the napkin beneath her glass. One corner bore the image of a pig in a red frock coat.

Goldie plunked her glass to the table. "But the plane crashed near the reservoir, right on land that belongs to your water agency."

Hank flung an arm along the top of the booth behind Rachel. "From what I hear, drug smuggling is so common that close to the border, the plane we saw crash may have been just a coincidence."

And Lonnie? Rachel was wondering. How did he fit in? She looked up to see Marty, just inside the pub's entrance, scanning the crowd. "Pop!" She waved. "Over here."

His hair looked straggly, but his eyes were snapping and bright. "And to what do I owe this extraordinary invitation to a toast?" Marty asked when Hank had put a glass of champagne in his hand. "You haven't by any chance struck oil beneath that parking lot?"

Rachel scratched her forehead where the stitches were beginning to itch. "Don't I wish."

"What's that?" Marty asked, forehead furrowing with alarm as he took in the exposed stitches. "What happened?"

"Just a couple stitches, Pop." She smoothed her dark bangs.

Goldie flashed a white smile. "Your daughter, here, had a little tussle with an ape."

Marty was still frowning. "I take it the other guy looks worse?"

"He's dead." Rachel leaned toward him and added quietly, "But don't tell anyone, Pop. I'm serious. I broke the law and I don't want to get caught."

Marty stared at her, puzzlement and fear seeming to rise and fall like waves across his face. His mouth worked at getting the words out. "You killed someone?"

Rachel held his eyes until he fell quiet. "I'm fine," she said. "The cops don't know I had anything to do with anything."

"You thought you were raising a debutante," chimed Goldie, "but she turned out to be a cross between a pit bull and a storm trooper."

Hank pushed the newspaper across the table and pointed to the cover story. "She had a hand in this."

"You don't say." Marty searched for his glasses, didn't find them, and held the paper at arm's length to read. "But this was about drugs. How'd you get involved in something like that?"

Goldie shot Rachel a look. "He's your dad. We can trust him, right? We can tell him?"

Rachel held her gaze until she was sure Goldie understood it was to be the sanitized version only. Then, "Okay. But keep your voice down."

When Goldie had finished, Marty shook his head. "Now I need a real drink." He signaled the waiter, ordered a double of Johnny Walker, drank it in three gulps when it arrived, then leaned over the table and hugged his daughter.

"It's over, Pop," Rachel said, voice muffled against his shoulder. "No way I'll ever get into anything like that again."

"If she does, I will personally chain her to her kitchen sink," Goldie said. "That's a promise."

Marty eased himself from the booth. "Sorry to cut this short, but I gotta get back."

"Sure, Dad." Rachel watched him amble through the crowd, then took a sip of her phony drink and put it down.

"How about we adjourn to Melrose?" Hank said. "I know a great little Thai place."

"You guys go ahead," Goldie said. "I gotta get to work. More important, I got to hit the ladies'," she said, and sauntered toward the rest rooms.

Hank was settling the tab when Marty reappeared, lips pursed with frustration. "Damn car won't start."

"You have Triple A?" Hank asked.

Marty shook his head. "'Fraid not."

Hank glanced at Rachel. "We'll drive you home. And we can look after the car tomorrow."

"I've got a better idea." Rachel took a ring of keys from her purse, extracted one, and handed it to Marty. "Take mine, Pop. It's down a block and around the corner on Wilshire. I'll get yours fixed tomorrow."

Marty looked at the key doubtfully. "Well, I am in kind of a hurry."

"I'll get your daughter home," Hank reassured him.

Marty thanked them and hurried off.

Rachel watched him thread his way through the crowd. *Late for a date with an almost full house that doesn't fill.*

The door closed behind Marty, then opened to admit another couple.

"There's one of your board members now," Rachel said.

Hank craned his chin over his shoulder. "Charlotte Emerson? The day must have been even worse than I thought. Never dreamed I'd see *her* at the Pig's Whistle."

"I could swear I've seen her here before," Rachel said.

A tall, slender black man was eyeing the crowd over Charlotte's head. The two made their way toward the back booths. Rachel gave a small wave as they approached.

"How nice," Charlotte said, sounding as though she meant it. "Good to see you."

Hank gestured to the seats across the table. "The place is pretty full. You're welcome to join us."

The older woman's smile was like that of someone on the *Titanic* who had given up a seat on a lifeboat. She looked around, then slid into the booth.

"You know Andrew," she said to Hank.

The two men nodded.

"Andrew Greer, our human resources director," Charlotte said to Rachel.

Either the shadows had hidden Rachel's bruises, or the older woman was too preoccupied to notice. Charlotte raised her voice over the crowd. "We were hoping to discuss a little business, but I suspect we chose the wrong place."

Rachel dropped the wad of keys into her open handbag. "We were just leaving. Really," she said over Charlotte's protests and nudged Hank to stand up.

"But I am pleased to run into you," Charlotte smiled warmly at Rachel. "Saves making a call."

Rachel tilted her head. "Yes?"

"About that business we discussed. I wonder if you would be willing to drive out to Riverside? I'm afraid I'm tied up for the next few days. But perhaps a week from Friday?" Charlotte was writing on the back of a business card. "My home address is on the other side. I promise some good wine and cheese. Shall we say six?"

"Of course." Rachel nodded and followed Hank out of the booth. At the door, she glanced back over her shoulder. Andrew had moved to the other side of the table and the conversation looked intense.

Chapter Thirty-five

In the passenger seat of Hank's Mustang, Rachel hugged herself, trying to forestall the barbs of pain that jabbed at her ribs when the wheels passed over a bump.

"You hurting?" Hank slowed and eased the car around a corner while the impatient driver behind him honked irritably.

"Just someone doing a bongo solo inside my head."

He put his foot on the brake, took the corner carefully and headed back downtown. "Can you hold out another fifteen minutes?"

She shrugged, then screwed up her face at another bump in the road.

Hank reached for her hand, didn't find it and settled for her knee. "Let's go down to one of those markets in Chinatown, pick up some stuff, and I'll make you the best Chinese dinner you ever saw, right in the comfort of your own kitchen."

When they reached her apartment and turned on the light, he stared at the purpling shadows on her cheeks. "You look like a refugee from Baghdad."

"Bruises don't show up right away." She stared at herself in the mirror, then took some ibuprofen.

He led her to one of the barstools at the counter, and with a big white dishtowel tied about his waist for an apron, chopped, sliced, and stir-fried while she watched. He set up a card table in the living room, covered it with three more towels and set out the food.

"For this we need chopsticks." She rooted four from a drawer.

Hank frowned. "I might cook Chinese, but I don't *eat* Chinese. How could a culture whose people eat with sticks ever amount to much?"

Rachel had already managed some quick bites. "Hey, this is fabulous! You are a good cook. But you gotta use the sticks."

They shifted on the way to his mouth, dropping rice into his lap. "No wonder you never see a fat Chinaman."

"Your fingers should be back farther. It gives you more control. Look." She demonstrated.

He reached over and touched her wrist. "Thank God you weren't hurt any worse. You going to tell me what really happened over there?"

"I already did." Goldie knew the real details, but the story she had given Hank and her father, the only others who knew she had been there at all, was that she had realized she had lost her watch in the lab. The security guard was not at his desk. She went upstairs and happened upon a drug-making operation. In the fracas, Harry fell through a window.

Hank had given up on the chopsticks and was making better progress with a fork. "Have it your way. But I get the distinct impression you're leaving something out. I think it had something to do with Jason and that damn car."

Rachel paused, food midway to her mouth, and dodged the subject with, "How well do you know Alexandra?"

"About as well as any business acquaintance."

"That's all?"

"You kidding? When that woman cries, chipped ice runs down her cheeks."

When Rachel had captured the last grain of the rice with her chopsticks, Hank stood, drew her to her feet, and looked solemnly into her face. "If you don't want to tell me what happened, fine. But give me your word you won't take those kinds of risks again," he said, and pulled her to him.

A tear puddled in the corner of her eye and dripped onto his collar.

The phone rang. Rachel sighed and hobbled to the phone.

"Is this Rachel Chavez?"

She agreed that it was.

"You related to a Martin Chavez?"

Her lungs stopped pumping air and her heart tried to fast-forward. "He's my father."

There was a pause on the line, then another voice. "Dr. Graham, County Hospital. I'm afraid your father has had an accident."

"How bad?" The words felt like shards of glass on her tongue.

"He's in surgery now. I'm not the attending physician. I'm afraid that's all I can tell you."

⸻

Above the flimsy hospital gown, Marty's face, what Rachel could see of it, was the color of putty, his eyes a flat blue-gray.

"Papa. What happened?"

His eyes closed. "Car's a mess. Sorry." The words were slurred.

"Papa?" Her eyes shot to the monitors, but she wasn't sure how to read them. Rachel pressed the call button and a short, round woman with gray hair cut shorter than most men's appeared.

She barely glanced at Marty before pulling the rubbery curtain until it enclosed the bed. "He needs to rest."

"But is he all right?" Rachel asked.

The nurse raised a finger to her lips, glanced at the three other occupied beds in the ward and gestured toward the door. "He needs rest," she said again when they reached the hall, then strode into the next room.

Before Rachel could remember the location of the elevator, the nurse emerged in the hall again and hailed her. "They'd like you to stop by the desk in the lobby on your way out."

In the lobby, Rachel found Hank sitting in a molded-plastic chair that looked designed for discomfort, reading an eight-month-old copy of *People*.

"How is he?"

She shrugged and jerked her thumb toward what looked like a window at the racetrack. "I'm trying to find out. Be right back."

When she gave her name at the desk, the man behind it—neat as a Mormon, hair shorn short, starched white shirt—punched at his keyboard. "Ah, there's the matter of financial responsibility." He pushed a clipboard toward her.

She was filling out the form when a police officer arrived at her side. She almost flinched at the sight of yet another uniform. She had never seen so many cops when she *wasn't* trying to avoid them.

He was short, stocky, with a cheery manner, and Rachel hated him on sight. "Sorry to bother you, Miss, but we understand you own the automobile driven by Martin Chavez?"

"Yes, what happened?"

"Hit a guardrail on the Long Beach. Paramedics got to the scene before we did. The doctor hasn't let us talk to him yet. The car's been towed, of course. Would you be the party to pay for that?"

Rachel closed her eyes and counted to three. He hadn't even asked if her father was okay. "Give me the number. I'll call them tomorrow."

He handed her a slip of paper. "And where can we find you?"

She gritted her teeth. "I don't know where I'll be staying." The hospital knew her number, that was enough.

The officer thanked her and bounced off toward the exit.

She handed the clipboard to the Mormon. "Who can tell me something about my father's condition?"

He glanced at his watch. "I'm afraid the admitting physician is off duty," he said in the voice of a church elder. "Perhaps you could call tomorrow."

"Look." Rachel wanted to reach through the window and grab his perfectly knotted blue-and-red striped tie. "I want to know his condition and I want to know now."

The man picked up the phone on the corner of his desk, dialed a few numbers, and handed it to her.

The fourth person she was transferred to told her Martin Chavez was treated for a fractured shoulder, lacerations, contusions, a suspected concussion, and a puncture wound. When she asked how serious and what sort of puncture wound, there was only silence, followed by a dial tone.

"I know why they put their desk staff behind those little windows," she muttered to Hank as the hospital door wheezed asthmatically shut behind them.

⌐⌐⌐

A short, rotund figure was pacing unsteadily back and forth at the corner when Rachel and Hank got back to the garage.

"That looks like Bruno," Rachel said. "I introduced you at the bar. Remember? I wonder what's wrong."

"You want me to stay?"

"No. I'm fine. Really. He's a good friend." She got out of the car and waved at the figure.

Hank shook his head, put the Mustang in gear, and drove off.

"Bruno," Rachel called, and limped toward the figure. "What's going on?"

He looked slightly forlorn and smelled of scotch. "Hope I didn't scare you, kiddo."

"Not a lot left that could," she replied, and told him about Marty.

Swaying a little, Bruno blinked owlishly and made a clicking sound with his tongue. "Jesus. What next?"

They made their way through the empty garage. In the elevator's bright light, he stared at her bruises. "What are these marks?" He threw out his chest and brought up a fist. "I swear to God if some bastard—"

"No, no. Nothing like that. Just a sort of accident. I'm fine."

"You sure don't look fine, kiddo."

"You need some coffee," she said pointedly, as she unlocked the apartment. "You aren't driving home tonight, are you?"

"Got to start work at three." Bruno's eyes had a hollow look of shock about them.

"If you left now, you'd barely be home by three." She selected two mugs from the pile of dirty dishes in the sink, and gave them a hurried scrub. "What are you going to do for sleep?"

He resumed the pacing he had been doing on the sidewalk. "What you're really saying, sweetheart, is you think I shouldn't drive."

Rachel shrugged and decided to stop mincing words and play it straight. "Okay. You shouldn't drive."

Bruno shrugged. "I've done it in a lot worse shape than this." He paced some more, on slightly unsteady feet.

When the coffee was ready, she set both cups on the counter, moved the stools apart, and sat down, carefully distant, a little wave of guilt lapping at her conscience. "So what's up? What's driven you to drink?"

His eyes wandered aimlessly about the room, then came to rest on her upturned face. "I tell you the truth, kiddo, it may not matter a tinker's poop whether I get to work tomorrow."

Her grandfather had once commented, admiringly, that if Bruno had broken both legs and all his ribs, he would still be up at three to work the packing shed.

"Can't be that bad," she said lightly, trying to drain the mounting tension from the air. "What happened? The wind take your farm and set it down at the North Pole?"

Bruno's shoulder's sagged. He took a sip of coffee, but didn't sit down. Wrapping his short arms around his barrel chest, he said dully, "Could be the wind might just as well do that."

"Enough riddles." A rising sense of alarm gave her voice an edge. "What's up?"

"I got a lot of land. A lot."

"I know that. Something like ten square miles, isn't it?"

"All but maybe ten percent has hardpan under it."

"That's not exactly news. You've always had to be careful about salt buildup." Hardpan, a sort of clay, prevented water from draining all the way through the soil.

"We should have been careful about the buildup of something else."

"What are you talking about?"

Bruno dropped his arms and heaved a sigh. "Selenium."

Rachel's jaw dropped and it was several moments before she found her voice. Then words rushed out like steam from a pressure cooker. "What the hell does selenium have to do with anything?"

"Well, you see, sweetie, the terrible monster farmers irrigate their fields. Irrigation is water. When it runs back off the land into the ditch, it carries selenium with it, along with other trace elements and salts from the soil. After that water has run by enough farms, it is just chock full of selenium, among other things. And where do you think that water goes?"

"To shallow ponds somewhere so it can evaporate."

Bruno dipped his head slowly in agreement. "That's the only thing you can do with it when the land is on hardpan—unless you run a pipe all the way to the ocean to dump it."

He paused and took another sip of coffee. "So there's stuff in the water. And yeah, some of it's selenium. And it gets soaked up by the plants and insects and fish, and then some ducks and frogs come along and eat those plants and insects and fish...."

Rachel was staring at him intently. Her mouth began to form into an O and the voice that came out of it was faint. "Those ponds that were on the news? Where they found the wildlife problems?"

Bruno nodded, tottering a little on his feet. "Full story's not out yet, but already the reporters are on us like a pack of dogs. I swear to God that water couldn't wash that much selenium out of the soil. It's flat-out impossible. But they'll make so much noise about the poor little birds, people will be spitting on us in the streets."

"What does that mean?"

"It just may mean that if I don't get to work tomorrow, it ain't going to matter. My land may be worthless. It just may mean that after thirty-two years of hard labor, I am about to go on welfare, kiddo."

Chapter Thirty-six

Charlotte Emerson gathered up the papers on her desk, placed them neatly in a folder, and put on her jacket. The trim rose-colored suit added a pale blush to her cheeks.

She closed the door and stepped across the wide hall. Today would be part of her legacy.

Yesterday, the board of directors had become a platoon of fools. She had almost lost sight of her own priorities. But with all the board members focused on finding someone to blame for the disaster in the water quality lab, with everyone tossing about the word "responsibility," it had turned out to be almost simple.

If there was an afterlife, she would consider thanking that frightful creature Hunsinger.

She left her office and walked briskly to the board room.

It was as grand as the U.S. Senate chamber and already filled with milling bodies, including the mayors of several cities. Fifty-five high-back swivel chairs were arranged behind tables in a three-tiered horseshoe. Microphone arms rose from the tables like poised snakes. Three enormous flags, for nation, state, and district, were draped behind the chairman's seat at the center of the highest tier.

Charlotte was almost giddy with the knowledge that this bastion of right-wing white males was about to announce the appointment of a black general manager.

Andrew's wife, Jackie, was at his side, smiling and gracious in a simple dress of cobalt blue, a beautiful woman whose features recalled some sultry isle in the Caribbean.

Charlotte shook hands until her jaw was stiff from smiling. Someone touched her elbow and she turned to find Alexandra's warm eyes on her.

"Interesting choice," Alexandra said with impeccable charm. "When can we talk? It's important."

"Of course," Charlotte nodded. *I'm sure it is.* "Soon. I'll ask Janet to set it up."

She left Alexandra chatting animatedly with Andrew and drifted up the steps, past the small desks, reminding herself that Andrew was a virgin in politics. She would have to help him.

Bruno Calabrese caught her eye and she nodded to him. *Poor Bruno.* The press was hammering the farmers unmercifully. She swiveled the chairman's seat toward her and sat down.

Alexandra made her way to the first row of seats and sat down next to Bruno. She was thinking it was a shame that the reporter from the *Chronicle* had singled him out as the arch villain. Alexandra had little fondness for agriculture, but as Central Valley farmers went, Bruno was the best of the lot. She put her hand on his arm and murmured, "Is Charlotte out of her mind making this Andrew Greer general manager? A personnel director, yet! He can't possibly know the business."

Bruno squeezed her hand. "Charlotte doesn't make many mistakes," he said carefully. All the same, he was feeling betrayed. And how could a beautiful woman like Alexandra, who should be home having babies, be destroying him?

Alexandra settled back in her seat. "I hear things are rough up your way."

"We give you free land, free water, you should be happy. Instead you boil it up and toss us poor farmers in it like poached eggs."

"The land was no good for farming, you know that. And you didn't give us water, you gave us drain water. You had to get rid of that anyway."

"We built the damn ponds for you, the ditches to bring the water. You think we get our jollies hurting ducks? What do you want? I know. Don't tell me. You want *us* to be dead ducks."

"It's your own drain water you'll drown in," Alexandra said sweetly.

"No way in hell that drain water could have washed enough of it out of the soil and into those ponds. Not even in decades. And you know it."

"Why don't you just give us the delta and we won't bother you again."

"Sure, I'll have the papers drawn up. How would you like it? By the acre or the farm?" Bruno masked his uneasiness with a laugh. *Jason gone and this Andrew…an unknown, like a joker in the deck. Andrew Greer had no power base. What did he know about politics, enviro nuts, or farming? The sharks would gut him by the end of the year. Unless….*

Bruno's eyes again roved over the crowd. He reined them in and forced them to focus on the flags behind the board's tables.

Andrew's fingers were cold. He'd shaken a hundred hands in the past hour, each time with a twinge of embarrassment that his were so cold. Some of those who had congratulated him did not make a habit of touching black hands. Now they would think all blacks had icy fingers.

For the ninth time, he straightened his maroon paisley tie, then drew Jackie to the seat reserved for her. Her eyes held his for a moment before he made his way to the chair next to Charlotte's. Tugging on the back of his grey suit jacket to keep it from buckling around his shoulders, he sat down. Yes, he had done all right, he had. He just hoped it wouldn't destroy his marriage.

At least they could afford to move into the city now and send the kids to private schools. Had he really made it to the top of the whitest old-boy system in the state? The sea of faces, many of the eyes seeking his, assured him that he had.

Awful, what had happened to Jason. And Harry Hunsinger. Odd. More than odd. They said things happen in threes. But perhaps he was only number two-and-a-half.

Alexandra raised her hand to be sure her hat was still in place. It was black and broad-brimmed and she was oblivious to the fact that it blocked the view of those behind her. Her hair was drawn back, making her neck, above the peacock blue dress, seem longer.

She was smiling to herself. Today, she loved the water industry. She was one of only fifteen or twenty women in the meeting hall, which held a couple hundred people. Not a frilly business, water. That was one thing she liked about it. These men were so ignorant, so used to disregarding anything in a skirt outside the bedroom or kitchen, they thought opening doors and talking over her head was all there was to it.

Bruno was another matter. But she could handle him.

Charlotte, of course, was an old warhorse, but Alexandra had amassed weapons that Charlotte had never dreamed of.

Jason had been a loose cannon. Andrew, she would have to study. Alexandra's eyebrows knitted slightly. She'd made the mistake of overlooking him, but what a stroke of luck he might turn out to be. When he sank in over his head in the raging sea of politics, he'd be needing a friend.

On the dais, Charlotte picked up the gavel. The noise of the crowd dulled to a buzz, then a hum, then silence punctuated by a few coughs.

Chapter Thirty-seven

By the end of the week Rachel's bruises were fading and Marty's condition was improving. After visiting him on Friday, she was back in her glass booth before noon.

She picked up the phone to postpone the meeting with Charlotte. Harry was dead. The car that killed Jason, or who checked it out when, didn't seem to matter much anymore.

Rachel's hand poised over the buttons to dial, then she put the receiver down. Charlotte seemed like a decent sort. She probably had questions she wanted to ask Rachel. Why not keep the appointment?

Until the panel truck had circled the parking garage for the third time, she didn't bother to look up from her paperwork. It was the sort of van used by plumbers, but sloppily painted a flat white like a billboard between advertisements. It seemed almost eerily amorphous.

Her eyes followed the truck as it again rounded the curve to the next level. A rash of car thefts had recently hit downtown LA. Was this a reconnaissance? When it passed her booth yet again, she stared after it uneasily, trying to read the license number, but the plate was covered with mud.

A few minutes later, she heard it again and turned. The driver was staring boldly straight at her. She glimpsed mirror-like sunglasses on a narrow face, dark hair, a pointed chin above a black jacket before he turned his face away. She waited, but he didn't return.

Rachel rubbed her eyes and rested her forehead in her hands. Would her life never be calm? The Harry business was certainly over, but her father was still in the hospital after his own mishap, and there was the totally preposterous news that selenium, the same ordinary mineral that had killed Lonnie, was ruining Bruno. Now a thief was probably casing her garage.

A few hours later, she turned the garage over to Irene and drove to Riverside. Her own car had been dead-on-arrival in the towing yard, but her insurance covered an economy rental.

After two wrong turns, she found the right road and drove slowly along it until she saw the mailbox marked *Emerson*.

At the end of a long, winding driveway, she turned off the ignition. In the rearview mirror, she could see that her face still bore the shadows of bruises. A mournful smile played about her mouth as she got out of the car. *Thank God it was over and done with*.

The evening air was warm. Santa Ana winds had been sweeping the hot desert air toward the coast. A big globe willow fanned out over a brick patio. A shiny brass plate with the numbers 4979 in black hung from chains on a post next to the tree. Rachel checked the address against the one on the card in her pocket.

The only window she could see was a long strip of glass about six feet up. Flowers cascaded from two big baskets that hung from hooks under the eaves next to the front door.

She wiped her feet on the doormat and rang the bell. A set of chimes responded. She rang again and waited. Had she got the date wrong? The time? She rang a third time.

The minutes stretched to five. Perhaps Charlotte was in the backyard?

Abutting the house to her right was a high wooden wall. At Rachel's touch, the gate of thick weathered redwood planks creaked a little on its big hinges and swung open on a lush garden. A huge mound of mums bloomed in the center.

In a white Adirondack chair sat Charlotte, her feet on a wooden stool, papers on her lap. The wind caught one of the papers and blew it toward Rachel. She fielded it.

Charlotte didn't look up. *Must have fallen asleep. After all, she's seventy-something.*

Rachel called softly. Still Charlotte slept. Another paper blew from her lap. Rachel put her toe on it, picked it up, brushed off the mark her shoe had made and called Charlotte's name again. No response.

A foot or two from the Adirondack, Rachel stopped, thinking maybe she should just let the woman sleep. She could write a note on the paper.

Something was dripping steadily. She glanced toward the sound. A tube descended the wall near the chair. Drip irrigation. Charlotte was not squandering water to provide herself with the abundant greenery.

Rachel changed her mind yet again. She was here. Charlotte would probably be embarrassed, but she would be embarrassed if she found a note. By waking her, at least they could have their talk and be done with it.

Rachel reached out and touched the woman's shoulder. No response. She shook her gently. Nothing. Then Charlotte's head lolled to the side, the face pale as the chair, mouth slightly open. The eyes were closed.

And directly over the bridge of the nose was a small crater.

Inanely, Rachel's mind bounced to photos she had seen of the moon. But this crater was red.

And behind the head....

"Oh, God." The words tore from her in a harsh whisper. She grabbed Charlotte's wrist. It was thin, the skin like tissue. Her own hand was shaking so badly she couldn't tell if there was a pulse. Steeling herself, she pressed her middle finger under Charlotte's jaw and held her breath. She could feel no throb. Eyes wild, she whirled and raced to the house.

The screen door rattled as it swung closed behind her. The kitchen was like a Sears display of gleaming, tiled cabinet tops. On the wall near the sink hung a white cordless phone. Rachel grabbed the receiver, then dropped it back in its cradle.

Three bodies in a few weeks? *My own mother wouldn't believe I had nothing to do with these deaths.* And this one so clearly a violent death. *Goldie was right. I'm the common thread!*

But what if Charlotte were still alive, the pulse too slight to feel?

She reached for the phone again and more steadily than she would have imagined possible, dialed 9-1-1. "I need to report that I heard a gunshot at...at...." She fumbled in her purse for the card Charlotte had given her the night before. "At 4979 Daimler Road." The voice on the other end had just begun its questions when she hung up.

❧❧❧

Rachel parked in the garage space she reserved for herself. She had only dimmest recollection of getting back to the car. Getting home had been like driving on some other planet. *Harry is dead, how can this be?*

Even her footsteps on the ramp as she made her way to her apartment sounded odd. She turned the key in the lock, flipped on the light, and the air in her lungs turned to lead, immobilizing her in time and space.

Everything she owned seemed to have leapt from its normal place and crashed itself on the floor.

Stupidly, her brain unable to process this information, she stood, gaping, trying to take in the scene. *But Harry is dead....*

Chapter Thirty-eight

It wasn't the sheets from the bed she had carefully made that morning, now bunched in a tangle on the floor, that horrified her so much as the mattress, slashed and spewing its stuffing. The image of Charlotte's dead face flooded her mind again.

Run. The thought hammered at her. *Get out of here. Now.*

She couldn't find Clancy. No orange ball of fur emerged from some hiding place in the rubble to answer her calls. She opened the door and called again, her voice coming back to her in eerie echoes.

Remembering that the possibility of a burglary had crossed her mind, and why, she found a chair to stand on and pried at the light fixture on the ceiling. Jason's cuff links and the packets of grainy powders from Lonnie's apartment and Jason's office tumbled out.

She pawed through the mess near the bed where she had stashed her father's old revolver, but couldn't find it. She could not stay here much longer.

Would she be followed? *Maybe.*

Why? For God's sake, why?

Never mind why, just figure out how to prevent it.

Hurriedly, Rachel changed clothes: a dark blue pants suit of raw silk, and over that a baggy, bright green jogging suit.

Into her scarred leather suitcase she flung as much clothing as would fit. At the door, she set the suitcase down. What if the people who had done this were lurking somewhere in the garage, knowing she would bolt, knowing she would take the powders and cuff links with her?

Opening the door, she listened intently for some telltale sound, then wrestled the suitcase down the ramp and into the trunk of the rental car.

Hyper-alert to every movement on every cross street, and watching her rearview mirror as closely as the road ahead, she drove toward the Glendale Mall and parked among the largest horde of cars she could find.

Inside the mall, she located a rest room on the brightly colored directory, then took one escalator up and the next down. She darted into the Lenscrafters' shop, selected a pair of demo glasses and took them to the counter.

"But you need a prescription," the clerk said. "Now if you'll just step over there for an eye test—"

"I need them for a costume. For a play."

He stared at her a moment, then took her money.

A woman in a flowered dress looked up from the sink as Rachel entered the ladies room. Startled eyes in a round face caught Rachel's in the mirror. Wisps of drab hair straggled along the woman's pale neck. A small green gemstone was snuggled on the right side of her nose. She glanced at Rachel's feet and gave a knowing smile. "In a hurry?" Four shopping bags were lined up under the sinks.

"A little." Rachel slipped into a stall, shed the sweatshirt and pants, stuffed them into a shopping bag, and smoothed the pants suit they had covered.

"Ah." The woman at the sink gave a short, low laugh and began rattling through her packages. Rachel ran a comb through her hair and sat down on the edge of the toilet. She needed a mirror. Would the woman never leave?

More parcels rattled. "You needn't wait, you know," the woman called sweetly. She seemed to be lacking a few wits, might not even notice the change of clothes.

Rachel left the stall, and with as much calmness as she could muster, washed her hands, then swept her hair back and pinned it high.

The other woman, rearranging her own hair, stared into the mirror at Rachel. Slowly one eye closed in an unmistakable wink.

Was she mad? A maniac?

As the woman bent over to pull one of the bags from under the sink, the edges of two more skirts peeked from beneath the hem of the woman's flowered dress.

Heart thudding, Rachel escaped toward the door. "Be careful of the shoes," the woman called after her. "They can be a dead giveaway. No one would ever jog in those black pumps."

Rachel was in the mall walkway before understanding hit her: the woman was a skilled shoplifter. And she was right about the shoes.

The crowd was thinning. No one seemed particularly interested in Rachel. She found a cash machine and tried to look bored while the man ahead of her conducted a lengthy transaction.

At the drug store she debated over hair color. She'd never tried to dye her hair, but there were directions. She made her purchase and left the mall by the street exit. A few couples wandered by on the sidewalk. Rachel stopped beside the door, waited five minutes, then slipped back inside the mall and, moving quickly, took the stairs instead of the escalator and exited two levels above where she had parked. A quarter-hour and many steps later she retrieved the car.

Freeway traffic was light. She took a sharp breath when, as she changed lanes, a dark BMW followed suit. Had someone been watching the car? She studied the rearview mirror intently. In the dark, all the headlights looked alike. When hers was the only car to take the exit for Burbank airport, she sighed with relief.

She parked in the long-term lot and, suitcase in hand, boarded the shuttle to the airport terminal, where she stopped at another cash machine, then found the row of car-rental desks.

In the offhand voice of a frequent flyer, she told the Avis clerk she'd forgotten to reserve a car. Did they have something available?

"Yes," he said, tapping a few keys on his computer keyboard. "What would you like?"

"Something big."

"A van? How many passengers?"

"Not a van." Too unstable, Rachel thought, if someone tried to run her off the road. "A big sedan. Something heavy. Any color but white." Her present car was white.

Apparently perfectly programmed to react neutrally to anything other than shouts of *fire*, he calmly tapped again on the keyboard. "How about blue? There's a nice blue Mercury."

"I'll take it." Rachel filled out the papers, paid with a credit card, and departed with the key.

"Another odd one," the clerk remarked to the woman at the Hertz desk. "That's the third weirdo today."

Rachel drove to LAX, parked, and replayed the same script she'd used at Burbank, this time renting a Pathfinder the color of metallic mushrooms.

An hour and forty minutes later, she had checked into the stately old Biltmore in downtown LA using the name Katharine Chase and paying a three hundred dollar cash deposit. "I just don't like leaving credit card numbers around all over the place," she murmured blandly to the clerk, who nodded his understanding.

With a firm grip on her brown leather bag, Rachel studiously ignored the bellhop and took the elevator to the top floor. The Biltmore was not a place for rushing. The decor seemed to imply that if you could afford to stay within such hallowed walls, you could afford a leisurely wander through the high-ceilinged grandeur. By the time she reached the bank of elevators in the hotel's opposite wing, she was wishing she hadn't packed so many clothes.

Descending again to the ground floor, she slipped out a side door where a taxi was discharging a group of Japanese businessmen. When they had paid, the driver looked at her quizzically. "The Bonaventure," she said, keeping her voice low. It was only a few blocks, but struggling with her luggage on foot would be slow and noticeable. She got into the back seat and sat, wishing the driver would hurry the job of stowing her suitcase in the trunk.

Registering at the Bonaventure as Melanie Whitaker, she again paid cash. She'd have to find another bank machine soon.

Having tipped the bellhop to take the suitcase to her room, she walked back to the Biltmore parking lot and moved the car to an underground city lot five blocks away.

Heading back to the Bonaventure on foot, she felt fatigue shoot through her legs. By the time Rachel reached her room, she was exhausted and the heel of one foot was blistered.

The carefully designed aura of a French boudoir had little appeal, but at last she could take off the damn shoes. She ordered dinner from room service, thinking that if no one were following her, this was costing an awful lot of time and money.

And what about the garage?

But Irene had agreed to look after things each morning, so Rachel could visit Marty in the hospital. The woman had proved amazingly conscientious, and something of a busybody, so she would probably take charge if Rachel wasn't about.

~~~

Waking late the next morning, groggy and aching all over, Rachel couldn't think where she was, or why. Then waves of anxiety descended on her.

Her mind fretted over every detail. For the first time she contemplated with horror the possibility that she might be wanted for Charlotte's murder. Her fingerprints would have been all over the phone in the Riverside kitchen. And couldn't they even take fingerprints from bodies now? She had tried to take Charlotte's pulse. Maybe her name was on Charlotte's calendar!

But by the time she finished a room-service cup of coffee and bran muffin, she had struck a balance between fear and triumph. At least she was safe.

When the maids came to clean the room, she went down to the lobby, bought a copy of the *Times*, found a back table in the coffee shop, and thumbed through the paper. On the eighth page a small photo of Charlotte smiled up at her under the headline: "Water Executive Commits Suicide."

The short article reported that Charlotte Emerson, Chairman of the Board of InterUrban Water District had been discovered by a neighbor who telephoned for paramedics. *"Suicide?"*

The waitress delivering her tea frowned, "Excuse me?"

Rachel looked up at her numbly. "Nothing, sorry."

She hadn't seen a gun anywhere near Charlotte. The poor woman could hardly have shot herself in the head, then put the gun away. But was there a gun? In her fright had she missed it?

She had been certain Charlotte was murdered, and that the burglary of her own apartment was somehow part of the murderer's plan.

But the car that killed Jason *was* checked out to Charlotte. Could Charlotte have been involved with Harry? The idea strained Rachel's imagination. If that was the case, suicide might be believable. Still, why would the woman kill herself just before Rachel was to arrive? *Did she want me to find her?*

When the maids had finished cleaning her imitation boudoir, Rachel called County Hospital and talked with Marty.

"I'm fine," he told her. "When are you going to spring me from this antiseptic prison?"

"Something has come up, Pop. It may be a few days before I can get over there again. Besides, the doctor told me yesterday that he wanted to send you over to rehab for a few days or so." She dodged his questions about what was so important that she couldn't visit.

A call to the garage brought a sprightly answer from Irene, who cackled loudly when Rachel asked if she could run the place for a few days. "Course I can, dear girl," Irene shouted. "Got yourself a fine gentleman, eh?" Rachel didn't deny it. She gave Irene a list of instructions, then added, "Do me a favor and put out some cat food. Clancy, my cat, is missing."

She dialed Hank's office. His voice buzzed in her ear. "Hank?" she faltered. The voice stopped, followed by a beep. Speaking slowly, knowing she sounded evasive, she told the machine she would be out of town a few days, would get in touch when she returned.

Did Charlotte commit suicide?

Rachel decided it didn't matter. Suicide or no, *someone* had torn her own apartment to shreds.

In the bathroom, she studied the hollow-eyed face in the mirror. Taking a pair of scissors from her cosmetic case, she began to chop at her hair.

She had to read the instructions on the hair-color package four times. The smell was beyond bad. Rachel dabbed the solution onto her hair, covered her head with the plastic cap, and sat fidgeting on the edge of the tub.

Restless, Rachel tried to read the newspaper, then went to the phone and dialed Goldie's number. There was no answer, and, not wanting to trust another machine, she hung up. Glancing at her watch, she leapt up and raced back to the bathroom, ten minutes overtime with the bleach.

The result was brassy, orange hair. No matter how many times she rinsed it, she looked more like an exhibitionist than someone who wanted to fade into the woodwork. The hair dryer turned it even brassier, and the eyeglasses from Lenscrafters made the whole effect even more comical.

She would have to dye that mess on her head back to some believable color.

She wrapped her head in a scarf and locked the door behind her.

A man was dawdling near the hotel entrance: dark, wiry, black jeans, black leather jacket with a pattern of chrome studs. Can't be a killer on every street corner, Rachel told herself as she traipsed the blocks to the pharmacy the room clerk had recommended.

With a box of auburn tint in a brown paper bag clutched in one hand, the other hand clenching the scarf, which wouldn't quite cover the brassy orange hair, Rachel was making her way back through the hotel lobby, when she saw the short, stocky man in a yellow knit shirt and black pants turning toward her from the hotel desk. She tried to turn away, but he saw her.

"Rachel, honey."

"Bruno!" She almost gasped his name.

He didn't seem to notice her consternation or her ridiculous appearance. "Big meeting called at InterUrban and I gotta see some people, so I came down early."

"Well, good to see you," she said blithely. "Sorry to rush off, but I'm in a hurry." She dashed back toward the elevator, then turned and called, "I'll phone you, soon. Promise."

His back was to her, so she hardly noticed the small man with reedy limbs waiting at the elevator. Then he turned, and she saw the black jeans and black leather jacket with chrome studs.

Whirling, she dashed back through the lobby. Bruno had disappeared. In the gift shop, without taking her eyes from the shop's doorway, she bought a pack of gum. Then she found a stairway and walked up ten flights.

The odds were ninety to ten that guy in the leather jacket was just some delivery guy, a repair man, or even a tourist, but Rachel decided she couldn't risk the ten. Yanking together her belongings, she stuffed them into the suitcase.

Hair uncovered and feeling about as inconspicuous as a bolt of lightning, she left the key on the dresser, and was relieved to find the elevator empty. On the street, a panhandler angled toward her. A rather pathetic chin, sporting a somewhat unsuccessful attempt at a beard, jutted above a dirty tee shirt.

"You really want some money?" she asked boldly.

His black eyes flashed. "My sister, she is very sick," he mumbled, dark eyes boring anxiously into hers.

"Carry this bag to the Biltmore for me and I'll pay you ten dollars." He gaped at her, and without another word, lunged for the suitcase. She paid him when they reached the hotel. He was staring at the bill so hard as he walked away that he almost fell off the curb.

Rachel reached the tenth floor only to realize she'd forgotten the room number. Dropping the bag she had carried from the drugstore, she dug through her purse for the key. Forcing a calmness she didn't feel, she walked down three flights of stairs and put her key in that door.

Once inside, she tossed the suitcase on the bed and picked up the phone. "This is Katherine Chase, Room 707," she said, trying to breathe slowly. "I'd like to stay over another night. I'll be down to pay shortly."

It wasn't until she had downed an entire can of Coke from the room's self-serve bar that she glanced out the window.

A man was leaning against the building across the street reading a newspaper. At that distance, she couldn't see him clearly, but he was dressed in black.

Chapter Thirty-nine

The man in black hung around on the sidewalk below for most of an hour, then disappeared.

Attracting stares like an electromagnet, Rachel ventured to the lobby to pay another night's lodging. The Biltmore room favored nouveau Victorian, with deep red carpets, drapes of maroon velvet, and a king-size bedspread of creamy satin. In her lighter moments, Rachel wondered if there was a buxom middle-aged woman with platinum hair and dangling earrings in the lounge whispering room numbers in the ears of lonely business travelers.

In her worse moments she would have welcomed a chance to exchange that scenario for reality. Her present hair color might serve her well in that context.

Then she realized she must have left the package of hair dye where she had searched for her key. *What floor was that? The tenth?*

She took the elevator up. But there was no abandoned bag of hair dye. Could it have been another floor? She checked every floor above seven. Nothing.

She would have to make yet another trek to a pharmacy to fix the dreadful orange hair. Rachel nearly groaned out loud. It would have to wait till morning.

Back in her room, she dragged the plush loveseat across the room and propped it against the door.

At two a.m., she awoke remembering something.

With a pair of chrome-rimmed mirror sunglasses, the man in the black jacket would be a dead ringer for the driver of the white van that had been circling the parking garage.

Rachel reached for a magazine, afraid she'd never get back to sleep. But obviously she did go back to sleep, because it was out of blankness that she snapped to full-blown alarm.

Something had pushed against the settee. She couldn't see it from the bed, but that something could only be the door to her room. She turned on the light. Immediately, there was a soft click as the door closed.

She grabbed the phone, punched the zero, and spoke loudly into it without waiting for the clerk at the front desk to answer. "This is...Katharine Chase, Room 707. Someone is trying to get into my room." She had to repeat it when the clerk answered, but two security guards quickly arrived.

The night manager followed with apologies and the offer of another room in a wing where the doors were unlocked by cards and reprogrammed after each guest. She took the offer.

An hour later, with an identical settee propped against the door of the new room, Rachel sat sleepless in an uncomfortable straight-backed chair, staring at the wall with unfocused eyes.

At five o'clock, she carried her suitcase down the back exit stairs. Every step she took echoed.

Annoyed, Dr. Paula Greenfeld slammed down the phone in the medical staff lounge. She had figured that a resident's life could not be nearly as bad as an intern's.

This was her thirtieth birthday, but her work had devoured the last pitiful fragments of her personal life, so nobody cared except her parents.

The nursing staff was getting surly due to some screw-up in scheduling and she herself had worked thirty-one hours out of the last forty-two. And now some idiot patient was claiming someone tried to kill him. He wanted to talk with the police. He probably wanted a guard.

Dr. Greenfeld's shoes squeaked on the imitation-marble linoleum. She thought she remembered the case, but she was too tired to be sure. Apparently he'd had a drink too many or was hopped up or had fallen asleep behind the wheel. At any rate, he had collided with a guardrail on the Long Beach. Her first guess was that he was probably trying to dodge a DUI by claiming someone was trying to kill him.

The nurse at the U-shaped desk gave her a terse smile. The doctor flipped through the patient files. There it was. Room 408. Martin Chavez, age fifty-seven. Blood alcohol level hadn't been all that much. A nasty concussion. Possible spleen contusions, a cracked shoulder. He was one lucky guy. Not fully alert until a few days ago and a real nuisance ever since. Well, the concussion could account for agitation and paranoid delusions.

She dodged a steel tray caddy that held breakfast remains and pushed open the door to Room 408, stopped short, and with thinly veiled irritation checked the file again. Had someone written the wrong room number on the file?

All four beds in 408 were empty. The bathroom door was closed.

She knocked. "Mr. Chavez?" It wasn't locked. The bathroom was empty.

Striding back down the hall, she passed Earl Downy at the nurses' station. Strongly built, with a coffee-colored face between the grizzled hair and the starched whites, Earl had been with the hospital for about a hundred years and was as reliable as the sun.

"Dr. Greenfeld," he called after her. And when she turned, "Any idea where the guy in 408 bed four might have got to? I came up to take him for a CAT scan but I can't find him."

～～～

Rachel's eyes blinked open, her brain foggily trying to remember where she was. She turned her head and hit her chin on the steering wheel.

Am I in a car?

Either that or a bed with a steering wheel.

But why? And where?

Reality was slow to filter in. She remembered returning the Pathfinder to Hertz and renting a Toyota sedan from Avis. Or was it the other way around? Whatever. Then she had bolted—had driven as far as she could. Finally she remembered pulling onto the shoulder of a side road, too exhausted to drive another mile.

Something tapped on the window above her head.

Adrenaline charging now, Rachel tangled with the steering wheel, finally managed to swing her feet to the floor and sat up. The guy outside wore a uniform. Relief at that wore off as soon as she remembered all the reasons the police might be interested in her, and how many times she had seen cops lately.

He tapped again.

She turned the key in the ignition one click so she could roll the window down a few inches.

"Can't sleep here, ma'am." Blue eyes, sandy hair, freckles, the gangly frame of an adolescent. A boy playing cops and robbers. Surely he was too young to be a trooper. Rubbing her face where the upholstery had left marks on her cheeks, she felt centuries old.

"Sorry," she croaked, her throat still full of sleep. "I was just too tired to go on."

"Can I see your driver's license?"

"May I see your ID?" she asked.

"Beg pardon?"

"I want to see your ID."

A perplexed frown and a finger pointed at his badge.

She shook her head. "Badges are easy to come by. Uniforms can be made, cars painted. I want to see a photo ID." She thought for a moment, came to herself and added, "Please."

Wide blue eyes studied her, then he took a leather case from his back pocket, opened it and held it to the window. *John Parsons, Jr.,* it said. And a number.

"Okay." She pulled her purse from the floor on the passenger side, extracted her wallet, rolled down the window, and handed him her license.

He gazed at it, then handed it back. "Can't sleep here, though," John Parsons said. "You okay, ma'am?"

"Fine. I was just tired." She started to close the window, then opened it again. "Do you know of any cabins for rent?" she called after his retreating back.

"Matter of fact I do." He traipsed patiently back to her door. "My folks own a real nice place they rent out from time to time...."

~~~

John Parsons, Sr., looked flustered when he answered the knock on his door.

Plump and bespectacled, he stood in the doorway blinking at a woman with bright orange hair, wrinkled clothes, and mascara half-moons across her cheekbones. "Eh?"

"Terribly sorry to bother you so early in the morning. Your son gave me your address," Rachel explained. "He said you could rent me a cabin."

"Ayah?" One of the suspenders that held up his light blue trousers was twisted. He was still blinking at her as if he thought she might be a mirage projected on his doorstep by some quirk of the early morning sun.

Rachel groaned inwardly, an ache in her neck making her irritable. "Will you rent me your cabin?" She said loudly, spacing her words evenly.

"Cabin!" He smiled benignly and added loudly, "Yes. Of course. Come in." He retreated into the house. The suspenders were doing a very good job. They held the beltline of his pants above his equator, making extra folds around the seat of his pants so that he looked as though he'd been hung on a hook. "Who did you say sent you?"

"YOUR SON."

"He did, eh? Well, where did you meet him?"

"JUST NOW, ON THE ROAD."

"Who is it, John?" Through a doorway behind him, Rachel saw a woman at the kitchen table, her face, the very twin of his, raised in curiosity.

"A lady wants to rent the cabin," Parsons called.

The woman hurried into the hall. "Of course," she smiled. "Pay no attention to him, he hasn't heard a sound in twelve years. Fell off a tractor. Hit his head on a rock. I'm Mrs. Parsons."

Rachel began her request anew.

Mrs. Parsons assured her they were pleased to interrupt their breakfast for an off-season renter sent by their Son-The-State-Trooper. She took a cash deposit and handed over the key.

Chapter Forty

Irene had scorned the isolation of the glass booth and was standing at the garage entrance waving as the cars arrived. The bird on her hat bobbed with each wave. She had moved her cart into the garage and built herself a nest to sleep there so she would be sure to have the gates open on time.

When the black sedan pulled off the street, she gave the man who leaned out the window and flashed a detective's ID her best smile.

"You know a Rachel Chavez?" he asked.

"Yes, sir," Irene said. "Believe I do, as she is the lady who owns this establishment."

"Where is she?"

"Can't rightly say. Could you move your car just a wee bit so you don't block the way?" A car halted a moment at the entrance, then pulled on through.

The detective moved his car a few inches, cut the engine, and eased his big frame from behind the wheel.

Irene thought he must be seven feet tall, and he looked every inch mean. She marched up to him and propped her hands on her hips. "Yes? And what brings you here, if I might ask?"

"When will Ms. Chavez be back?"

Irene's round shoulders rose and fell. "Don't know."

"You must know something if she owns the parking lot and you work here."

"What's this all about?" Hank had come up behind Irene.

The detective's neck was so thick he seemed barely able to turn his head. "Rachel Chavez. Know her?"

Hank frowned. "Why are you looking for her?"

"Couple questions we want to ask her."

"In connection with what?"

"Nothing much. Seems like she might be the last person to see someone alive. Leastwise her fingerprints was all over the place."

"Who?"

"I'm not at liberty to say."

Irene had lifted her chin high to peer into the cop's face. "You saying Rachel did something wrong?"

"Not at liberty to say that either."

"I'll give her the message," Irene said firmly.

"Think maybe I'll just wait around."

"Well, she's not here. And you're still blocking traffic." She pointed to the stream of cars edging through the space behind the black sedan.

The man gave her a steely glare.

Irene decided he couldn't run her in for sleeping in the street. Not now he couldn't. "You get on out of here. Shoo!"

He stared a moment longer, then ambled back to his car. "Tell her I'll be back."

Hank and Irene watched the cop drive off.

"No good for business, police hanging around," Irene said. "No good at all."

Crawling along a road fit only for the hardiest four-wheel-drive, dodging rocks and getting her head slammed into the roof of the Toyota, Rachel finally found the cabin.

With its redwood siding hugged by a cedar-shingled gambrel roof, the little house looked wonderful. And safe. A quarter-mile farther down the road, she parked the car on the shoulder and walked back.

The furnishings were no-nonsense pine, doubtless hammered together by Mr. Parsons and painted with enamel. In the parlor a worn corduroy sofa and a faded chair squatted shapelessly next to the hearth like beloved old dogs.

In a canister on a shelf over the stove, Rachel found some coffee. Both the can and the shelf had been covered with red and white contact paper. The coffee she brewed was harsh and acrid, but she drank it anyway and tried to think.

Something had trimmed her life expectancy to practically zero. But her sleep-starved mind buckled under the effort to comprehend why.

An old black telephone sat on a pine table in the parlor. Surprised to hear a dial tone, Rachel dialed. She listened to the message, then called into the mouthpiece, "Goldie! Pick up!"

The line buzzed. "Holy shit! Where you been, girl? "

"I'm still among the missing, or I sure hope I am," Rachel said and told her about the apartment and the ransacking. "I'm in a cabin in the mountains."

"You're where?"

"In the mountains. Near Lake Arrowhead." Rachel rushed on, "You said your brother had some friends on the force."

"He had a buddy who's a rookie now in South LA," Goldie said.

"Any chance you could ask him a favor?"

"I don't know him real well, but I guess I could. Lemme get a pencil," Goldie sighed. "Okay, shoot."

Rachel described how she had found Charlotte.

"Jesus, that's three dead people!"

"Four if you count Jason," Rachel said.

"You're like a one-woman death camp!"

"Please, Goldie. I need your help to figure this out."

"Like how?"

"The point is, I didn't see a gun anywhere near Charlotte. How could she shoot herself and then get rid of the gun? You think your brother's friend could talk to someone with Riverside police and find out why they think it's suicide?"

"He'd have to give some reason for asking."

"Maybe he could say that some informer told him it was murder? It's important." Rachel rubbed her eyes and pinched her nose where the phony eyeglasses had been. "Please."

"Okay, okay. Get up off your knees. Give me your number."

"It may not be a good idea to talk much on the phone," Rachel said. "I mean it's probably okay now, but I don't know for how long."

"I know you're not saying I got to come up there."

"I need help figuring this out," Rachel said again.

Goldie groaned and Rachel could hear her pounding on something. "Okay, okay. How do I get there?"

Rachel recited the roads. "Memorize it. Then tear up that piece of paper."

"You sound almighty paranoid."

"I am." Rachel described the attempt to get into her room at the Biltmore and the man in the black leather jacket.

When she finished, there was a long pause on the line before Goldie spoke. "Girl, I'm not sure I want to be in the same room with you."

Chapter Forty-one

The first day in the cabin was easy for Rachel. She felt safe and it almost seemed like a vacation.

She was asleep that night when a loud thud jarred her awake. She assured herself it was just a branch falling on the roof, but could sleep no more. Wrapped in a blanket, she prowled the rooms, every nerve alert, flinching at the smallest sound. Rain began peppering the roof and daylight came slowly.

Rachel peered bleakly out the window at the leaden sky, the cheerless landscape, its color gone grey to match the haze.

Is someone looking for me?

How long before they find me?

She tried to light the heater on the wall. It wouldn't cooperate.

Jerking a change of clothes from the closet, she sent the hanger clanking to the floor, and barely resisted an urge to twist it into some unrecognizable shape. She was bone-deep cold.

There was the fireplace, but she didn't want to unlock the door to get to the wood pile. Besides, the cabin was safer if it looked deserted. Smoke coming from the chimney would give her away.

She picked up the phone and called Irene, whose voice immediately dropped to a conspiratorial level. "What kind of trouble you in, dear girl?"

"What makes you think I'm in trouble?"

"I took a look-see for that cat of yours. Figured he got locked in your place upstairs. Just used the key on the ring here. Not a pretty sight up there. No sir, not at all pretty. And a giant-size copper came 'round looking for you." She paused.

"Tell me true now, dear girl. You in trouble with one of them mob types? 'Cause if you are, I got to find me some other line of employment."

"No. It was a burglary. I'll clean it up when I get back."

"And when might that be?" Irene asked.

"I'm not sure."

"Did they find what they were looking for?"

"I don't know," Rachel said.

"You're sure it isn't some kind of gangster you're hiding out from? Irene can handle most anything else, but curs like that, they got no morals, no morals at all. You never know what they might do."

"I swear it has nothing to do with gangsters." Rachel hoped that was true. "Did you find Clancy?"

"Who?"

"The cat."

"'Fraid not. He wasn't up there, and the food I put out here ain't been touched. He may have run off, dear girl."

"Keep putting out the food, okay?"

"Don't you worry yourself about that," Irene promised.

Rachel was placing the receiver back on the hook when she heard the low hum of a motor. Tires crunched on gravel, the motor stopped, doors slammed.

With trembling fingers, she lifted the edge of the faded green-and-orange drapes, sighed with relief and thrust open the front door. Goldie was picking her way along the long path from the driveway. Behind her was Hank.

"You sure you weren't followed?" Rachel kept her voice barely audible.

Goldie shook her head. "Not unless they were flying over our heads. Not a soul on the road behind us. God's wonder we found this place at all. How'd you get here? In a space ship?"

"Where's your car?" Hank asked from behind her, brow furrowed, eyes tense.

"Parked down the road," Rachel whispered, gesturing with her chin. "Maybe you should do the same."

Hank's scowl deepened. "Are you that scared?"

"Yeah. I am." Rachel heaved a sigh. "Thanks for coming."

He eyed her for a moment, taking in the ragged blanket around her shoulders, the mussed orange hair. "I'll move the car." He turned and jogged back to the driveway.

Rachel hugged Goldie. "My brain is out of gas. I don't know what to do."

"All you got to do is get inside. I sure as hell didn't drive all this way to hang out in the cold rain. You get struck by lightning? Is that what did that to your hair?"

Rachel put her hand to her hair. She had almost forgotten. "It's cold inside, too. I guess it's the altitude."

Goldie inspected the cabin room by room. "Orange hair, no heat, no hot chocolate. What kind of a welcome is this?"

"The wall heater doesn't seem to be working."

"There's a half ton of firewood out there," Goldie said over her shoulder as she flipped open kitchen cabinets and drawers. "You ain't gonna get warm standing there, honey. Sure to heaven you didn't come up here without a coat?"

Rachel stared at her blankly for a moment, then put on the red parka she'd thrown over the back of the sofa. "Don't know what's the matter with me."

"Guess you had yourself a couple big shocks. Shit happens. It just ain't a real good idea to wade around in it."

"So what's this all about?" Hank was standing in the doorway.

"That's what I need to figure out," Rachel said. "But I haven't been able to think."

Goldie squeezed her shoulder. "Thinking never did make anybody warm. You get some wood in."

"You figure it's safe to have a fire? Someone might see the smoke."

"Frostbite," Goldie said, "is sure enough not safe. I'm going into town to get some real groceries. Then we will sit down and you're going to talk.

"I know, you just moved the car," Goldie said to Hank. "Give me the keys." He tossed them to her. "Maybe you could take a look at that furnace," she said.

Rachel followed Goldie out and reappeared cradling two logs, her chin steadying a wobbly third. She stacked them in the corner, then brought three more.

Hank was tinkering with the heater. "These things usually work better if you light the pilot," he said, striking a match. A ring of blue flames flared. He adjusted the burner and sat back watching Rachel stack the wood.

"It was damn scary when I found out you'd disappeared," he said. "Why didn't you at least call?"

"I tried. Kept getting the machine." She tried to smile but the effort only tightened her lips. "I was afraid to leave a message."

By the time Goldie returned, Rachel had made an attempt at cleaning the kitchen and Hank, sweatshirt sleeves pushed up, was using an old paper sack to coax a trio of rain-dampened logs to burn.

"This is more like it." Goldie slung the first of five bags of groceries onto the counter. "And what I got here will make it even better. Never mind the coffee. We're going to hot up this cider."

Rachel shrugged and went to sit stiffly in a chair near the fireplace. In an earlier life, the chair's upholstery had boasted huge blue flowers that had now faded almost to white. The generous stuffing had shifted over the years so that it tended to swallow its occupant.

Whishing and clanking sounds issued from the kitchen until Goldie appeared with cups balanced on an old bar tray and joined them by the fire.

Rachel recited again how she had found Charlotte, the mess she came home to, almost breaking down when she got to Clancy's disappearance.

"This whole thing is wearing thin enough to read the newspaper through it," Goldie muttered.

All three stared into the fire. When a drop of sap exploded like a rifle shot in the silence, Rachel almost spilled her cider.

A look passed between Goldie and Hank, who cleared his throat. "I'm afraid I have a couple of things to add to the events of the past few days," he said, his face lost in the shadows in the darkened room.

"We were going to wait till you were in a better mood," Goldie added, "but looks like we might be too old to remember by then."

Feeling like a bit of dust in the path of a broom that was relentlessly sweeping her to hell, Rachel slid her eyes toward Hank. "Is it Clancy?"

Hank and Goldie both shook their heads. Hank propped his feet on the cracked-vinyl hassock. The laces of his scuffed hiking boots were knotted in several places. "The cops are looking for you, too," he said finally.

"I know that," Rachel said. "I talked to Irene. Probably something to do with Lonnie, or the garage."

"Afraid not," Hank said. "Something to do with fingerprints. Apparently yours were all over the place at Charlotte's."

The long stream of air that escaped from Rachel sounded like a punctured bicycle tire.

"But why, if they think it was suicide…?" She turned to Goldie. "Your brother's friend have any luck in Riverside?"

"They told him there was a gun, registered to Charlotte herself, in her lap."

Rachel stared at her. "No way. There was *no* gun. Certainly not in her lap. I was upset, not blind. I couldn't have missed that."

Hank leaned back and closed his eyes. "Why would they take prints at all if they were so sure it was suicide?"

Goldie put her feet on what passed for a coffee table. "My brother's buddy, Sammy, talked to some detective in Riverside. The dick said there was some doubt that the prints on the gun were consistent with someone shooting himself. Sammy's a little edgy now because they want more information about his 'informant.'"

Rachel drummed her fingers on the chair arm. "But Harry is dead. Why would someone kill Charlotte? This doesn't make any more sense than that plane disappearing."

"I keep forgetting about that damn plane," Goldie said. "You think it's connected?"

"Not necessarily," Hank said. "Might just be a failed smuggling job."

"You never saw the pilot?"

Hank and Rachel both shook their heads.

"Seems like a pretty good chance he mighta seen you, though."

Rachel slapped her hand over her mouth. "I think I lost my key out there. Maybe that's how my apartment got trashed."

"We have to go to the police," Hank said. "You have to tell them that."

Rachel gazed at the rough beams of the cabin ceiling trying to conjure up the scene of the crash. "We can't even prove there *was* a plane."

The cabin's atmosphere seemed to whir with thoughts from all three.

"There was a granular powder spilling out of one of those boxes on the plane," Rachel mused. "It looked a lot like the stuff I found in Lonnie's kitchen."

"The same as what was in the envelope behind that guy Jason's toilet?" Goldie asked.

Rachel nodded several times. "I think so."

"Too bad you didn't take a little handful of it," Goldie said.

"I did. It got ruined. I put it in the trunk of my car and a bottle of bleach leaked all over it." Rachel was staring at the fire as if answers might rise from the flames. She shifted her gaze to Hank. "I saw a long, flat building by that reservoir. What's in it?"

"At Coyote? Just a place to stash equipment and supplies."

"Any staff there?"

"On a regular basis, just one guy, I think. He lives there. We send out others from time to time. There are two or three houses on the other side of the lake. Most of them haven't been used since they finished building the aqueduct."

Rachel frowned, her eyes far away.

Hank looked back at the fire. "Why did Charlotte ask you to go to Riverside?"

"I don't really know," Rachel said. "I'd been asking her about records that might show who had driven that company car the day Jason was killed, but I didn't figure that mattered any more after Harry did his swan dive."

"So who killed Charlotte?" Hank asked.

"Or did she off herself?" This from Goldie.

"I'd stake my life there was no gun," Rachel reflected to no one in particular. "Someone had to put it in her lap after I left. Unless...." She paused, staring into empty air as if seeing something. The words exploded from her: "Someone saw me there."

Chapter Forty-two

Goldie looked as if she had seen a snake. "You think you walked *in* on a murder?"

Rachel pulled her legs up under her in the chair. "Kind of sounds like it, doesn't it?"

The silence stretched out as all three tried to fit another piece into the puzzle.

"I give up," Rachel said and turned to Hank. "But you said there were a *couple* of things."

Hank tipped his chipped cup and swallowed the last of his cider. "When I couldn't find you, I thought you might be at the hospital with your dad. The hospital staff was real evasive when I called, so I went over to the hospital. I said I was his son, and I wanted to see him."

Rachel stared at the cartoon image of a reindeer on the side of her cup.

Hank went to reconfigure the burning logs. "Finally an administrator took me into a private office," he said over his shoulder, then paused.

Finally Rachel asked softly, "Why?"

Hank straightened and looked at her. "He said your father has disappeared."

She leaped out of her chair. "My God! When? How?"

"They don't know."

Rachel's fingers twisted the coarse orange hair that didn't seem to belong to her. She reached for the parka she had discarded in the fire's warmth. "I have to find him."

Goldie grabbed Rachel's arm. "You can't. An hour ago you were scared to open the door, now you're a Green Beret?"

Rachel gaped at her. A burning log punctuated the quiet with a hiss.

Goldie's matter-of-fact voice bisected the silence. "Listen, girl, for the past hour you've been saying someone is trying to kill you!"

"And now they have my father!"

"We don't know that," Hank cut in. "All we know is the *hospital* doesn't know where he is."

Rachel sank back into the ample lap of the chair. "Jason, Lonnie, Harry, Charlotte, and now my father…Pop never even met the others."

Goldie nodded. "According to you, neither did Lonnie. But…they all knew you."

Rachel was looking at them, but her mind was somewhere else. "Pop struck a guardrail," she said, in the voice of someone in a trance. "On the Long Beach. A *one*-car accident. Not the cop at the desk, or anyone at the hospital said anything about his blood-alcohol. He had a couple of drinks with us, remember? But that was all."

"Look," Goldie said, "I know he's your dad, but maybe he stopped somewhere after that."

"He's no saint," Rachel said, "but the cards were more important to him than booze. He never drank much when he was playing. Said it affected his game. The point is, he was driving my car." Her voice rose, razor thin. *"Did someone run him off the road?"*

Hank said, "You mean someone was trying to kill you and got him?"

Goldie's cheeks puffed up as if she were blowing out candles. "Jesus, Mary, and Martin Luther King!"

The three argued, pondered, and solved nothing.

After they had gone over it for a fourth time to no avail, Goldie rose and put on her jacket. "Almost forgot I've got a job. You just stay put," she motioned to Rachel. "I'll be back as soon as I can get away. And I sure enough got to find some hair dye. You look like a neon sign in a red-light district. Promise you'll call if anything happens."

Rachel agreed. She was getting sleepy.

Hank was reaching for his own jacket.

Goldie swung her eyes to him. "Any chance you can stay here?"

Rachel looked at the floor.

Hank looked startled.

"No use pretending this isn't bad business," Goldie went on. "Real bad. They just might be looking for you, too, Hank. You been hanging around that parking lot, you were at the hospital with Rachel, you saw that plane crash."

"I didn't bring any clothes," Hank said.

"So go down to Gorman and buy some. Supermarkets even sell clothes these days."

"I'll be fine by myself," Rachel said. "I'd rather be alone."

Hank hesitated, then took off his jacket.

"Good." Goldie opened the door.

Rachel locked it behind her and turned to Hank. "Look, I know we're…but…."

"Just go to bed. I need to do some thinking." He sat down again in front of the fire.

～～～

The black-triangle head of the snake rose above the water. Its eyes, two tiny beads of light, were trained on something: a tiny tortoise, mouth wide with panic. And behind the tortoise floated her father's face, the eyes dead. Saliva cascaded from the snake's inch-long fangs. Little sobs from the tortoise crescendoed into a shriek.

"Rachel. Rachel." The voice was saying her name over and over, louder and louder. "Rachel!" Strong hands shook her shoulders.

The huge dark triangle wove back and forth. A light behind it prevented her seeing the eyes. She tried to get up. To run. The snake wound itself around her. She tore at it but it held her down until she stopped struggling.

A dim yellowish light began to seep through the edges of her mind like water into a tent. The face above hers was silhouetted against the light from the door.

"That must've been one hell of a dream."

Her tongue seemed made of sawdust. She swallowed, then tried to sit up.

"Lie down," Hank said, his voice was almost a whisper. Arms gathered her to him and she clung to his shoulder—a bird clinging to a branch in a wind storm.

—⁓⁓⁓—

Bacon crackled and popped in the pan as Rachel turned over the strips. "Good morning." Her voice ended in a chuckle as she watched Hank stagger from the bedroom, squinting against the sun that flooded through the open windows.

"Can't remember where the john is," he rasped in a sleep-thick voice.

She pointed at the door with a fork. "Breakfast coming up."

"I can't eat this early in the morning," he mumbled, sagging onto a chair at the kitchen table. The chair seat had been clumsily covered with dark green plastic.

Rachel put a cup of coffee in front of him. "It's six-thirty already."

"Oh, God," Hank moaned. "An early riser." He propped his forehead in his hand. "A sanctimonious early riser."

"As soon as you're awake, I've got some ideas."

"Not the strenuous sort, I trust." He took a gulp of coffee and choked. "I'm not the type who wakes up whistling and pawing the ground."

"Could've fooled me."

Mournfully, he took another swig of coffee.

Bacon, eggs, and a quart of coffee later, Hank was pacing the room while Rachel, in jeans and an old black wool turtleneck, squatted on the floor in front of the fireplace scraping up ashes.

"Maybe we're trying too hard to tie everything together," she said. "Maybe some of it was just coincidence." She brushed her hair from her forehead, leaving a smudge of ashes. An unwelcome thought crept through her head, leaving a trail of ghostly cold in its wake.

She swiveled to face Hank and sat back on her heels. "Jason, Lonnie, Harry, Charlotte, Pop." Her voice quavered on the last. "You knew all of them, too, except Lonnie, and maybe he was a coincidence."

Chapter Forty-three

"You think *I* had something to do with all this?" Hank's voice almost squeaked.

"Did you?" Rachel asked bluntly.

"No! For God's sake! How can—?"

She cut him off. "How long have you been with InterUrban?"

"Why?"

"It's a simple question," Rachel said.

With each word, the lines in her forehead deepened until the mistrust hung like a spiderweb in the air between them.

At length he said, "A long time. They took me on as a diver when I was fresh back from Brazil and the Peace Corps."

"A diver?"

"Someone has to go down in the reservoirs to check algae and stuff. That was my first job."

"And then?"

Hank examined a spot just over her head. "And then I finished school, moved into plant operations, then to headquarters as a lab tech in water quality."

She studied his face. Something there seemed to still her suspicion and she asked more calmly, "What was Jason like?"

Hank sighed and brought his eyes to hers. "You keep asking that. He was a mixed bag. When he wanted to, he could charm a rattlesnake. But he could go mean in an instant and turn on you."

"That ever happen to you?"

"Once. He wanted me to jigger water supply statistics."

"When was that?" Rachel asked.

"A couple years ago."

"Did you do it?"

Hank shook his head. "I wouldn't do it myself, but I went along with it." He glanced at Rachel then down at his feet.

"Jason did this sort of thing often?" she wanted to know.

He seemed intent on examining his shoes. "Not often, I guess."

"But that wasn't the first time?"

Hank sank onto the sofa. "Water is not a squeaky-clean enterprise," he said. "There are a lot of dirty hands."

"Like who else?"

"The farmers."

Rachel blinked at that, but said nothing.

"The greens," Hank added. "About a year ago, they were after Jason to join them in some big campaign against agriculture."

He paused, then went on: "We are approaching a time when there just won't be enough water to protect everything from minnows to kangaroo rats, and still grow food, run industry, and water landscapes down here where it doesn't rain six months at a stretch."

"Did Jason climb on the environmental bandwagon?"

"He had other ideas. He had us documenting a lot of statistics on all the endangered species that really weren't endangered, starting with the snail darter that killed the Tennessee project. He compiled thirty years of data on every time the EPA screwed up."

Rachel gnawed at her lip. "Not exactly a Ben & Jerry's kind of guy."

"He was an attorney. I guess he was mounting a defense. Or an offense."

"Nice business," she said.

"No worse than a lot of others."

"Maybe not." Rachel frowned at the glimmer of something just beyond the view of her mind's eye. "Better than running drugs, I guess."

The floor creaked under Hank's feet as he crossed the room to peer out the window. "If you think you'll be all right here till tomorrow," he said, "I could go home and pack and call in sick."

She was staring at the ceiling beams, her mind quietly opening—an oyster exposing a tantalizing pearl.

"Hey." He snapped his fingers in front of her.

"Sorry," she said, her voice small, like a little girl's. "Yes. Go ahead. I'll be fine."

Chapter Forty-four

Late sun was slanting across the dusty desert road, leaving its shadows in the ruts. The Toyota's underside bounced twice on rocks, skidded into brush once, but the wheels kept crawling along. According to the topographical map Rachel had picked up from a sports shop in San Bernardino, the road ended at Coyote Reservoir.

At what seemed about the right distance, she wrestled with the steering wheel, persuaded the complaining automobile to turn around, put it in park, and set out on foot.

The lake was still out of sight, but she figured it couldn't be far. In her pockets were the small flashlight and a wedge of ground beef wrapped in butcher paper. She hadn't forgotten the dog.

Sandy soil sucked at her feet, tiring her legs. Tall tufts of coarse grass had taken over most of the landscape. As she rounded a bend, the top half of what appeared to be a long, windowless wall hove into sight.

Three strands of barbed wire blocked the road, which had become little more than a wheel-rutted path. She squirmed through with only a minor scratch. Now she could see that a vast opening in the wall was sealed by an enormous metal panel, a giant blind eye facing the sunset.

A human-size door was at the far end. Rachel's pulse sped and stuttered as she contemplated what she had to do.

Feeling obvious as a solitary ink blot against snow, she moved past the pale walls of the warehouse to the door. It was locked, but at the bottom was a metal plate with hinges and a hook-and-eye lock. She stooped to examine it. Once the hook was removed from the eye, a nudge from her hand swung it inward. A doggie door.

Kneeling, Rachel pushed her head through the opening. Huge, angular shapes squatted in a jungle of darkness. Fighting down a fear of getting trapped, she wormed her way through the opening and waited for her eyes to adjust to the darkness.

The flashlight beam was limited, but strong enough to prove she had found what she expected to find. A dark, brooding hulk took up most of the space.

Even in the dimness its identity was obvious: the mangled carcass of a plane. Pointing straight at her, in the pale light from two windows high in the wall, was a very broad wing.

But what did it prove? She and Hank knew they had seen a plane crash. They both knew the cargo was drugs. And everyone in Los Angeles now knew the water quality lab was full of drugs. But what did all of that mean? Was the plane smuggling the drugs the lab made *out* of the country? Not likely. And it was too small a craft to take them any great distance on this side of the border.

Containers stood about the dented corpse of the plane like passengers about to board. Not knowing what she was looking for, Rachel searched the hodgepodge of boxes, then slowly scanned the rows of cartons that had been stacked along the walls. The boxes she had seen in the plane's cargo were relatively small, probably to make it easier to scoot them across the border from Mexico. The drugs themselves would be long gone, maybe already on the streets.

Having found exactly what she figured was there, she was strangely disappointed. *What did you expect? A neon sign pointing to the guilty?*

She glanced toward the dog door, then decided that as long as she was here, she might as well have a look inside the plane.

The rungs to the cockpit were blocked by boxes too heavy to move, but behind the wing stood an aluminum ladder, all four legs splattered with paint. It screeched against the warehouse floor as she drew it closer, and wobbled as she mounted. Rachel inched along the damaged wing to the cockpit, lowered herself into the bucket seat, and swept her light around the cargo space behind it. The floor looked as if it had been swept.

Running her hands along the floor behind the cockpit, her knuckle struck a small solitary carton wedged under the seat. A heady excitement flooding through her, she wrestled it free and ripped it open. But a plastic lining stubbornly resisted her efforts to reach the interior, and the beam of the flashlight merely bounced off.

She searched the cockpit for something sharp, found nothing, tried again to puncture the plastic with her fingernails, but with no success.

The light was growing perceptibly weaker. She berated herself for not having bought fresh batteries and switched it off. Darkness descended like a dense cloud. The box weighed only a pound or so, she would just take it with her. It might prove nothing, but at least it was something tangible.

Rachel twisted and writhed back through the cockpit window and slithered along the wing. Hanging on to the box made her efforts awkward. She reached the ladder and started down. Her left foot was blindly seeking the next rung when a snarl erupted from the darkness below.

Something lunged against her leg. Pain blazed from her heel to her hip. The ladder teetered, dumping her suddenly to the concrete floor. The dog gnashing at her shoe backed off when the ladder crashed to the cement with a clanging crescendo.

As the noise faded, Rachel could hear the dog's panting breath somewhere to her left and knew he would soon size things up and be back.

Hastily righting the ladder, she snapped the crossbars down, crawled into the conical cage it formed, slammed one open side against a tall box and pulled a large carton toward her until it blocked the other side.

The pain in her leg had dulled. Her trembling fingers found a gash in her calf, but it was small and the blood was already clotting. Rachel swept the floor around her with her hands. Where was the box she had taken from the plane?

Big, and blacker than the shadows, the dog began snuffling at the spaces between the ladder's rungs.

Scooting back, Rachel bumped her elbow against a cardboard corner. She reached behind her and brought out the box, its plastic lining still intact. From the pocket of her jeans, she took the soggy packet of meat. Mashed to a thin, ragged blob, it was warm from the heat of her body.

At the smell of it, the dog began butting the ladder. If she tossed it to him now, he'd just gobble it on the spot. She wrapped it again and shone the flashlight full into the canine eyes. The beam wasn't strong enough to back him off more than a few inches, but her eye caught a sharp pucker of split metal where one of the ladder legs had buckled in the fall.

Grasping the open carton, she twisted a little of the plastic between her fingers and raked it across the barb of broken metal. On the second try, it punctured. The spilled contents were soft and grainy, like beach sand, and even in the dim light she was suddenly certain what it was.

Rachel ripped away some of the lining, folded the plastic around a small handful of the powder, tied the corners twice and slipped it into her pocket, then reached for the meat and kneaded the mound of spilled powder into it.

How much would it take to stop a dog? Or would it stop a dog at all? It might be just some harmless substance, a detergent maybe, tossed into the plane by someone too lazy to store it properly. But Rachel didn't think so.

She tossed half the chunk between the rungs of the ladder.

The dog snarled and with a harsh bark snapped up the hamburger, then lay down, watching the place the food had come from. The back of the ladder had only two crossed strips of aluminum. If he veered in that direction she wouldn't be able to protect herself. She worked a little more of the powder into the remaining glob of meat.

The dog's jaws clamped around it before it hit the floor. He lay down again, watching.

Please let it be a nice, good poison, Rachel prayed and sat down. *And please let it be quick.* The dull throb from the wound in her calf made it agonizing labor to sit still on the cold concrete.

On the underside of the wing, she could dimly see narrow steel piping. Very slowly, she stood up, training her eyes on the dog, whose head was lowered, still watching her. When she glanced at the wing from this angle she could make out small nozzles arranged at intervals along the piping.

Where had she seen this before? On the farm? No....

Yes. Recognition snapped into place. This was a crop duster. She remembered Marty calling her, when she was about nine, to watch the plane sweep down and over their fields. It was very risky, he told her. And the pilot had to be an artist. Only test pilots and stunt pilots matched the skills of the duster pilot.

Rachel remembered being mesmerized by the rhythm of it. The plane's belly seemed to snuggle to the earth, only to drown it in fog. The way a squid cloaks its prey, she thought now. It was like a long, slow dance. Up, a graceful turn, then the leisurely dive. The closer to the unsuspecting earth, the better. There had been something disturbing about it too.

An ideal aircraft for smuggling, she realized. No one would notice a crop duster moseying up to the border and slipping across. Once over the vast farmland in the Imperial Valley, there are probably as many crop dusters as cars.

The dog seemed less alert, his breathing slower, but when she moved her arm quickly, he growled. Slowly, she sat back down. To pass the time, she studied the plane. Behind her, the fuselage jutted. Near the end, a row of large numbers was stenciled in black. She recited them to herself. Once, twice, then tested her memory.

She could no longer hear the dog breathing. She snapped her fingers. Clapped. He didn't move.

But now another sound edged its way into her consciousness. Muffled, businesslike, almost angry thuds that faintly jarred the earth beneath her.

In the cage of her own creation, Rachel froze.

A key clicked in a lock, a bolt scraped, and air whooshed over her face. Between the boxes she could see bright light thrusting through the open door framing a large, thick man. The buckle on the wide belt that shored up his potbelly gleamed in the sun.

"Max," he shouted. "Here, Max." The dog didn't move. "Fine damn guard dog," he muttered. "Where the hell are you?" Then, after a pause, "Prob'ly chasin' a damn rabbit." The man lumbered back through the doorway and slid the bolt home.

Chapter Forty-five

It was nearly full dark by the time Rachel began her clamber through the tiny opening in the door. Max had been totally silent for what seemed like hours, unconscious or possibly dead. But not knowing where the man might be, Rachel had stifled her desire to bolt and forced herself to wait.

Fear drummed a tattoo in her ears and shortened her breath to puppy-like pants until she was free of the door.

Then she ran.

The wall of the warehouse seemed to stretch into outer space. The western horizon was a purplish bruise where the sun had been excised. The stars were already clear. Her jacket snagged when she dove under the barbed wire. Rachel jerked it free. When she could run no longer, she stumbled as fast as she could along the road between the tire grooves.

At last the car appeared and terror began to give way to elation. She was breaking into a run when a shot sounded behind her and dirt spewed from the ground a few feet ahead. She threw herself to the ground.

A harsh voice rang out behind her. "Stop!"

Rachel pitched herself to her feet and tried to run toward the car. Her energy was gone. She stubbed her toe, lurched to one knee, rose and forced herself forward again.

The car didn't seem to be getting any closer.

Another shot hit a rock to her left, spewing fragments of stone. One bit into her cheek. She started to drop to the ground, thought better of it, and instead dodged in the direction of the rock, then right again.

Trying to work the key out of her pocket as she ran, she hurled herself one way, then the other. Don't make it a pattern. The thought drummed through her head. Keep him guessing. Four steps right, five left.

Another shot churned up dirt a few feet to her right. She ran on, thanking God she had turned the car around before she parked.

Pain seared through her left arm just above the elbow. She dropped the key.

Frenzied fingers searched the ground. The key gleamed among a dozen dirt-imbedded stones. She snatched it up and ran again.

A bullet struck metal somewhere close ahead. If he managed to disable the car, she was dead—or as good as.

But the Toyota seemed relatively unharmed. Rachel plunged under the bumper. More shots pierced metal. The shooter wasn't far. And he would be watching the driver's door.

Key in hand, she slid out beneath the passenger door, rose and jammed the key into the lock. Seconds later she was in the driver's seat and the motor was running. Darkness was moving in fast. Unable to see much of the road, she turned on the headlights, then quickly thrust them off again.

A bullet slammed into the passenger seat.

A web of cracks had appeared on the windshield near the upper right corner.

But the car was moving, complaining loudly, jouncing hard against the rocks. The Toyota was not built for this, but it was moving.

The left front wheel careened off a rock, and for a moment she thought the car would roll. But it righted itself. A quarter mile later, the surface under the tires went smooth. She had reached the main road. Blindly, she turned the steering wheel left and gunned the engine.

Forty, fifty, sixty. She wasn't sure when the shooting had stopped. Had there been a car nearby, hidden in the brush? Was he behind her even now?

The moon was bright, but she was barely able to see the road. Her foot hovered over the brake. Red rear lights would be glowing bull's-eyes.

But a blind crash, if it didn't kill her, would strand her with her pursuer.

She stomped down on the brake. The car fish-tailed, skidding sideways, but held the pavement. No lights showed in the rearview mirror. If he was back there, he wouldn't be able to see either, and his vehicle would probably be a pickup or a four-wheel-drive. Neither was built for speed. The Toyota would fare better on the open road.

She turned on the headlights and floored the accelerator.

Chapter Forty-six

Rachel wrestled the steering wheel, the pain flaring through her arm, bringing beads of sweat to her upper lip The car almost foundered in a chuck hole. She slowed her speed and cautiously probed the area near her left elbow. Her fingers came away damp. She wiped them on her jeans.

The desert here was flat and filled with moonlight and shadows. She passed no cars, saw no lights until she reached the main highway.

A car sped down the hill toward her. Past her. Another followed. Ordinary people living ordinary lives. The gas station where she and Hank had called the sheriff was closed. Eight miles later, Rachel pulled into a brightly lit Shell station and stopped at the full-service island, leaning her shoulder against the inside of the door so the attendant wouldn't see the blood on her torn jacket.

"What happened?" He pointed at the spider's web of broken windshield. His hair, long in back, had been shorn to the scalp on the sides. His pants were slung so low he looked like a child whose dirty diaper was weighing him down.

"Attacked by kamikazes," she said, and left him trying to figure out what a kamikaze was.

In the rest room, Rachel shed her jacket, rolled up the sleeve of her tee shirt, and examined her arm in the mirror. The blood had begun to cake around a diagonal gash that began just below her shoulder. She washed it carefully, wincing at the cold of the water and sting of the soap. She unrolled the toilet paper and, careful not to touch the sheets, covered the wound.

By the time she reached the cabin, the moon had disappeared. Unable to keep her eyes open a moment longer, she broke her own rule and parked in the driveway. She was turning off the engine when weariness gave way to panic.

A light was showing through the crack between the drapes. A light she was certain she had not left on.

And a figure was moving through the shadows toward her.

Chapter Forty-seven

"What the *hell* do you think you're doing?" The hoarse voice hurled the question like a rock.

For several seconds, Rachel sat immobilized, clutching the steering wheel, unable to do anything but blink.

The figure reached the driver's door and shook the handle.

"Rachel! Are you all right?" The familiar voice finally penetrated her numb mind. Hank.

She tried to get out of the car, but her knees buckled.

She felt herself being carried, but beyond that, could not connect with reality except to note that the room was brightly lit.

Blue sheep marched across the top blanket of the pile of bedding that covered her. They were very like the blue sheep on the blanket that had covered her childhood bed. But those sheep had been pink.

Rachel rolled over. She was wearing little beyond one makeshift bandage on her arm, another on her leg. Stretching, she was surprised that there was little answering pain from beneath the bandages. Then she noticed the two crushed pillows were stacked against the headboard next to her.

And someone was frying bacon.

"About time," said Hank from the doorway. "It's almost noon."

Over her third piece of toast, wrapped in the blanket of blue sheep, she explained.

Hank's face grew grimmer with each sentence.

"So I did a stupid thing."

"Not stupid," he said. "Insane."

"But I got the…oh, God, where is it? I tied it up in plastic."

"Over there." Hank pointed at the kitchen counter. "It fell out of the car about the same time you did."

"What does it look like?"

"Morton's salt."

"Where are my clothes?"

"Where all the good little clothes go when they die. In the trash."

"But I don't have many others here," Rachel wailed.

"They look like you wore them in the front lines in Iraq."

"I don't think so," she said. "I didn't have that much gas."

His blue eyes glared at her and her flippancy fled. He began clattering dirty dishes into the sink.

Clutching the blanket around her, she crossed the kitchen and put a hand on his arm. "I didn't expect you back so soon. I should have left a note or something. I'm sorry."

Suds-covered hands gripped her shoulders. His voice was hoarse and harsh. "I don't want to lose you." His hard and insistent mouth gentled when it met hers.

The blue-sheep blanket slipped. She again felt herself being carried. This time, she was connecting very well with reality. "The bacon will burn."

"I turned it off."

Her bare toes touched the floor by the bed. Kind, clumsy fingers tugged at the blanket.

Chapter Forty-eight

"Of course, it never entered your mind you could have been killed," Goldie sputtered. They were in the cabin kitchen dyeing Rachel's hair.

"You'll drip that stuff all over me and it'll never come out." Rachel's words were muffled by the towel she was holding at her hairline.

"You should have called me before you left," Goldie shouted.

"You would have told me not to go."

"And sure as God made little green grasshoppers I would have been right. That was the world's dumbest move going down there alone. You not only deserved to get shot at, you deserved to get hit."

"It wasn't much more than a scratch. What do you make of the plane being a crop duster?"

"Just goes to show how sly folks can get when they're huntin' ways to put their paws on millions of bucks." Goldie wrinkled her nose. "This stuff smells like it came from a mortuary."

Rachel lifted the towel and gasped for air. "You think it smells bad up there, you ought to try it down here."

"I have more sense than to give myself orange hair." Goldie dabbed at Rachel's head. "Ooh, I bet that feels good, just one cold drip at a time going down the back of your neck." She turned to rummage in the drawers next to the sink. "If we had a plastic bag and a rubber band.... What the pink and purple hell are these?" She held up three paper packages marked *Terumo ½ cc* that obviously held syringes.

Rachel peered from under the towel. "Looks like hypodermic needles."

"What the hell are they doing in that drawer?"

"Don't look at me. I may have some bad habits, but shooting up was never one of them. Someone must've left them here. Some former guest was a doper? The owner's a diabetic? How would I know?" Rachel retreated again beneath the towel.

"Put that little orange head of yours in the sink. Well, it ain't exactly orange any more."

"It's supposed to be brown," said Rachel. "Dark brown."

"Well, let's see now. Looks kind of green to me."

Rachel's head came up out of the sink, eyes wide.

"That's a real interesting expression. The white is showing all the way around your eyes." Goldie rinsed Rachel's hair and handed her a fresh towel.

"Hank took the stuff I found in the plane to the same chemist who analyzed the others."

Goldie planted her back against the kitchen counter and crossed her arms, scowling.

With no warning, Rachel burst into tears. "How can any of this be? What's happened to Pop? And Clancy?"

Goldie put her arms around her until the sobs subsided.

Rachel wiped her eyes with a corner of the towel. "If that number I gave you is some sort of serial number, we can find out who owns that plane."

The phone rang. Twice, then twice again. Both women froze, staring at the black instrument on the table until it began for the third time—the signal she had arranged with Hank.

Rachel picked it up. "Goldie's Dye House," she announced into the receiver, then listened intently. "You're kidding…but that's crazy.… No, I'm not going anywhere. Goldie thinks thumbscrews would be a suitable punishment if I so much as open the door.… Okay." She hung up.

Goldie was looking at her expectantly.

"The lab test. He got them to rush it."

"And?"

"It's sodium selenate. The same thing that killed Lonnie, the same stuff that was in Jason's envelope. And here's maybe the oddest thing. Selenium killed a bunch of ducks at a wetland over near Salinas. My friend Bruno thinks he's going to lose his farm because of it."

Goldie shook her head when Rachel finished explaining. "This gets weirder by the minute."

They hashed and rehashed things until every possible explanation was limp and tasteless as old chewing gum.

"Selenium has to be an ingredient," Rachel said, "in whatever Harry Hunsinger was concocting in the lab. And that plane must have been smuggling selenium."

"Selenium's not illegal," Goldie said. "Why bother smuggling it?"

"Because they were using so much of it someone would get suspicious if they bought it?"

"You could be onto something there," Goldie agreed.

"Maybe we should try to get hold of someone at the water agency. See if they have any idea why someone would be after me."

Goldie wasn't sure. "Making drugs, hiding plane wreckage. Too many people at that water agency were in on that deal. Say we call the wrong person and he passes the information along to whoever's hunting you."

"Damn," Rachel said, and was silent a long moment. "But I know someone over there who I would bet wasn't involved in that scheme."

"Of course Hank wasn't," Goldie said. "But he's already doing all he can to find out what's going on."

"Hank doesn't have the clout to ask the hard questions. This guy does."

"Who?"

"Andrew Greer. He's just been appointed general manager—Jason's job. Hank and I met him at the Pig. He was with Charlotte."

Goldie was pouring two glasses of orange juice. "That woman who killed herself? Or didn't?"

Rachel nodded gravely.

"He's new? They hired this guy since everything happened?"

"Nope," Rachel said. "According to Hank, he was manager of human resources or something like that."

"Then what makes you so sure he's not mixed up in it?"

"Because he's black."

Goldie took a swig of orange juice. "I hate to tell you this, honey. There actually are one or two seriously bad black guys."

"This Andrew Greer didn't work in the field, or in the lab. Harry didn't need him. Aside from that, only about a dozen blacks park in my garage. And most of them are women. One black guy among all those whites—they wouldn't have trusted him with even a hint."

Goldie thought about that. "Okay, maybe you should call him, tell him what's in that so-called warehouse. But don't tell him where you are."

"Why should he believe me? Especially when I begin with 'You don't know me and I can't tell you who or where I am....'"

"Maybe Hank could talk to him."

"I'd rather not ask him," Rachel said. "For one thing, he's been calling in sick. Sort of odd if he suddenly turns up saying bizarre things. For another, InterUrban is Hank's whole career. If this guy Greer turns out to be a jerk, doesn't believe him, Hank could lose his job."

Goldie put her hands on her hips. "So why we discussing this if it's impossible to talk to this guy?"

"Because there is someone who could talk to him."

"Who?"

Rachel nodded to Goldie's raised eyebrows. "You."

"You gotta be kidding. 'Hello, I clean toilets at the water agency and I just thought you might like to know you've got a drug smuggling plane in your warehouse and maybe a killer or two on your payroll.'"

"Goldie, he'd listen to you *because* you have no connection except the wastebaskets."

"I couldn't keep it all straight in my head. I'd forget something."

"I'll go over it with you. We can make notes."

"How do we know this Greer guy would even talk to me?"

"You could go see him face to face."

"Honey, you seem to be attributing a whole lot of virtue to being black."

Chapter Forty-nine

Marty was awake and wearing real pajamas. Navy blue ones with white piping. That was reason enough to do it, he told himself. He had a horror of dying in a piece of blue-dotted cotton that tied in the back.

The early morning sun was just beginning to seep in under the dingy curtains. He'd slept better than he had in the hospital, but now he had to do some real serious thinking.

He tried to lever his feet to the floor but pain spiked from his side to his shoulder and back again. He nodded stoically. Cracked a rib or two and probably your damn skull, Marty told himself and tried again. This time he made it, but his face was pale from the effort. He glimpsed himself in the mirror and grimaced.

You can do it. He'd been telling himself that since he had lowered himself one step at a time on a back stairway from the hospital's third floor, then forced himself to limp another two blocks before he called a cab.

In the cramped little kitchen, he ignored the sink full of dishes from God knows when, and bent, wincing, to remove a three-pound can of Chase and Sanborn from a cabinet. Having measured and poured, he leaned against the cabinet, scratched the bald spot that was beginning on the top of his head, and listened to the water chug itself into coffee.

When the machine had given its last chug, he poured a cup, limped to the living room and sank into the homely, worn, wonderful chair in his dusty, rumpled living room. Thank God he was home. But he couldn't stay there any more than he could stay at the hospital. And he had to find Rachel.

He pulled the phone toward him and began dialing. It was barely six-thirty.

⌐⌐⌐

Rachel awoke with an amorphous memory of something terrible. It was still dark. The moon had found her through the top of the window, enveloping her in a pale circle of light. The fear that swept her along like a dry leaf in the path of a hurricane seemed to have been with her forever. She could hardly remember what her life was like before.

She kicked the twisted blankets loose from the mattress and lay there puzzling it over, watching the moon-shadow trees tease the cracks in the ceiling until they faded with the rising sun.

⌐⌐⌐

"You look glum," Hank said that night. "Is that what happens when it's your turn to cook?" They were eating dinner in the cabin's tiny kitchen.

Rachel's movements were like those of a windup doll. All evening, the only sound had been dishes scraping against each other and the clamor of a rain that had begun in earnest.

Her hand descended on the table, making the knives and forks chatter. "I can't take much more of this," she said, voice almost a sob.

"I know." Hank took a sip of tea. It was watery and lukewarm, and a few fragments of tea leaves swam on the surface, but he barely noticed.

"Why is it happening to me?"

"It sort of fits together, that maybe someone saw you take something from the plane wreckage and didn't know it got ruined by bleach in the trunk of your car. Except why would anyone be smuggling sodium selenate? It's not an illegal chemical."

Rachel was carefully examining the cracks in the kitchen table. "Three other things don't fit. Big things. Monstrous things. Lonnie and Jason and Charlotte."

Hank's normally affable face had the look of someone who has waked one morning to find the sun going down. "I know," he said for what seemed like the trillionth time. "Charlotte didn't have anything to do with the drugs."

"Why not?" Rachel asked. "Appearances can be deceiving. Not every drug lord has a mustache."

Hank rubbed his chin. "Charlotte hated anything to do with drugs. Her daughter OD'd on PCP or some such thing and died."

"How awful. You're right. That probably rules her out."

The ate in silence until, a bite of dinner halfway to her mouth, Rachel dropped the fork to her plate. "My car was parked on the road near where that plane crashed. If the pilot saw me around the wreckage...." She reached for the phone. Dialed information. Then dialed again.

"Sheriff's Department, Milligan." The female voice that answered sounded vaguely offended.

"Do you log calls requesting license plate checks?" Rachel said quietly into the mouthpiece.

"Maybe."

Rachel took her checkbook from her purse, studied its calendar, then gave the date and her own license number. "Did you run a check on that license that day?"

"I can't give you that information."

"Why not?"

"Not public information."

"All I want to know is whether a check was made. No details." The phone line buzzed with static. Rachel pressed on: "Either a check was made or it wasn't. Nothing private about that. You guys use radios that can be picked up by anyone."

"Hang on." Computer keys clicked. "1SQZ753? Sure enough," the voice drawled. "My shift. Must've done it myself. Oh, yeah. They said somebody found a key belonged to the guy with that license number."

~~~

Goldie sat at the steering wheel while the cleaning crew climbed into the van. They had worked hard that night, had even covered for her because her mind just wasn't on polishing floors. Now, with the job done, the van was rocking with leftover energy.

"Quiet!" she yelled. She couldn't go see that Andrew Greer. Sure, Hank had a career to worry about and all she had was a job. But what if Greer called her boss?

She tossed some scraps of paper and a brown and shriveled apple core into the bag that hung from the dash. Fingers plucked at her sleeve and she turned to see Peter's placid round face turned up to hers.

"Stop it," she said peevishly. "You think I can drive with you pinching me? Get back in your seat."

He dropped his eyes and obeyed.

She started to pull the van into the street, then backed it again along the curb and turned.

"I'm sorry," she announced. "I'm just in a rotten mood. Anybody want some ice cream?"

Amid a chorus of giggles, she parked at a Dairy Queen and took orders.

When she returned with a cardboard tray of cones, Peter was still eyeing her warily. "I said I was sorry."

Solemnly, he reached for a cone. "You won't be mad if I show you something?"

"Of course not."

"I think maybe you should see it. Maybe I shoulda throwed it away, but it was in such a funny place. Maybe I shoulda put it on the desk, but that lady isn't here anymore."

"What lady?"

"The one that's gone. I was running the sweeper in the pretty office, and you know how it sometimes messes up the rug. This time it pulls the rug way up and way far underneath was this." He took a sheet of paper from his pocket, unfolded it and handed it to Goldie.

She stared at it and dropped the tray of cones on the pavement.

<p style="text-align:center">~~~</p>

Virginia Wexford was not amused. It was hard enough to suddenly have a new boss. Not that anyone could be as demanding as Jason had been.

She'd been up half the night, holding her little granddaughter's hand while the child threw up, while her own daughter snored away across the hall.

She had told Barbara not to marry that idiot electrician. He drank and she knew he drank before she married him. A wonder he hadn't electrocuted himself. Good riddance. Her daughter was a good looking, intelligent woman. She could have found a good husband. She could have joined the church singles group.

Virginia separated the papers on her desk into neat stacks. She'd built her career on orderliness, ninety-two-words-a-minute typing speed, and the ability to wear the same expression through tragedy, comedy, and past everything in between.

Andrew was a very nice person. He just had no idea how to run InterUrban Water District. Virginia would have to get him trained fast.

And now, unannounced, without a proper appointment, was this woman in jeans—jeans yet!—demanding to see him. And Virginia probably wouldn't get out of the office until seven. This was not the way things were going to happen. No, sir.

She looked at her watch. Andrew was off the phone. Her feet made no sound on the thick carpet she had helped Jason select when he first became general manager. New ones always wanted to redecorate—like dogs doing their business on a fire hydrant, was Virginia's opinion. She had survived three general managers. She would survive a fourth.

She cleared her throat, moved to Andrew's elbow and spoke quietly. If you didn't sit. If you made them look up at you at close quarters, they almost always gave in.

"Who?" Andrew asked.

Virginia repeated the name. "She doesn't have an appointment."

"What does she want?"

"She wouldn't say. I told her you probably couldn't see her, but she insisted—"

"Excuse me. Sir." Goldie was standing in the office doorway. Her eyes pinned Andrew's surprised ones. "It's urgent."

Andrew leaned his white shirtsleeves on the arms of what he still thought of as Jason's chair and looked hard at Goldie. "I hope it won't take long," he said. "I really don't have a lot of time."

Goldie quickly took the chair directly in front of his desk. Virginia was still standing at his elbow. Goldie gave her a small smile and said in a voice as low and controlled as Virginia's own, "Please close the door."

When Goldie finished, Andrew was peering through his gold-rim glasses at his hands. The half moons on his nails were very pink against the rich molasses brown of his fingers. His face betrayed nothing. He was wishing he could get up, walk past the machine in the lobby that still held this morning's newspapers, and forget what he'd just heard.

He looked up. "I'll look into it," he said, trying to conjure up a smile and failing. He was thinking of the firestorm of reporters and his promises to the board of directors.

～～～

"You're out of your mind!" Rachel pulled her hand away from Hank's on the sofa and stood, staring down at him as if his neck had suddenly sprouted a second head.

Hank looked away from her, the straight hair, bronzed by the light from the fire, masking his eyes. "I think it's possible."

"Bruno is a friend. A lifelong friend. He would never be involved in this. Never. Why would you think such a thing?"

He tossed the hair from his eyes and held her gaze. "Sodium selenate was involved with Jason and with Lonnie, and when the lab said the sample you took from the plane debris in the warehouse was the same, you said there had to be a connection. You said two incidents could be some wild coincidence, but not a third."

Rachel's face was stiff with shock. "I said selenium. I didn't say Bruno."

"That lab report is actually the fourth time selenium entered the picture. That's what poisoned Farwell Ponds. You know that as well as I do."

"That's from the drain water. Everyone says so. That one has to be a coincidence. Are you sure the lab didn't get something mixed up?"

"Labs are incredibly careful about that. But I don't know...." Hank's shoulders under the slate blue chamois shirt lifted tensely, then fell. "Unless...."

The little patches of hair on his hands looked red against his whitened knuckles. "I do think something is wrong with the water analysis figures from those ponds," he said. "The concentrations are just too high. It doesn't seem possible that so much selenium could have just washed out of farm soil."

"That wetland refuge was Bruno's baby. He helped set it up. You can't think he's doing something to those ponds himself."

Hank turned his hands palm up. "It's not impossible."

"But Bruno is a farmer. No farmer would deliberately do something to get himself accused of destroying wildlife with his drain water...." Rachel trailed off. She was seeing Bruno in the hotel lobby the morning before someone tried to break into her room. He had not asked what she was doing there. He had not asked why her hair was orange or why she was wearing those silly glasses.

"I've seen him in action at open board meetings. Bruno Calabrese is a tough old bird," Hank was saying. "If he thought the end justified the means...."

"But his entire life, every dime he has, his very being, is his farm," Rachel said. "And if selenium is washing out of that soil like they say, and poisoning wildlife, land values are probably already dropping like a rock." She walked to the window and pulled the faded drapes more firmly across the glass.

"Unless he sold his land just before the news hit," Hank said softly.

Rachel turned, looking as though she'd been kicked in the stomach. "It wouldn't be long before he could buy it back pretty cheap."

Chapter Fifty

Saturday morning Andrew Greer, brand-new blue-and-grey Izod windbreaker open over his white Jantzen golf shirt, mowed his lawn even though the landscape maintenance people were due in two days. He liked mowing grass and he wanted to get away from his wife's accusing eyes. The wind was up and his cheeks were rosy.

The mower zigzagged and the wind blew the clippings. Andrew had missed little Jennifer's piano recital last night, his wife Jackie wasn't speaking to him, and his son had greeted him at the breakfast table this morning with 'What are you doing home?' followed by the sort of blank thirteen-year-old stare that made Andrew long to prevent the boy from becoming fourteen.

Maybe Andrew could manage to get one of his feet under the mower blades and hack it off. Then he wouldn't have to go back to that horrible quiet office where the carpet was so thick his secretary could sneak up on him.

He wished the electric mower with its bright yellow hundred-foot cord made more noise. He was tired of thinking.

One more swath brought him to the big weeping willow at the corner of his property. He turned the mower, brought the handle up, leaned his elbows on it and looked back at the house.

Some house, he thought. The white stucco walls under red Spanish tiles seemed to go on forever. Five bedrooms, three bathrooms, and now he could afford even better.

And his face was hanging on the hallowed wall in the Inter-Urban entry with the eight white men who had preceded him as general manager.

But your wife won't speak to you, your kids have forgotten what you look like, your sister thinks you're an Uncle Tom. And you don't even like yourself very much.

Andrew wished he hadn't listened, wished he didn't know, wished a lot of things. But it was too late. It had been too late ever since he'd let that smart-mouthed female who reminded him of his sister into his office.

He trundled the lawnmower to the garage, thinking that the amiable reign of InterUrban's first black general manager was likely to be shorter than expected. He was almost looking forward to Monday.

⌒⌒⌒

The smell of old papers made Rachel sneeze. Despite the long, tiresome drive, she was ecstatic just to be out of the cabin.

The courthouse clerk frowned and tugged at his yellow vest.

Rachel returned his frown, thinking this dried-up little man probably wished his ledgers could be left alone to rot, in perfect numerical order.

Between audible sighs, the clerk handed Hank the records requested and reminded them that the courthouse closed in less than two hours.

Checking land sales quickly became drudgery. Even the light from the huge fixtures that hung from very high, very dirty ceilings subtly discouraged browsers by wandering off before it quite reached the tables.

Absently, Rachel chewed on the eraser of her number two pencil. "Could he have used another name?" she whispered, although there was no one there to disturb but the clerk. The whisper seemed louder than normal speech.

Hank's eyebrows climbed comically. "They frown on the sale of land by people not named on the deed."

"Are you sure these are all the companies he owns?" She pointed at the nine names Hank had written down under the heading *Calabrese Corporations*.

"I'm not sure of anything."

They returned to studying the records.

"Good God!" Rachel's voice resounded from the walls. The clerk scowled at her and she ducked her head like a second-grader. "That's a lot of land," she whispered, running her finger down the lines. "But Bruno hasn't been selling. He's been buying."

"So where does that leave us?" Rachel asked Hank as they got into the car in the small parking lot behind the courthouse. "Seems like we're right back to square one. If Bruno's been *buying* land, he can't be poisoning the ponds."

Hank sat, the car keys dangling from his hand, which was propped on the steering wheel. He didn't answer.

"They say there's going to be a huge earthquake this afternoon," Rachel said loudly. "The earth will open and swallow this car for a late lunch."

Hank turned a puzzled face to her. "Huh?"

"Were you planning on spending the afternoon in the parking lot of the Merced County Courthouse? I want junk food. Genuine, bonafide junk food."

❧❧❧

Andrew turned on the lights and sat down in Jason's big black leather chair. He had come in early to beat the traffic. On Monday the freeway was always a bear.

He leaned back and stared at the desk. Then, very slowly, he put the heel of one size eleven-and-a-half spit-shined black wing-tip oxford on top of the desk, brought the other up and rested it on the ankle. He was still sitting there when Virginia looked in at eight.

"Call a board meeting," he said in a soft, even voice.

"But…but…," Virginia squawked like a hen.

"The general manager has the authority to call a board meeting. Do it."

Someone was shaking Rachel's shoulder.

"Stop it, Hank. Let me sleep."

She rolled over, but the shaking got rougher. Someone called her name in a voice that bore the same lilt as her father's and, wanting to go to him, she blinked open her eyes.

But it wasn't her father.

Her hands flew to cover her face from a blinding light. Her heart drag-raced from sleep to panic as she realized Hank had gone down to LA to take care of some business.

She jerked forward, half sitting, knees to her chin, making herself as small as possible against the bed's plain pine headboard, like a torture victim.

"Get up, lady. Get dressed." The voice came from behind the light that was trained directly on her eyes.

Rachel wrenched at the covers until they came loose from the foot of the bed, and pulled them up around her naked shoulders.

"May I have some privacy?" Her voice was steady. If they intended to kill her immediately, weeping would not deter them. If not, she would need her wits about her.

At first there was no answer, then, "Three minutes," came out of the darkness behind the flashlight. A different voice, also male.

"We will wait outside the door." The first voice again. "And someone is outside the window. Please, you will not do anything stupid." The door closed, blotting out the light, pitching the room into a void of blackness.

How had they found her? No one knew where she was except Hank and Goldie.

Rachel staggered to the closet and fumbled at the clothes. Afraid that if she turned on the light they might burst into the room again, she dressed like the blind, by touch and memory. Her eyes had adjusted to the darkness by the time she opened the door.

Again the hammer of the oversize flashlight beam struck her.

"I can't see when you do that," she said calmly.

"This is the complete point."

They didn't search her, blindfold her or even tie her hands. They just put her in the back seat, then climbed in on either side of her.

Both men were Mexican, young, but already running to fat, potbellies straining at their belts. Rachel had never seen any of them before. They muttered and grunted, but didn't say much. The driver, much smaller, had a look of meanness about the eyes that only short men can achieve. He had wielded the light, so she hadn't seen his face and couldn't see much of him above the car seat. All three wore dark jackets.

Forty minutes later, the driver pulled into a dimly lit office parking lot in a town Rachel didn't recognize. A small yellow light shone above the steel-door entrance.

The two who had hemmed her in the back seat now pushed her toward a door to the building. "*El Jefe* is waiting. He does not like waiting."

The door opened silently as she approached, and an arm reached out to usher her inside.

A light shone behind the desk across the room, casting the man who sat there as a mountainous shadow, dwarfing everything around him, his demeanor that of a wrestler.

"Come, sit." He pointed at a chair. His voice was kind enough, but something in the tone warned that if its owner decided, Rachel could be diced like a cucumber and tossed in a salad.

Figuring at least one of the men who had abducted her was outside the door with a gun, she did as she was told.

El Jefe leaned his elbows on the desk. Only his hands were clearly visible, and she was surprised to see they were neatly groomed, the nails even polished.

The room was chilly, the air like lead. Rachel's neck was aching, her head pounding. She tried to swallow, but her mouth was too dry. If she tried to speak, she was sure her voice would quaver.

The silence stretched like an overtaxed rubber band. When she thought she could trust her voice to be steady, she stared at him as squarely as one can stare at a hulking shadow. "So you're the boss."

He laughed, as though she had passed a test.

She said nothing, eyes trying to find the man behind the shadow, trying to measure his meaning.

The voice came again: "You have a little Spanish. Very good. Marty did not let you grow up without it."

Chapter Fifty-one

Rachel's chin jerked up, her eyes intense. "You know my father?"

"*Si*, child. Of course." Footsteps were crossing some adjoining room and *El Jefe* lifted his hand carelessly. "About time you got here, Marty. Your lovely daughter seems a little suspicious of me."

Rachel leaped from her chair and Marty's arms closed around her. "Oh, Pop!" The words came out in a half-sob. "I thought, when they said you were gone from the hospital.... God, I'm glad to see you."

Marty brought out a handkerchief, dabbed at his eyes, then handed it to her. "I wasn't sure I'd ever see my girl again." He pulled a chair next to hers and sat down, not letting go of her hand.

"No one knew where you were," Marty said. "Some crazy old woman is at your garage. She wouldn't believe I was your father, wouldn't let me into your apartment, said she didn't know where you were. What happened?"

Wondering if they were both now caught in the same trap, Rachel glanced toward *El Jefe*, then back to Marty. "You first. What happened in the hospital?"

"I had to get out of there or they would find me."

"Who would find you?"

"Rachel, believe me, that was no accident. Someone on the Long Beach Freeway was trying to kill me. He kept ramming my car, ramming and ramming." Marty's voice grew thin and he paused. "I didn't remember at first, but then it came back."

"You don't know who it was?"

He brought his palms up in a shrug. "Not a clue. I don't even owe anyone. Not much anyway. Of course, you meet a few bums at the tables, but I didn't think I had an enemy in the world."

"You probably don't, Pop. You were driving my car."

Marty's troubled eyes held hers. "You think someone was trying to kill you? But why? What have you got yourself mixed up in?"

She tipped her head toward *El Jefe*, who had leaned back in his chair and was gazing at the ceiling, now in full light. She was surprised to see he wore a three-piece pinstripe suit, a white shirt, and a beard as neatly trimmed as his fingernails. He was older than she'd thought and looked nothing like a wrestler.

Marty read her look. "I guess you could say *El Jefe* is an old friend."

The big man barked a laugh. "We are both old, and we are friends. I will tell her myself." He turned to Rachel. "Your father is a good man. My son Emilio got it into his head a few years ago that he was such a hotshot poker player he should not waste himself on college. But he was not quite so great a player as he thought. Emilio lost a large sum to your papa, here."

A smile played about Marty's mouth. "Only royal flush I ever held. Spades."

"A very large sum," *El Jefe* went on. "His entire tuition to Stanford."

"The boy was shattered," Marty said. "He could hardly stand up from his chair."

"He knew he could not both pay your father what he owed and go to college as I expected. To make it short, your papa did something no one I ever heard of would do. He did not know Emilio was mostly afraid I would find out. Your papa believed Emilio had lost his entire future."

"Can't say I blame Emilio for being afraid of you," Marty chuckled.

"Your papa was maybe a bigger fool than Emilio. He gave the money back." *El Jefe* shook his large head like a Saint Bernard. "My son was a fool, but he was not as dishonorable as this sounds."

"Emilio told me he owed me his life," Marty said. "And that if ever, *ever* I needed a favor I should look him up."

"More than six years ago and I never knew of it. Of course Marty here did not know what sorts of favors Emilio could produce." The big man nodded with unconcealed pride.

Marty scratched his nose with his thumb. "I heard things here and there over the years."

"My son is no longer afraid of me. And me, these days I am maybe a little afraid of him. He's going to be a damn fine lawyer. But he knows there are things I can do that he can't." Somewhere in the building, a door slammed.

"How did you find me?" Rachel directed her question at Marty, but *El Jefe* answered.

"Your friend with the Mustang, Mr. Sullivan, lost us the first time, but he is—pardon my saying this—a beginner."

One of the owners of the potbellies that had escorted Rachel slouched across the room to the desk and said something in a low voice. Little of what the big man replied was audible beyond the way he chopped off each word, spitting them out like cherry pits.

When the messenger had slouched his way back to the corridor, *El Jefe* turned to Rachel. "No one followed you here. We had someone behind. You are safe for now." Then to Marty, "I will leave you. Your daughter, I think, does not like to talk in front of me and she is right. Trust no one.

"When you are ready to return, Jose and Felipe will see to it," he said to Rachel, then got up and lumbered across the room. At the door, he turned and pointed a thick finger at her. "Good luck."

She looked at her father and whispered, "Who is he?"

"Never mind him, he means us no harm. I called in his son's debt. He honored it. Now what the hell is going on?"

Rachel rubbed her temple with a forefinger. "I wish I knew."

"Just begin at the beginning."

"I'll try," she said, and for more than an hour they mulled over the details, with Jose and Felipe strolling through the corridor from time to time, casting glances through the open door that spoke much of impatience but little of curiosity. At this stage in their careers they listened to no words but *El Jefe*'s.

Rachel's exhausted brain spun like a wheel in sand, almost, but never quite, grasping an elusive something that would convert what she was saying to sense.

"Maybe *El Jefe* could help," Marty said, when she had finished. "I'll ask him."

"No way, Pop." Her lips were dry. She ran her tongue over them.

"But he could protect you."

"It's pretty obvious he'll never be nominated for Citizen of the Year," Rachel said. "A couple of friends are helping me—you met them at the Pig's Whistle, remember?—I think I'm better off with them."

"They seemed like nice enough people, but not exactly the sort who can give you any real protection. Whoever is threatening you wouldn't mess with *El Jefe*," Marty pointed out.

"For all we know, he could be part of it," she said firmly.

⌒⌒⌒

The tires of the old blue Ford seemed to crunch over the gravel forever before they got to the end of the driveway. Whistling an off-key tune, Goldie turned off the motor and stowed the key in her purse, thinking Rachel was going to find this very interesting.

Goldie would have bet her paycheck that wishy-washy Andrew Greer would cop out. She had been flabbergasted when he telephoned to thank her and say he was calling a board meeting. He hadn't sounded like the same man she had talked to in that office.

And there was Peter's discovery of that strange sheet of paper beneath the rug in the Emerson woman's office. Rachel would be interested in that, too.

Grasping the arm of the rusty, blackened knocker from the cabin's front door, Goldie tapped it against the plate and waited, gazing down at her feet, thinking her shoes looked like the Mexican army had borrowed them for a million-mile march. She'd have to stop by Kmart for another pair.

Lifting the knocker again, Goldie slammed it hard against the plate. Where was Rachel? She banged on the door with her fist. No response. She tried the knob. It turned.

The door swung inward. Still no sign of Rachel.

Brows a sharp line above her eyes, Goldie stepped inside. The living room was dark and empty, drapes closed, fireplace cold. She went to the bedroom and yanked open the closet door. It banged against the wall. Eight empty hangers swung a little on the rod. No clothes. On the floor of the closet, like a pool of blood, lay a red scarf.

Chapter Fifty-two

Hank had been adamant. "I don't want to hear any more about it," he had said, a muscle jumping along his jawline, as it had since he'd heard Rachel's story. "I'm glad your father is okay, but we are clearing out of here."

He'd wanted to leave the rental car behind. "Whoever was shooting at you out there by Coyote got a good look at that Toyota."

"But when you go into town or whatever, I'll be trapped without a car. I need to be able to escape," Rachel had insisted.

Hank had relented, had even paid extra to park it in a closed garage.

Now he set the suitcases down in front of the furnished condo on the outskirts of San Jose and tried a key in the lock of the unfamiliar front door. Late-morning sun drowned the blue of the sky. The lock didn't open.

"We have to call Goldie right away. She thought she might drive up this morning. If she did, she's probably called out the Special Forces by now. Why did we have to come here?" Rachel muttered while Hank tried the second key, which worked.

"It was my fault," Hank shouted. "Okay? The subject is closed."

"This guy could have offed me a dozen times. He didn't," she said, following Hank up the inside stairs.

"Look," he pointed. "There's even a fireplace."

Ignoring him, Rachel marched to the kitchen. When she had unloaded the plastic bags she'd brought in, she brought her fist down on the sink and burst out, "I hate condos. There are twenty-two of these exactly alike. You have to count the doors to figure out which is yours."

"Of course. There should be a sign: Rachel Chavez is hiding here." Hank touched her shoulder. "You aren't moving in for the rest of your life."

"I was just beginning to get used to that cabin." With morose flips of the wrist, Rachel opened each cabinet, not really bothering to look inside. "I want a salad. I'm sick of frozen peas," she said, knowing it sounded childish, but unable to stop herself.

"Rachel...." Hank touched her cheek. "Believe me, I do understand. It's got to end soon." He pulled her toward him.

A tear flowed over the inside corner of her eye. "I know it sounds silly, but I miss Clancy. He's been my friend for a lot of years. No place is home without him. I just want this over," she said quietly and moved away.

Hank left Rachel to unpack, made a list of staples they would need, and left to hunt out a grocery store.

Her spirits sank from doleful to wretched. Was her father really safe, or did this man they called *El Jefe* have some stake in the horror that engulfed Rachel? Was he playing his own game?

Dismally, she took her few belongings from the suitcase and stowed them in drawers, wondering how long it would be before another frenzy sent her to rush them away to yet another drawer in another town. What had she done to land herself in this predicament?

A paper-wrapped something, the shape of a pencil, fell to the floor as she yanked the last pair of jeans from the suitcase. She picked it up. One of the damned syringes. She must have scooped it up with the rest of her things. She wished she had some mind-altering drugs to go with it.

Hank returned. Without lettuce. She didn't even mention it.

When they had emptied the sacks and put things away, he put his arms around her and studied her face. "You look like a lost child."

She only shrugged.

"I know it's been rough on you," he said. "We've got the rest of the day. What would you like to do?"

"You're asking me? You're not just going to lock me up in this contemptible place?"

"You can lie down in the back seat until we're sure there's no one following us. And we can't go anywhere we might be seen. But—"

"I'd like to see the ocean," she cut in, already giddy with the thought of a little freedom. "Is that too far?"

He thought for a moment. "No, I guess we could do that."

By the time they got to the tiny beach, it was nearly dark. The sun's scarlet halo marked where it had drowned in the Pacific, and to the east, wisps of clouds were flirting with the rising moon.

Hank found a place where a rock blocked them from the casual observer but allowed them a view of anyone who chanced upon the beach.

"I feel like an old time gunslinger," Rachel said. "Always sit with your back to a wall, your face to a door." She took off her shoes, exulting in the feeling of still-warm sand under her toes, and ran fingers through hair that felt coarse from all the bleaching and dying.

"Aren't you going to take yours off?" She pointed at his shoes, then dropped to the sand, grabbed one of his feet, and when he toppled, whisked off his loafers and ran toward the water.

"Don't you dare," he yelled, dashing after her, grabbing her about the waist and tickling as she poised to toss one of the shoes into the sea. They both crashed to the sand in a giggling heap.

Rachel writhed, then reached her hands to the back of his neck and brought his mouth to hers.

"This is a public beach," he said when they drew apart.

"I was going to speak to you about your wanton behavior," she said, rolling over and propping her chin on her hand. The waves were making soft fizzing sounds a few feet from their heads. "There's some brush over there," she added solemnly.

"Are you serious?"

"Well, okay, here will do." She pulled him back down on the cooling sand, and watched moonlight dance across his slightly bewildered face as she unbuttoned his shirt.

They lay, bare legs still tangled, the breeze beginning to cool the air. Hank rubbed a five-o'clock-shadowed chin against her hair. "When this is all over—"

She cut him off, "It will never be over."

"Yes, it will. All things pass, even this, and when it is—"

"No." She drew a finger across his lips. "Don't."

"Why not?"

She wanted to say, *Even if this is ever over, I'll still be an alcoholic. You don't know that, do you? Alcoholics aren't very stable people. We live from one AA meeting to the next, and I haven't been to a meeting in weeks.* Instead she said, "Just treasure the moment. Never mind the future," and turned to gaze at the sea. Far away, the lights of a boat bobbed with the waves.

She stood, dressed, and began walking. The sand beneath her feet was cool.

"Where are you going?"

"Back to the car," she said, her voice was so low it was almost a croak.

When, after a few steps, she looked back, he was still staring at her, the ache of confusion written in his eyes.

Rubbing the back of her hand across her lips, she returned and sat down again. "Remember when you said it's funny how sour things can become? Well, it isn't. It isn't funny at all."

After a time, Hank rubbed his thumb across the back of her hand. "What are you thinking?"

A small tear left a damp streak in its wake as it slid down her cheek. "That plants always try to bloom when they think they're going to die."

Chapter Fifty-three

The next morning arrived wrapped in a fog that pressed itself against walls and crept under the doors.

They slept late and rose reluctantly. After a haphazard breakfast, Rachel reached for the phone to call Goldie. Hank took it out of her hand.

"But I don't know if she's picked up her messages. She's either been to the cabin or she's been trying to call. By now she'll be certain someone is boiling us in oil." Rachel reached for the phone again.

"Better not make any calls from here."

"It's just to Goldie."

"Maybe especially Goldie. If that Mexican Mafioso could follow me, how do we know someone isn't tapping her phone?"

"What about your cell phone?"

"I'm not sure how, but I think someone could get a fix on that, too," Hank said. "I need to run some errands in town. I'll call her from a pay phone and tell her everything's okay."

"I can't stand being cooped up like a prize pig."

"I know. I know. That's why we got away yesterday."

"It wasn't enough. It made it worse."

Hank put his hands on her shoulders and shook her a little. "Don't go out." He said the words slowly, then turned and moved toward the door. "Don't," he said again, then left.

Twenty minutes later Rachel was flinging her crossword puzzle across the table, eyeing her watch and craving lettuce and tomatoes and blue-cheese dressing. For the second time, she checked the refrigerator and cabinets, banging the doors. Nothing looked fit to eat. And she had forgotten to ask Hank to pick up some salad makings.

Outside, the fog had slunk away, leaving a bright, cloudless sky. *Hank is paranoid,* she thought, dropping the kitchen curtain back in place.

If I'm stuck here even five more minutes, I may start screaming and not be able to stop. If only I had my revolver—or any weapon, even a knife maybe.

She went to the kitchen and opened a drawer: only three knives, all pitifully flimsy and hopelessly dull. Then her eye caught on the syringe packet she had tossed in with the knives.

She did have a weapon.

⌒⌒⌒

Checking her rearview mirror every thirty seconds and eyeing all cars with cold suspicion, Rachel drove into town, located a supermarket, and left the Toyota down the street at the back of a McDonald's parking lot. Hoping no one would notice the car's several bullet holes, she walked back half a block to the grocery.

Rachel selected three different kinds of lettuce, then added some spinach. Looking for the checkout, she found herself in the liquor section. She reached out and touched a bottle of Napa Valley Chardonnay. *Why not? I'll probably be shot in my sleep or gunned down in the street anyway.* She placed the bottle in her basket.

Leaving the store, a sharp wind caught the grocery bag, nearly wresting it from her fingers. She set it down to get a better grip. When she looked up, a young man, probably out of his teens but still in search of manhood, was making his way between the cars toward the store entrance. He swung his gaze in her direction, then ducked his dark head, protecting his face from the wind. As he reached the store entrance, the silver rivets in his black leather jacket caught the sun.

Was he…? She was certain he was. Had he recognized her? Rachel didn't think so.

She backed down the street toward McDonald's, eyes fixed on the grocery store entrance. She got into the car, put on her sunglasses, and brushed her hair forward. The man in the black jacket was still in the store. She started the car and waited.

The automatic doors busily opened and closed, spitting out basket-pushing shoppers. But no spindly guy in a black leather jacket. Had she somehow missed him? No, there he was, thin arms in black leather sleeves, one hand thrust in a pocket, the other carrying a plastic sack.

She craned her neck to follow his passage to an aging panel truck, the body a blotchy white. Rachel was certain she had seen that truck before: circling her garage the day her apartment was burglarized.

And its driver was a dead ringer for the guy who had hung around her hotel.

He turned, seeming to stare in her direction as if seeking her out. Then he climbed into the van and drove slowly along the street toward her.

Was he going to stop? Say something to her? But no. The van rolled on by.

Easing her car onto the road, Rachel stayed a block behind as he drove casually, at moderate speed, taking the freeway north several miles before exiting onto a state highway. She settled into the easy pace, thinking that following someone was really quite easy.

Eight miles later, as she topped a rise, she was dismayed to find the panel truck had disappeared. She examined every vehicle ahead of her. Not one was a white van. She had blinked at the wrong time.

By the time she noticed the small county road that ran east, she had to cut the wheel sharply, spilling some of the groceries, to turn onto it. But yes, a quarter-mile or so away was the van. Slowing, to put a little more space between them, she glanced at the groceries that had spilled on the floor. An orange tag dangled from the spinach: *Organically grown*.

Something gnawed at her.

Organic farming.

When Hank had talked of his time in Brazil, he had mentioned that organic farming didn't work because of the insects and they had to resort to dusting. Crop dusting. He had taught the native farmers, had flown a crop duster.

Like the drug-smuggling plane that crashed?

She tried to remember exactly how he looked, what he said, when she confronted him in the cabin with the fact that he knew all the people who turned up dead. Except Lonnie.

Hank had been indignant. And she had believed him because she wanted to.

Dear God! It couldn't be Hank alone, but is he involved in some diabolical scheme?

Was that why he kept moving her around? So no one would know where she was? How much did she really know about him?

Was that why Hank had come on to her, become her friend, and more?

But why?

Because she knew something.

What do I know?

She began to recite in her head everything she thought she knew—about the car that killed Jason; about the crop duster that crashed, disappeared, and reappeared in a warehouse. That Charlotte had not committed suicide, but was murdered. That Lonnie had died from an overdose of selenium.

Selenium.

The same substance that was killing wildlife at Farwell Ponds.

Could enough selenium be sprayed from a crop duster to kill wildlife?

But why would anyone want to kill wildlife?

Money. It had to be money.

It couldn't be Hank by himself. He must work for someone who would stand to gain a lot of money by...by what? Killing wildlife? How would that produce money?

By ruining farmland. Buy it cheap, stop the selenium dusting, and in a year or so, with new soil analyses to prove the problem was gone, sell the land at an enormous profit.

Exactly as Hank had led her to suspect Bruno of doing.

Mind in a sickish spin, Rachel lost sight of the vehicle ahead.

The road ended abruptly in a small, level parking area, but no splotchy-white panel truck was in sight. Had she missed a turn-off somewhere? She parked the Toyota in a cluster of cars.

Through the open gate of a chain-link fence a wind sock was writhing, trying to escape its pole. Half a dozen small planes sat like dogs at a pet show, eagerly awaiting their owners' command to fetch.

Was the guy in the black jacket involved, or was his appearance in her parking garage that day just a coincidence?

Was he one of *El Jefe's* men?

Whoever Black Jacket was, he seemed to have disappeared.

Her racing thoughts slammed into something else: *Goldie. I have to warn her about Hank.*

Chapter Fifty-four

Rachel was exhausted, as if she had reached another planet where gravity was greater. With cold, jittery fingers, she opened the car door, got out, and headed for the cinder-block building that seemed to be both waiting room and office.

The pay phone was just outside the glass door. Clumsy with haste, she extracted a phone card from her wallet and began dialing the endless numbers needed to make a call. She miscalled and had to start over. When the ring on the other end finally came, Goldie didn't answer. And there was no answering machine.

Leaving the phone, Rachel glanced down the row of parked cars. The panel truck was there, stopped directly behind her Toyota, trapping her car. Preventing her from driving.

Deliberately? Had to be. But why?

Maybe it was just coincidence.

Above the chain-link fence that lined the airfield, the sky was cloudless except for a black speck moving toward a strip of land shaved bare among the perpetual crop rows. A whirring sound rose as the speck became a plane that touched down gracefully and rolled to a stop some 20 yards away.

The pilot appeared. A woman, slender and agile, with hair like smoke. Alexandra Miller was making her way toward the building. She caught sight of Rachel and stopped. "What a nice surprise!"

Rachel fumbled for her manners. "Yes. Good to see you."

"What are you doing here? You look upset."

"It's nothing, really. Well, maybe I'm a little jumpy. Someone is blocking my car."

Alexandra's eyes darkened as they skimmed Rachel's flushed face. She patted her shoulder, then took a cell phone from her pocket, flipped it open and pushed a single key with her thumb, turned away and said something into it.

She took Rachel's arm and began walking quickly. "I have an idea. Guaranteed to change your mood."

"I'm okay, really."

"You don't look okay. You look miserable. I seem to be making a habit of finding you when things are going badly."

Rachel managed a smile. "I guess I'm a little unstrung. And yes, you sure rescued me from those muggers."

"Let's have a quick cup of tea," Alexandra said, opening the door to the small waiting room. An urn of hot water sat on a card table. She took two Styrofoam cups, filled them, tore open two teabags, dropped them into the water, and handed a cup to Rachel.

They moved to the window where several people were watching the airfield. "So, what has unstrung you?" Alexandra asked.

Rachel was wondering what Hank would do when he returned and found her gone. She took a sip of the tea and winced as it burned her tongue. "Nothing much." She blew gently on the tea and took another sip. "Well, there are some problems. Someone I really trusted...."

Where could she go now? What should she do?

Alexandra shot her a look. "Bad idea trusting anyone."

"Too late now."

"A man?"

Rachel nodded, thinking Alexandra couldn't possibly imagine the degree of betrayal. "I need to find a place to stay for a while."

"That's easy. Come with me."

"Oh, no," Rachel said. "I couldn't."

Alexandra was gazing at the airfield. "Of course you can." She turned to Rachel. "Look, do me a favor."

"What?"

"Just let me rescue you again. I have a wonderful idea. I guarantee it will change your mood."

Alexandra crossed the room to the door. Rachel followed her into the unpaved parking area. The van was still blocking her car. A pickup truck was pulling away, throwing dust.

"This will be perfect," Alexandra said as she reached a black Jaguar.

Rachel was thinking that might be true. Alexandra's place might be the perfect place to hide for a while.

They got into the car. "Not afraid of heights, are you?" Alexandra asked.

"A little." *Oh, no.* She had forgotten that flying was Alexandra's favorite way to unwind. The last thing she wanted was another plane ride. "I don't think—"

Alexandra cut her off. "Trust me."

Rachel wiped sweaty palms on her jeans. "Okay."

Alexandra backed the car in a semicircle, then it sprang forward like the cat it was named for. A few miles later, she pulled off the road into an open field where two pickups were parked.

The field seemed nearly filled by an enormous pool of bright yellow.

Alexandra laughed at the expression on Rachel's face. "That's Delilah. My hot-air balloon. Ever been up in one?"

"No." Rachel didn't want to now, either. But Alexandra seemed so pleased at the prospect, and the woman had offered her a place to stay. The least she could do was humor her. It was probably perfectly safe. People went up in balloons every day. And maybe she could tell Alexandra the truth. Maybe the two of them could figure out what to do.

"I was planning to go up," Alexandra was saying. "Pure luck that you caught me."

The balloon's basket seemed oddly small against the sea of yellow. Alexandra strode toward it. Four men who had been sitting on the grass rose and followed.

The pool of yellow became a huge bubble.

Alexandra climbed easily over the side of the basket. Rachel followed clumsily. Her companion was studying the small array of valve handles and gauges on the console.

Pulling a glove onto her right hand, Alexandra called, "Never mind the safety chute. We're in a hurry."

Rachel turned, searching what she could see of the road. A cloud of dust was moving along it.

A whooshing sound rose. The bubble began to rise. The basket followed.

After a moment someone shouted, "She's up."

Another whoosh, like a furnace igniting, was followed by a series of short, hissing blasts, like air being pulsed into an enormous tire. The basket rocked, then slowly followed the balloon into the air.

Rachel stifled an impulse of panic as the ground quietly fell away. This was probably the safest place she'd been in weeks.

It's perfect. No one can get to me here.

Then she saw that a white van had joined the two pickups.

Backing away from the edge of the basket, she asked, "Who is that?"

"Where?" Alexandra asked from behind her.

"There. The guy in the black jacket getting out of that van."

Alexandra glanced at the ground. "He works for me."

"He works for you?"

The words congealed, almost closing Rachel's throat as she turned. The barrel was very short but it belonged to a gun and it was pointed at her face.

Alexandra's glove was gone. The long fingers looked as elegant gripping the derringer as they would holding a teacup.

Chapter Fifty-five

"If you so much as move a finger," Alexandra said conversationally, "you will die. There will be no warning. So do keep your hands still."

Her words hung in the air like birds that had stopped flying but didn't fall.

The hissing sound continued for what seemed a long time. Then there was silence but for a wheezing sound, like the breathing of an asthmatic, and a feeling of floating.

Rachel fought a wave of dizziness.

Above them was only sky, and ropes that led to a huge, open, yellow mouth.

"Lovely, isn't it?" Alexandra asked, as if they were two chance passengers on an airliner.

Adrenaline surging now, Rachel's senses hit red alert, nerves and muscles demanding action. But there was nowhere to flee. Struggling to slow her mind enough to think, she said nothing.

Alexandra moved toward her with the deadly grace of a panther. "My compliments. You have been very slippery."

Rachel only stared—an animal caught in onrushing, lethal headlights. The wheeze came again and the huge yellow orb swayed above them like the head of a giant adder.

Gazing at the sky behind her prey, Alexandra said in a tone one hears at cocktail parties, "Pity you've never gone ballooning. Nothing compares. Hang gliding should, but somehow it doesn't. Planes conquer nature. Balloons join us *to* nature."

Rachel was thinking that she was shorter, but probably the stronger of the two.

"Of course the main advantage of the moment is that there's no need to file a flight plan. No record of balloon flights at all. And the flying is quite simple. The air heats, the balloon ascends." Alexandra said the words slowly, as though teaching a rather dull child. "Pull the rip line—that cord over there—the deflation panel opens, the warm air escapes, and we descend. Direction, of course, is the problem. So much depends upon wind. And wind is so capricious."

"How…how do you get back to the same place?"

"We don't. The ground crew will follow us in the truck. Isn't this a splendid view?"

"I can't see much."

"Of course you can't. How thoughtless of me. Turn around. But do it very, very slowly."

Rachel eyed the gun's muzzle. The last thing she wanted to do was turn her back on it.

"Go ahead," Alexandra was saying. "The basket is quite sturdy. Quaint, isn't it, to use a basket. A throwback to the era of the bustle. There's even champagne. If a farmer takes offense at your landing in his field, you can invite him to a party. Now, slowly, turn around." The gun barrel moved ever so slightly, indicating that this time, it was a command.

The floor of the basket was surprisingly stable, but Rachel's legs wouldn't hold her. She staggered against the wicker wall.

Something rigid pressed into her ankle. For a moment, she couldn't think what it was.

The air had become noticeably cooler, and very quiet. Not even the sound of wind disturbed the silence. She pulled her jacket around her.

"There's no wind because we're traveling *with* the wind," Alexandra said, as if she'd read Rachel's mind.

Mountains purpled at the far side of the valley. Rocks showed between the tufts of trees that climbed the hillside. Stretched between the mountain ranges was a patchwork quilt—squares of brilliant greens, a few yellows, a few browns.

"It's simply delicious to drift." Alexandra's voice was dreamily sensuous. "Look."

Rachel cast a quick glance over her shoulder, wondering if this was a ploy to divert her attention before the kill. In the distance, three ponds glittered in the sun, roundish chunks of scattered mica amid row upon undulating row of naked farmland. The drainage ditch, betrayed as man-made by its precise straightness, aimed directly at the ponds.

Alexandra was gazing at them. "Bruno's great hope for a truce with Mother Nature."

"What does Bruno have to do with this?"

A small smile flirted with Alexandra's mouth. "With this? Not a thing." Her eyes had drifted lazily over the scene. Now they pierced Rachel's. "Remember that drought a few years back? It was phony. Jason trumped it up with bogus statistics. He got in bed with agriculture. Jason and the Farm Bureau were going to set the environmental movement back thirty years."

She gave a low, harsh laugh. "Fourteen million people saving the dishwater for the roses and paying four-ninety-five a pound for the tomatoes that could still be irrigated. People don't forget that in a few short years. Jason and the farmers thought they had bought fourteen million votes for more dams, more canals, more destruction.

"But the final part of the plan was even worse—more evil than I could have imagined." Her eyes riveted on Rachel's. "You know what they intended to do?"

Rachel could only stare as Alexandra's mouth twisted with rage.

"They were going to privatize it. Put our water in the hands of a corporation. Our water. At the mercy of profits and profiteers.

"Even now it's being whispered that water will become the *oil* of the coming century."

Rachel's head swam. She gazed at the other woman thinking that despite the threat to herself, Alexandra was not entirely wrong. Her methods were appalling. But her reasons were sound.

"They thought they had me cornered." The words floated on the clear, smooth oil of her now almost serene voice.

"Jason was putting together a mountain of twisted information to show how we," Alexandra's eyes hardened, "how *we*, the environmental community, had lied to the public. He wrote the proposition and had the signatures to put a peripheral canal on the ballot in November. It would have killed the delta. And privatizing it would kill much more than that. It would kill the environment. It would kill California. And maybe, eventually, America."

"So you killed him," Rachel said, voice raw in her throat.

"For a while, I hoped Charlotte would. I think she just couldn't bring herself to arrange it. But then Jason found something in his own water quality laboratory. Not the drugs," she said to Rachel's look. "That was Harry's own little game. Dear Harry was full of tricks. But the only one I cared about was that he obliged me by acquiring the sodium selenate."

Rachel's eyelids flicked closed, then opened slowly. "So you could poison your own ponds," she said, more calmly than she could have imagined. She was thinking that at least it was not Hank who had betrayed her. "How did you do it—get the poison into the ponds? Just send a dump truck?"

"Good heavens. That would have been clumsy and crass, and far easier to discover." A slow smile bloomed like a toxic flower across Alexandra's lips. "I used a crop duster. It was so simple. And truly thrilling to have such ultimate power. Over plants, over insects, over bacteria. Over life itself."

Rachel ran her tongue across dry lips. "They used a crop duster to smuggle the selenium and, I guess, other stuff Harry wanted, across the border."

"Is that right? I can't say I've ever done any smuggling, but the duster worked very well for my purposes."

"Selenium isn't illegal. Why did Harry have to get it for you? Couldn't you just purchase it outright?"

"But you see, I needed a quite a lot. The quantities might have seemed curious, especially since Friends of the Earth doesn't have a lab. Regardless, it would have left a paper trail. So Harry got it for me. Far as I knew, he got it from a chemical supply company."

"I suppose he didn't want a paper trail either," Rachel said. "So he had it smuggled, maybe a little at a time because the dollar value wouldn't have been worth enough for an entire load. And some of it probably was delivered to him by helicopter—through me. Lonnie must have carried one of those packages to the lab, thought it was something else, and snitched some."

"Lonnie?"

"Guy who worked for me. Poisoned himself with sodium selenate. Or did you kill him, too?"

"Never heard of him," Alexandra said. "But Harry did mention receiving a damaged package. He thought some of the stuff was missing. He was quite squeamish about it—went frantic when the pilot of that plane that went down with his shipment in the desert said he saw a woman take a box from the wreckage. Of course, at that point, we didn't know the woman was you."

"When did Jason find out?"

"He knew something, I'm not sure how much." Alexandra glanced up at the yellow mouth, then her eyes shot back to Rachel's. "Harry was crazed about Jason maybe discovering his sweet little multi-million-dollar scheme. Charlotte was suspicious when Jason was killed, but I think she was relieved. She felt almost as strongly as I did that Jason should not be allowed to ram through this ballot proposition."

"Why didn't she call in the cops?"

Alexandra's laugh tinkled in the still air. "I would guess it's because she discovered that the car that assisted Jason into the hereafter was checked out to her that day."

"But Charlotte wasn't driving it."

"Of course not. That wouldn't have been her style."

"So what did happen?" Rachel's voice sounded cold compared to Alexandra's conversational tone.

"There was this mundane little press tour of one of Inter-Urban's facilities. I drove out with Harry—I sometimes went along so that if Jason made some outrageous statement, I could contradict it before it got on the air. Charlotte had some minor car trouble, and she was worried about getting back. Harry decided to brown-nose. He offered to drive her car and gave her his. Harry is—or was—a rotten driver, so I insisted on driving." Alexandra recited it as if giving a report.

"And there was Jason by the side of the road." She couldn't control a smile.

"It was just too perfect. I couldn't resist."

Chapter Fifty-six

Numbed by Alexandra's ability to smile, Rachel gawked at her. "Harry knew? He was in the car?"

"Of course. But there was no way he'd say anything. I knew too much about him. I confess I didn't think you'd ever enter into it, much less add any of it up. But then there was that ridiculous tie tack." Alexandra's mouth pinched at one corner and she shrugged.

"Tie tack?" Rachel asked. "What do you know about a tie tack?"

"That afternoon you and I went flying. Your purse spilled. Remember? And there it was," Alexandra said, again smiling. "A tie tack, an odd design with a tortoise. I knew a Mojave jeweler who used that design, but it wasn't common. And I had seen Jason wearing it. That was troubling."

"And all the time, you were poisoning the environment you were supposed to protect."

A pained look flitted across Alexandra's face. "In some ways it was easier to kill Jason than it was to do that."

"Then, why?"

"Sometimes a few have to be sacrificed to save many. In mere months, the most devastating proposition this state has ever seen would have been passed by the voters. I needed a hammer. The rest was a simple bit of barter."

"Barter," Rachel repeated the word. Her mind flashed to Alexandra's tale of her grandmother. Barter, negotiation, and the Mojave who lived in harmony. *Does she believe* that's *what she's doing?*

A pair of nearly black eyes fastened on Rachel's. "The delta will be returned to nature...."

"It will never happen," Rachel said. "There are tens of thousands of acres of farms in the delta that need it for irrigation."

"But not that many farmers."

"Meaning what?"

"The voters are in the cities. They care nothing about farming. They can be made to understand that everything in the delta is a losing proposition. Many of those farms are below sea level. For their very existence, they depend on eroding levees that cost the state a fortune to maintain," Alexandra said.

"Not to mention the dozens of fault lines—one little well-placed earthquake and the ground would liquefy. Imagine thousands of miles of levees tumbling down like a house of cards. Sea water would rush all the way to Sacramento. The state would bankrupt itself trying to repair things."

Alexandra's eyes made it clear she would enjoy that scenario. "The public will see that it's better to concede to Mother Nature what is hers before she takes it by force."

Rachel was shaking her head. The longer the woman talked, the more time the other part of her brain had to think. "It won't work."

"When people see what the farmers have done to baby ducks, in living color...." Alexandra's face was sublimely enigmatic.

"At the ponds," Rachel said, her voice husky.

"Yes. The ponds. You have to understand: nothing, and I mean nothing whips up fervor for the cause like failure."

"Failure of what?"

Alexandra frowned as if Rachel was dim-witted. "Failure of the environmentalists to protect, of course. Donations have poured in since the news hit the press. Charlotte was one of the few who understood that."

"Was Charlotte in on all this?"

Alexandra frowned again. This time there was impatience in it. "Of course not. Charlotte did try to stop Jason, so I delayed, just in case she succeeded. You see, Charlotte was afraid if water flowed too freely around the delta and south, developers would destroy her beloved Southern California, would turn it into one gigantic bumper-to-bumper city."

"But Charlotte lost."

"The rest of the board was backing Jason." Alexandra gave an annoyed tap of her foot. "Charlotte didn't give up easily. She mapped out a whole new approach. She called it the Delta Plan. She made sure the general manager who followed Jason was so weak he would do anything she wanted. Andrew Greer was a stroke of genius!" Alexandra fairly beamed.

To Rachel, it looked like the grin of a hyena after a kill.

"Did you kill her? That was no suicide."

Alexandra's smile faded. "She knew I had driven back with Harry and if that was the car that had hit Jason, I had seen it. She never dreamed that Harry wasn't driving. She called, wanted to know why I hadn't said anything."

"And you said?"

"I went out there. Told her we needed to sit down over a cup of tea and discuss it face to face."

"And then you murdered her."

"I should have known it would come to that. Like with you. I didn't want to. I am not quite the monster you think me." Alexandra's voice was soft as feathers on a pit viper. "Charlotte was clever to the end. She told me how much you knew, but not that you would be joining our little chat."

"You were still there when I arrived."

"You gave me quite a fright." Alexandra was leaning forward, eyes like black marbles that seemed to read Rachel's expression with a special kind of Braille that could feel her thoughts.

"So, that is the story." Alexandra's voice took on a faintly apologetic tone. "Now, I'm afraid we have to finish it."

The sky was showing the first pinkish hints of dusk. Eyes vying with Alexandra's like arm wrestlers, Rachel willed the muscles in her face to blankness, not at all sure she could do what she must do.

Slowly she shifted her right foot. Inside her boot, a long, thin shape against her ankle.

She was not without a weapon. There was the dog Max, and there was Lonnie. Sodium selenate was obviously quite lethal.

Before leaving the condo, she had unwrapped the syringe, dissolved some of the powder in a small amount of water, drawn the solution into the hypodermic, removed the eraser from a pencil, and stabbed the needle into the soft rubber. Then it was simply a matter of wrapping it in tissue paper, slipping it inside her sock and easing it into her hiking boot.

The balloon was drifting very close to the ponds, which now looked like mirrors that had melted into one another.

Alexandra was watching her. A strand of hair like a streak of coal dust fell across Alexandra's face—a beautiful face, not marred, as it should have been, by the twisted mind, more like the face of a messiah.

Half mesmerized by the sun bouncing off the ponds, Rachel tensed her right arm.

"I hope," Alexandra was saying, "that you won't make this any more difficult for either of us than it has to be." The gun in her hand was at full attention, a well-trained animal waiting to be unleashed. She stroked the side of it with her thumb. "Come over here. Trust me. It will be less painful if the placement is right."

"Even if you manage to hide my...my body, eventually, someone will put the pieces—and all the bodies—together."

Alexandra shook her head slowly. "Next spring, some farmer plowing his field will be somewhat astonished. But by then the forensics will be limited to guesswork."

Rachel tried to take a step forward, then crumpled to the floor with an anguished cry.

She waited for the bullet. If it didn't come now, there would be one very small chance.

It didn't come.

"Ankle…I think it's sprained…." Slipping her fingers into her boot, Rachel grasped the syringe and flicked the eraser from the end of the needle.

"Get up!" Alexandra blazed, eyes like chips of black diamond.

Slowly, as if under water, Rachel staggered to her feet.

"That's better." Alexandra's voice was cajoling again. "Move over here. Now."

Rachel took a step, folded her ankle inward, lurched against Alexandra, and jabbed the needle through Alexandra's sleeve into the upper arm. Breath coming in rasping gasps, Rachel pushed the plunger, praying the poison would be quick enough.

The woman clutched her arm where the needle had entered. "What did you do?!"

Rachel grabbed at the pistol. It went off, the bullet driving harmlessly through the side of the basket. She seized the derringer.

As if with some blind, animal desire to maim with claws and teeth, Alexandra lunged, pinning Rachel against the basket railing. She wrested the gun from Rachel's fingers.

Inches away, the black eyes glittered as Alexandra jammed the muzzle of the little gun beneath Rachel's chin.

"Shoot," Rachel said. "For God's sake, get it over. Kill me." The balloon wheezed.

"In my own good time," Alexandra spat. "Not yours." Her head began to sway. Slowly, the glittering eyes faded to dull coal and she seemed to wilt, her elbow touching the floor, then her arm, finally the cloud of black hair.

Rachel looked up at the huge yellow mouth that gaped above her. She had not the faintest idea how to land a balloon.

Chapter Fifty-seven

The dials on the console told her little. What had Alexandra said?

The air heats, the balloon rises. What else? Pull a rope—yes, there it was—a hole opens and the balloon descends.

Over the suede rim of the basket, Rachel examined the landscape. The ponds were close. Very close. Did a balloon go straight down? How fast? How deep were the ponds? What about the poison-laced water?

On the ground to the left, a light flashed. A road snaked toward the ponds. A black pickup truck sat beside it like a forgotten toy, sun glinting from its windshield. The ground crew. Alexandra had said the ground crew would follow in a truck.

Rachel knew she must do it now: pull the rope before she drifted closer to the ponds and the truck.

The cord was quite long. She looked up at the balloon's circus-tent-like interior and, forbidding herself to think further, pulled the cord hard. High in the fabric, a hole opened and the balloon began to sink. Fast. Then faster. She eased the tension on the rope and the descent slowed. If she let go, the air would be trapped and the balloon would rise again.

Still gripping the cord, Rachel dropped to a crouch, head to knees, arms protecting her head, trying to remember the in-case-of-crash diagrams in the seat pockets of commercial airplanes.

An air pocket bounced her against the side of the basket, wrapping the cord around her wrist and opening the hole wider.

The balloon began to plummet like an out-of-control elevator. Rachel's insides screamed, sending her stomach into her
throat.

The impact was hard and fast. The basket tipped, throwing her
to the floor. For a horrifying moment, Alexandra's body bounced
toward her, then danced away.

Pain pounded through Rachel's shoulder, then her entire body
blazed with it. Slowly she moved one arm, agonizing with the
effort, then the other, then her legs.

She had lost the cord. The hole in the fabric had closed.

The envelope, brilliant yellow against the sky, began to rise.

Struggling to unsteady feet, Rachel pitched herself over the
basket wall. Her throbbing shoulder struck the ground.

In the distance, a vehicle motor thrummed toward her. The
ground crew? Did they know she was supposed to be dead?

Staggering to her feet again, she demanded that her legs run.

Every breath seared her lungs. A red-hot blade stabbed at
her shoulder.

Tall plants on the left. A sorghum field. If she could get to
that…. Rachel lost her footing again. She crawled the last few
feet and pitched herself among the stalks.

Grayish-green leathery leaves rasped against her flesh, rustling
like a Victorian skirt. She flattened herself and lay still. An acrid
smell tilted her already queasy stomach toward severe nausea.

A vehicle braked to a standstill close by, much too close by.
A lizard ran over the fingers of her right hand. She jerked away,
then lay still again.

Footsteps scratched along the pavement, eight steps, then
nineteen more, then a brushing sound. Then, for a long time,
nothing. Finally, the unseen feet took eleven more steps and a
door closed.

A tiny albino worm inched its way up her arm, but Rachel
lay utterly still. The sound of the motor dimmed to nothing.
She compelled herself to remain motionless, for what seemed
hours. When she began to crawl toward the road, it was almost
full dark.

In the dim light, the highway, when she found it, sliced the world into two farm fields.

Headlights approached but the driver didn't slow. It was many minutes before two more headlights appeared. Rachel stepped out onto the road. When the pickup stopped, she began to sway, unable to keep her feet.

A door opened. Hands grabbed her shoulders. She cried out at the pain, tried to wrench away, flailing with her fists.

"Stop. Stop dammit." The voice was gruff, the face in the headlights obscured by an unruly bush of a beard.

Her arms went weak. She could feel the sobs coming.

Hands picked her up, thrust her through the open door of the truck, past the steering wheel to the passenger seat. He climbed in beside her and started the truck. In cowboy boots and faded, baggy jeans, he looked like a barrel with a beard.

"Who are you?" she asked, voice quavering.

"Lady, it don't matter a red hot damn who I am, you are goin' to the hospital."

Chapter Fifty-eight

Rachel, Hank, and Goldie sat strewn about the furniture in the condo's living room like the dregs of an audience at an overlong play.

Aside from a sprained shoulder and too many bruises and lacerations to count, the hospital staff had pronounced Rachel without serious injury.

Now, huddled on the sofa, wrapped in bandages both elastic and tape, shoulder trussed in a sling, legs wrapped in a blanket, she was reciting everything she could remember.

Hank swore softly when she stopped. "Jesus. You thought it was me?" He fed another log to the fire.

Rachel pulled an apologetic face. "What can I say? It seemed to make sense. Who would think an environmentalist would kill? People, maybe, but wildlife?"

Goldie had used her entire stock of expletives three times over, but for the moment she was speechless.

"Will that balloon just float into outer space?" Rachel asked, her voice hoarse. Her head was beginning to throb as weariness flowed into the places vacated by fear.

"I don't think so. It probably didn't go far," Hank said. "But there's a lot of farmland out there and not many roads. It may be a while before it's found."

Rachel pulled her knees up to her chin. "With Alexandra's body and a gun and my fingerprints." On the street, a car sped by.

Hank got to his feet and began to pace. "Self-defense is so obvious. I can't imagine a DA would even charge you." They all considered that.

"You're right," Goldie agreed, then turned to Rachel. "You'll never guess what Peter found under the Oriental rug in Charlotte's office."

"Something called the Delta Plan."

The black woman stared at her. "How the hell do you know that?"

"Amazing what you can learn when you're trapped with a murderer."

"Why was that worth all this killing stuff?" Goldie wanted to know.

"Three-quarters of the state's population," said Hank, "is dependent on water from the delta. More than twenty million Californians would have been at Alexandra's mercy...."

Goldie shrugged. "I'll take your word for it, but before all this froo-fra, I'd hardly *heard* of the delta." The fire spat and flared. "Anyway," she went on, "I've got everything together to give to the cops. We need to get hold of the border patrol, drug enforcement, LAPD, the San Bernardino Sheriff—"

"I don't see why we have to call any of them," Rachel cut in. "Alexandra's dead, Harry's dead. We'd just be tying ourselves up in an investigation that probably wouldn't prove much, especially about the poisoning of those ponds."

"You may be wrong," Goldie said. "That Andrew Greer looked down the back of his shirt and seems like he found a spine."

Hank nodded. "Andrew can check the records on how much selenium the lab bought. I'll bet they were buying as much as they figured they could without attracting attention. Smuggling alone is not exactly a reliable way to go. And there's Charlotte's Delta Plan." He lowered his chin. "This time, Rachel, we have to."

Rachel squeezed her eyes tight, then nodded, as if giving something up after a long fight. "I guess so," she said slowly. "But I'm almost as afraid of the cops as I was of Alexandra."

"I never understood why," Hank said.

She turned to face him. "Because for a very short, unpleasant time I was in jail. For drugs. I would have been there a lot longer if Bruno hadn't got me a good attorney. I wasn't a dealer, in case you're wondering." She paused and took a deep breath. "But I am an alcoholic. And I came so close to falling off the wagon this morning that I actually bought a bottle of wine."

Hank had not moved.

Rachel stared at an empty chair across the room. Somewhere in the back of the house a timber creaked. The silence became heavy with its own weight.

Goldie broke it. "Well. Think I'll turn in. I'm beat. Seems like you could have hidden out closer to home. Took forever to get here."

The black woman started down the corridor to the spare room, then turned back. "Almost forgot. Irene said to tell you she owes you a fortune. That old gal is pretty sharp. I wouldn't be surprised if she had one."

Rachel gave a half smile. "She doesn't mean money, she means palm-reading, tarot, even a crystal ball for all I know. Maybe I'm ready to take her up on that offer."

Goldie shrugged and ambled back down the hall.

Hank turned to Rachel. A slow, lopsided grin crept over his face. "Be right back. I left something in the car. Actually two things." And he was out the door.

When he returned, she could hear him wiping his feet much longer than necessary on the welcome mat.

"I don't know if this is the right time," he muttered awkwardly, closing the door behind him.

Avoiding her eyes, he sat down on the sofa next to her and held out a small, square jeweler's box.

Rachel stared at it, not knowing what to think.

"It's not real," he said. "I mean not an engagement thing or anything."

"Well, that's good. I never believed in engagement things."

"When I got married last time," Hank said, "I hardly thought about it. It was like we happened to be at the right place at the right time and marriage, well, that was just what one did."

"I guess it happens to a lot of people that way."

"I don't think like that anymore. I think it has to be thought about. A lot."

She took the box and opened it. The ring was silver, an Indian design. It reminded her of Jason's cuff link, except there was no tortoise. Blinking, she looked up at him.

"It will be a while before it's legal, but I sent the papers to a lawyer in Brazil a week ago. When it's over, I'd like to think about…well, whatever…."

With her good arm, Rachel drew him to her, pressing her cheek to his chest.

"Careful," he said as his mouth sought hers.

Something squirmed inside his jacket. Rachel drew back, bewildered.

Hank's face split in a broad smile. "He turned up at the garage. Irene found him." Clancy's orange tiger-striped head emerged over his jacket zipper, licked Rachel's chin, and began to purr.

To receive a free catalog of Poisoned Pen Press titles, please contact us in one of the following ways:

Phone: 1-800-421-3976
Facsimile: 1-480-949-1707
Email: info@poisonedpenpress.com
Website: www.poisonedpenpress.com

Poisoned Pen Press
6962 E. First Ave. Ste. 103
Scottsdale, AZ 85251